What They're Saying About The Goldberg Variations:

"Jamie is like the rest of us, full of contradictions. He is funny, angry, sad, sassy, brutally honest and refuses to be quiet. In *Slings and Arrows*, we see Jamie on his twenty-second birthday, thrown out of his home, penniless, and sinking into greater despair and self-loathing. When a series of incidents at school, with gay rights organizations and with many others takes him on a journey of self discovery he ultimately develops the self confidence to know himself and pursue what he wants. Searingly honest, it is Jonathan A. Taylor's best work yet.
—Kunal Mukherjee, author of *My Magical Palace*

[In *Volume 2: The Redemption of the Damned*] Jamie begins to develop a reputation for promiscuity after an incident involving his crush, Casper Tyres, and he starts to explore—sometimes willingly, sometimes not—the world … of male sexuality. It's made all the more difficult by the fact that he still has not yet reckoned with the act that initiated his sexual life: the rape he suffered as a young boy. As Jamie's sex life quickly escalates to new heights, he realizes that he hasn't found himself by coming out of the closet. In order to realize who the real Jamie Goldberg is, he still has a lot of work to do. Taylor's prose is smooth and often striking, creating memorable images that will stick in readers' minds…
—*Kirkus Review*

"Heartbreaking and hilarious, provocative and romantic—in *The Rites of Passage*, the first book in *The Goldberg Variations*, debut novelist Jonathan Taylor drills down till it hurts in a coming-of-age and coming-out story tailored to our times."
—Linda Watanabe McFerrin, author of *Namako: Sea Cucumber, Dead Love,* and *The Hand of Buddha*

"*The Rites of Passage* is like encountering a gay *Portnoy's Complaint* in its distinctive blend of Jewish-ness, sex, moral panic, and maternal dominance. And it's painfully realistic in its depiction of what 'coming out' is, its alternation of moments of euphoric liberation with moments of renewed shame and sorrow, as if life were a coin God is flipping and can never be better than half right, but not always the same half. I've spent many pages and many hours with Jamie, and I still want to know what happens to him."
—Patrick Mulcahey, seven-time Emmy Award-winning screenwriter of *The Bold and the Beautiful*

"Reading *The Rites of Passage* reminded me of the fragile time in one's youth when one may or may not mistakenly believe that all information is somehow related to one's self. … Reading it became addicting. If *The Rites of Passage* doesn't remind you of yourself, it will certainly remind you of someone you love."
—*René Capone*, gay figure painter and author of multiple graphic novels, including *Legend of Hedgehog Boy*

The Goldberg Variations: Volume III

Slings
and
Arrows

Jonathan Arnowitz-Taylor

ArnoLand Press, LLC
601 Van Ness #443
San Francisco, CA 94114

Cataloging data:
Slings and Arrows
By Jonathan Arnowitz Taylor
Library of Congress Control Number: 2025933785
ISBN: 978-1-7342957-5-7

Cover design: Michael Arent
Cover illustration: "Reluctant Grace" by René Capone

Excerpts from *Hamlet* by William Shakespeare and *Tristan und Isolde* by Richard Wagner are in the public domain. The adaptations and translations are by the author.

Dedication

For my dear friend, Lawrence Brown

To the memory of

Morris Lyle Taylor:

"The rest is silence."

All normal things
Are now just a symbol
Here inadequacy
Becomes fulfillment
The indescribable
Here is accomplished
 —Jamie's interpretation of the
last lines of Johann Wolfgang von
Goethe's *Faust*

Variation: New Path

January 1982

Chapter 1: The Lost Path

I was through with sex. Debauchery, anonymous sex, faceless tricks, grim orgies, and diverse venereal diseases all had failed to save me. I had taken a long descent. A descent meant to bottom out and cleanse me via an imagined trial by fire of sins so dark that I began to accept that this cleansing could kill me.

In this quasi-suicidal slide into the seamiest sexual underworld, I came out … alive. Not exactly cleansed as I had hoped. I found there was no bottom. I was always able to go lower and lower until finally, even with my self-hatred, I couldn't take it anymore. I came up for air only to realize I had submerged myself in sexual mistakes too numerous to count—until I did: forty-three in the span of a few months. Realizing the futility of my actions, clarity finally emerged from the dark, ecstatic waters as I gulped for air. The first moment I realized this was in the filthy restroom of an orgy darkroom. There, staring at my emaciated face in front of a mirror, I yelled to myself, "I give!" It was an impulsive and uncontrollable scream.

I admitted for the first time that I had blocked out but never forgotten my brother's friend Gary. At first glance in that dirty mirror: staring at my face reflecting months of abuse and poor nutrition I remembered him. At that moment I felt so dirty, my mind went back to when I was just a bullied little kid. One day after school, I was surrounded by four kids while another kid pushed me to the ground and kicked dirt on my face and in my hair. The boys started to close in when Gary drove by honking his horn. He walked outside his car with a baseball bat, and rescued me. Then I had thought of Gary as my hero. Remembering, the word *hero* is when I screamed, "I give!" to the mirror; because I also remembered when, out of gratitude, or what I had thought was loyalty, or maybe even love, I followed his orders to do things to him sexually I could not handle or understand. I did these things for a while, even in my home. Then, he had abruptly left, and I felt rejected and broken. I had always blamed myself up until then; but now, in that bathroom, for the first time, I had enough self-compassion to recognize I wasn't to blame. After admitting it to myself, it felt like a huge burden of guilt were suddenly lifted. But it left a gigantic hole inside of me. The blame lifted but not the self-hatred that had grown around it. I never felt so alone. I had no friends who would listen. I had no family I could tell—I felt way too ashamed.

The only one who would listen was my mentor and theater professor, Mr. Arthur Nathan. Unlike many aloof faculty, he didn't like to be called doctor or professor, especially with his visceral teaching style. In our classes, because he used dramatic acting and such strong language, I knew he was not easily offended.

I clearly remember Mr. Nathan demanding from a dumbstruck playwriting class: "What was Stanley thinking about during the confrontation with Blanche in *A Streetcar Named*

Desire?" When no one said a word, he abruptly blurted out with rage, "I am going to *fuck you,* and then you will know who's *in charge* of this house!" Then he quietly added, "That's what Stanley's thinking. Or do you have other ideas?" No one did.

Still, I felt stupid when I finally dared to admit the abuse and how I had permitted it. I needed to extract the memory like a tumor from my body. Thank God Mr. Nathan, my father confessor, told me: "Resign yourself to the fact that this Gary play of yours isn't going away. You can't burn the book, you can't censor the parts you don't like, and you can't ban the play."

"I can't?" I asked.

"How you dealt with it and how you remember it is part of your integrity."

I had loved, even worshipped, Gary. This love, which was now repulsive to me, stuck in my brain like a glass shard. I couldn't get over the obstinate self-accusation that I had wanted him to sexually use me. At the same time, whenever I felt hatred or anger toward Gary, I felt shame: He had loved me—he told me so. He cried once on my shoulder. Yet he left me a broken boy with a poisoned feeling in my heart.

I also felt guilty because my parents banned him from the house. I felt doubly guilty because, at first, I hated my parents for what they did. I didn't realize it at the time, but they were protecting me. I hated myself from so many angles, it was overwhelming. The blame rested only on me, I was sure.

But Mr. Nathan helped me to understand that I was just an innocent kid. I couldn't possibly realize what was going on or what I was doing. I burst out crying at the thought that I had once been an innocent child. It was a sobering realization: There was still some innocence within me, something worth salvaging. From this innocent kid within me, I learned I had to have real compassion for myself. I needed to pick myself off the floor and do something else, but I didn't know what.

Cleaned up and cured of venereal diseases, I decided I would never have sex again. I just wanted to be comfortable as a gay man. In order to protect myself from—well, myself—I had to keep on the straight and narrow. I would dedicate myself to public service. And through this asceticism, I could regain some self-respect. I just didn't know how to start.

So I returned to the one person who knew everything I had done and hadn't rejected me: Mr. Nathan. I knocked on the door to his office, but he wasn't there. Rather than just leave, I read the notice on the door: the official cast sheet of the Detroit State University production of Shakespeare's *Hamlet*, where I had, surprisingly, survived the auditions:

Cast Announcement for *Hamlet*,
Theater 831, Winter Term 1982,
Director Dwight Griss
Set Design Casper Tyres
Lighting Eula Meyer

Hamlet Benjamin Geln
Claudius Alexander Morgan
Gertrude Barbara Jackson
Ophelia Leslie Henderson
Laertes Simon Garvey
Horatio James Goldberg
...

I was both relieved and a little horrified to see that after my confession, Mr. Nathan had still cast me in the role of Horatio—not because I didn't trust him, but from my own overwhelming self-revulsion. It wasn't just the business with Gary, but I had also confessed I'd hidden from myself that I had been raped when I was fifteen. I say *raped*, but I don't think it was clear to the perpetrator what exactly he was doing. Later, a doctor told me, quite unsympathetically, I was raped. I had met a male prostitute who must have thought it was a favor to me. I didn't put up much of a struggle. Not even Gary had prepared me for that. I was left alone afterward to figure out whatever had happened, and I didn't do a good job of it. I still had these confusing love-hate feelings for Gary, an even stranger empathy for the male prostitute, and utter bewilderment for what it meant to be raped.

At least it was all out in the open now. I had been so ashamed that I had buried these things deeply inside, pretending to forget, pretending they had never happened, only to end up re-creating that abuse over and over with anonymous sex partners. I had lost family, friends, and lovers along the way—and I was only twenty-one years old.

I was about to knock on Mr. Nathan's door again when I heard from behind me, "He isn't in."

I turned to face the string of dark oily curls that circled Dwight's pudgy face. He was the director of *Hamlet*. I stiffened when he looked at me with a disturbing leer he seemed to save just for me.

"Hi, Dwight."

"Hey, boy. Thanks to me, we're working together."

He wanted me to feel indebted to him for winning the part. He didn't know I already knew that Mr. Nathan had actually drawn up the cast.

"Thank you, Dwight. I appreciate you giving me the chance," I lied. "Now, I need to—"

"No thanks needed; the best actors got the parts. Though you get a little special consideration, if you know what I mean … You ready?"

"Right now?" I asked a little too sharply.

"Calm down. Just learn your lines, and you'll have nothing to worry about, kiddo. I can help you—you know—in my room."

"I know my lines. It's just, saying them in the large theater is intimidating … stage fright."

"That's what I'm talkin' about. Don't worry about it; we can start small. First in my dorm room—don't look at me that way. It's just a recital. And then, you know, we'll do it in steps. Our readings start in the studio hall."

"What studio hall?"

"You know, the small theater where you helped Casper out on *Long Day's Journey*."

A flash of shame heated my face. That overwhelming feeling started coming back. Once, I had thought love could be innocent. Casper was the reason why: He had been love at first sight. I was still closeted when I had fallen for him—this blond-haired, blue-eyed Adonis. He had a little twitch in his left eye that made him even more adorable. After many false starts, I summoned up the courage to volunteer to help Casper on the set of *Long Day's Journey into Night*. I was thinking of love.

But not Casper. He had other ideas and more or less intimidated me into sucking him off. Somehow most of the school knew about it, though Casper swore he had never told anyone. Dwight's reminder was not without its hidden agenda.

"I remember that job—"

"I bet you do."

"I mean, it was my first job—for the Theater Department."

"And I heard you were like a pro—"

"Don't say that!" I snapped a little too impulsively.

"Touchy. I just heard you did a great job. Why do you think you got the part? Come on, I'll show you. If you're too scared to come to my room, then let's go to the small theater and I'll ease you into the early rehearsals. The rest will be easy."

"Really? Dwight, you'd do that for me?" I felt compelled to be nice even though I saw warning lights flashing in my head.

"Of course. It's my job. I'm your director. Come on, let's work on it."

I followed him reticently to the small theater. Inside, it was dark. Everything within me was telling me not to do this, but a part of me felt I had to. Every step down the stairs seemed toward a judge's sentence on what an unlovable whore I was. I wasn't naive anymore; I knew what would happen. In the past, ignorance had driven me to self-destruction. Now it was something else. I didn't know what, but the feeling pushed me to keep following Dwight.

"Get on the stage, Jamie. I'll turn on a spot."

I tripped on the small half step to the raised platform of a stage and fell on my side. "Oomph!" I squealed.

"Bravo," Dwight deadpanned. He walked straight back into the tech room.

I decided to try and impress him with Hamlet's famous soliloquy in hopes that it would make this a professional encounter. I scurried to get up and placed myself where I thought the spotlight would be.

I waited. Dwight started moving things around in the tech room; it seemed to be taking a while.

"Do you need any help?" I asked impatiently.

"Finally. I thought you would never ask. Come back here a moment!"

A sense of dread immediately came over me. I felt a desire to run, matched only by my desire to mollify Dwight. I walked back to where he stood in the dark, in the back of the booth. I started to shake.

"Come on," he urged. "I need your help."

"No!" I involuntarily screamed. Then I fell silent.

This was the exact spot where Casper had me suck him off. Suck and run, to be precise. It had ended up destroying any hope of a relationship with him.

"Sorry?" Dwight asked. "What did you say?"

"Nothing." I had just forsworn from doing anything like that anymore—particularly never again with someone so repulsive as Dwight. Despite that, I could sense the creeping self-destructive urge to humiliate myself. I realized I was in the exact situation that I never wanted to be in again.

I looked at Dwight. "Sorry. I never wanted to come back here again."

"But you're here now … It's a good thing. No one's going to bite you. Jesus."

Even in the dark, I could see his erect cock in his pants. "Dwight, come on. We can't do this."

"Whaddya mean? Come on. It's safer here than where we used to do it."

"Used to—what are you talking about?"

"Oh, come on. You're gonna tell me you don't remember?"

"As a matter of fact, I don't. I know we never ever did anything—did we?" My newfound moral outrage quickly gave way to uncertainty. I had traveled such a long path of sexual self-destruction, a path taken in so many varying degrees of consciousness, that it was possible: We might have gotten together before.

"Don't get all high and mighty with me."

"Palmer Park?" I asked weakly.

Dwight nodded.

"Whatever might have happened, I am not like that anymore, Dwight."

"What, you no longer dig men?"

"Not that. I don't do … I mean, whatever we did—"

"Oh, come on, faggot! Who are you kidding?"

"I don't want that kind of thing anymore." With a grisly flashback, I recalled a creepy guy going after me in Palmer Park, a scene of my more drunken sexual debauchery. I suppressed the desire to say in disgust, "Don't tell me that was you." My heart sank.

In a panic, I began to do the calculations in my head: This was a sticky situation—and potentially literally so. Dwight unzipped his fly. He could make life miserable for me. But why had I come here? I tried to assess what the right response was. That was when I realized how far I had already progressed. I was not automatically submitting to my sense of low self-esteem. I seemed to be submitting to something else.

"Come on, do me," he commanded, pulling out his cock. "Don't get all snooty with me. You're the biggest slut in the department."

What he said triggered a deep humiliation. It flicked the switch. I felt the torrent of bitter self-hatred. A self-hatred I had hoped was long gone. I looked at the revolting sight of Dwight with his cock protruding from his pants. It made me nauseated to think of what I'd done. Then a vague memory of Gary and an incident with a male prostitute came back to me. Self-care started to clash with self-hatred. Given the tumult in my mind, I could barely think through the cacophony of emotions.

Dwight made it easier by grabbing my shoulders and forcing me to the floor. I felt my knees bending in compliance. Soon I was kneeling on the same floor where I had been with Casper, but instead of being with the love of my life, I was with this ugly guy. His cock stuck out right in my face.

"Well, what are you waiting for?"

My mouth widened, and I leaned forward, putting the semi-hard cock between my lips. I felt something moist at the tip of his penis that tasted musty on my tongue. I jerked back at once and scraped him a little with my teeth.

"Ow! What are you doing?"

I stood up. "I can't. I … sorry." I started backing out. "I gotta go, Dwight."

"What's the matter? You're suddenly getting so high and mighty with me."

"This never happened. I just … can't do this kind of thing anymore," I said as I started backing out of the tech room. "I gotta run. But don't worry, I won't tell anyone about this. Might look bad on your résumé. Bye."

"You son of a bitch!" he hissed.

Out of the tech room, I turned and stumbled from the dark theater and finally out the door. That was when I felt it: a reluctant twinge of a smile and something I dared to call the beginnings of pride. I even laughed, remembering my "Might look bad" comment.

I started to run. I ran so hard I eventually had to stop to catch my breath. My lungs heaving, I thought, *I need to figure this out before it kills me.*

Chapter 2: The Detritus of Things Past

Nightmares aren't really nightmares when they actually happen. Yet regrets or even bad memories don't fully describe the haunting thoughts that were lodged in my brain. In one of those memories, I did a face-plant in the middle of the street while running away from a psychotic homophobic killer. Well, at least that was who I thought he was. He had caught me in bed with his housemate, Bud.

To keep it short, Bud had picked me up from a bar and taken me away from another date who had assaulted me in the bar's men's room. Luckily, the night was a blur so I can't go into details. The only thing I remember is my date trying to rob me in a toilet stall. I bent over to give him my wallet from inside the pocket of my pants, which were on the floor. Just as I bent over, someone opened the bathroom door, which hit me on the head. The guy who opened the door was the bartender.

I guess this won't be short. I could hear he had a baseball bat by the way he struck the bathroom stall with it. He then proceeded to throw my date out on the street. What happened next was an even bigger blur, as the next thing I knew, I found myself in Bud's dilapidated house on Detroit's east side, a place I rarely ventured. I ended up in bed with him, and he was extremely needy and cuddly. But with the combination of the head injury, too much to drink—and I guess I left out the mysterious pills my date had given me to swallow—and the awkward position I was in on Bud's single bed, I just couldn't really sexually perform as I had been accustomed. Adding further to my confusion was the fact that Bud was apparently a male prostitute and asked me for money I did not have. It wasn't such a surprise, at this stage in the game, to end up in a prostitute's house. But I was broke from buying my long-lost date's Long Island iced teas.

I explained my almost complete lack of funds as I emptied my pockets. As if I was watching television, I watched him pocket the few dollars I had. I could not help but wonder how I was getting home from wherever Bud lived. Overcome with guilt, I decided to do what I thought was the right thing.

"I gotta go home," I said, panicked, trying desperately to put on my pants, which were hopelessly entangled.

"Just stay awhile, man." At this point, I tripped over my pants and fell on the floor. "You're crying."

"Huh?" I then felt the tears running down my cheeks. I looked at Bud, forced a smile, and burst out bawling.

"Don't cry, man."

"I'm not crying—I mean, I am. But not because of you. You're beautiful. I can't help you, but I should, somehow," I babbled.

Bud turned beet red and bent over me. I raised my hand and caressed his cheek. He had also teared up, which I found incredibly moving. "Are you okay?"

"Yes, of course. Why are you asking?" Bud whispered. "I'm hoping you're okay." He added sadly, "You don't like me."

"Yes, I do. You are a special person. Look me in the eyes, Bud. I am not better than you are. I don't think that for a second. If you only knew what a shit I am. I wouldn't be alive if it wasn't for you. I am very lucky you came to me. Look, I know this isn't about money, but if I had more than three bucks, I would give it to you, easily."

"You gave me sixty."

"I did?" I mulled over how to ask for cab fare. "Well, you're worth it. Thank you for tonight. I'm just sorry I am me—I mean, I'm sorry I'm the way I am. At the moment, I'm not feeling okay." I realized there was no way to communicate how I felt or why.

"Right." He stared at me.

"Did I really give you sixty dollars?"

"Yes."

Not knowing what else to do, feeling horrible, and knowing no words could put this aright, I pulled him to the floor and kissed him. His lips were surprisingly supple. My tongue felt like it had to possess his mouth, and we tightly embraced. I stretched my tongue into his mouth and caressed his teeth. I hoped this would make him feel better, as I was confident this would not cost me more money. He knew he had taken everything I had—even cab fare, apparently.

When I judged the meter was up, I clumsily arose and got dressed in the dark. I was about to leave when an untimely sense of obligation came over me. I said, "Goodbye, Bud. You deserve love." I kissed him again—this time a peck.

He looked at me very tenderly. "You're the nicest person. Take care. I think Jesus brought you to me tonight."

"He did?" I wanted to say, *No, you have been my savior.* What had I done that was worthy of such impossible gratitude? Me, the lowliest sinner, evil itself, and Jewish to boot—yet apparently, I had done something right.

"Oh my God, Bud. Look, I gotta go. You are really lovable. You're not damaged goods like I am." I didn't know what else to say, so I blurted out, "Jesus loves you."

Just then, we were interrupted by the sound of a slammed door and someone shouting obscenities. Bud jumped in horror. He grabbed me and put his hand over my mouth.

"Oh shh! He owns this place," Bud whispered, keeping a painful muzzle on my mouth. "Don't make a sound. He said he wasn't coming home. He's violent; he just got out of jail. If he hears you in here, he'll go berserk."

Fear aside, I didn't know how to tell him this painful grip on my face was totally unnecessary. Outside the room, the movements were heavy and boisterous. Inside, my jaw locked as Bud dug his fingernails into my cheeks. I was terrified. I wanted to break free and make a run for it.

Bud must have sensed it because he grabbed my arm with his other hand. "Don't move, man."

Rashly, I broke free of Bud and shot out of the room. I headed downstairs and ran like a maniac.

Once outside and assuming someone was in hot pursuit, I tripped in front of a moving car that came to a screeching halt. My face landed right into the rough street pavement. I looked up terrified. It was a police car. The cops ran out of it.

"Don't move, man!" I was told for the second time in less than an hour. The police had their guns drawn.

Here comes the end, I thought. *Armed police officers are going to kill an unarmed liberal Jew fag. Goodbye, world!*

"What are you up to, kid?" one of them demanded. Then the other one took a closer look at me, a bloodied, disheveled kid on the pavement. "Hey, Ralph, look at this guy."

They looked at me quizzically. Both lowered their guns.

"Buddy, you okay?" one of the cops asked.

In a moment of grace, they offered to take me home. On the way, I realized I had to be at work. They dropped me off at four in the morning in front of the Bagel Factory for my Sunday morning shift.

◆◆◆◆◆◆◆

Around noon, I got to my dilapidated student apartment and could finally flop down onto my mattress and get to sleep. Unfortunately, my roommate was playing loud R & B, which was usually a sign he had a girl inside. I checked the door, and there was the rubber band on it. That meant I had to wait outside until his sexual activities with the woman of the week were through.

I staggered around in the freezing cold, not daring to walk in. I was disheveled, beat up from earlier that night, exhausted from work. By now, I was wearing a Brooklyn Bagel T-shirt that my boss, Sheldon, had given me because you can't make food wearing a shirt stained with a variety of bodily fluids. I felt hungover from last night's alcohol and drugs. I leaned against the door. It opened and I almost fell in.

"Jamie? What are you doing out here? It's freezing. Get in."

"The rubber band on the door."

"Get in here!"

I settled back on the familiar carpet next to Dave and a naked woman whose name Dave kept forgetting. With a little push from a small feeling of drug-instilled pride, I finally had the guts to confess to my roommate. I had never even told Dave I was gay, let alone all that was going on. But this time, seated with him on the blue shag rug in the living room of our cold student digs, Dave's appropriately deviant Sly and the Family Stone record playing in the background, I went through the entire list of things I had done that night.

One thing that really helped was the cloud of marijuana that hung in the air. The other thing was my constant underestimation of how much Dave liked me. After I gave too many details of that night's sexual nightmare, Dave did not seem to feel in the least self-conscious hugging me. I was so relieved. I had thought if I admitted I was gay that he would throw me out like everyone else had, especially because he was pretty free with the fag jokes.

"So I guess you know that I'm gay now," I said, bracing for the worst.

"The part where you kneeled in front of a guy in the bathroom stall was a bit of a giveaway, it's true."

"Do you want me to leave?"

"Leave? You're kidding me, bro."

"I thought if you found out—"

"We've known for a long time, didn't we, Shelley?"

"Yes, but my name is Sally."

"Sorry, I knew that. I did."

"You knew I was gay?"

"Well, it doesn't matter anymore. Tonight I decided I'm never going to have sex again for the rest of my life," I confessed.

"Just like a priest," Sally said.

Dave chuckled. "They're havin' sex all the time."

Chapter 3: Platonic Ménage à Trois

My roommate was more than just a stoner who had sex and listened to R & B all the time. He was also a brilliant psychology grad student who had this irritating ability to analyze me really well.

Just back from the incident at the theater with Dwight, I came into the house, where Dave was on the shag rug cuddling with—for a change—a fully dressed Sally. Dave once told me, "Good music is good music no matter where it comes from," so it was no surprise he was blaring some classical music I had never heard before. I took a spot on the rug opposite the cuddling pair. We preferred the floor, as we were increasingly suspicious about what was infesting our couch.

"Groovy music," I quipped. "What is it, Mahler?"

"No, this is Bruckner's third."

"New one to me. The recording sounds tinny."

"It's an old, underground recording. He's a great conductor, Sergiu Celibidache, and it's a great performance. Everyone is crazy for Herbert von Karajan, but this was the conductor who should have replaced him."

"Celibi—I've never heard of him." I listened to the mesmerizing violins. "Oh wow!" I exclaimed after the orchestra suddenly exploded and then lulled like a musical roller coaster.

"You can always tell the difference between Mahler and Bruckner," Sally said. "Mahler searches the soul and Bruckner searches the cosmos."

"Far out," Dave said as he pulled Sally closer and their arms further entwined. I felt a twinge of jealousy at their easy intimacy.

"In that case, I should listen to more Mahler." Then, with another orchestral musical eruption, I added, "Sounds like a great performance. How did they make it?"

"Someone smuggled out a rehearsal tape, but that's not what's bothering you," said Sally, turning to Dave: "Sounds like you're needed."

"The doc is in, kiddo. What's up?"

She turned down the music. Since coming out to them, Dave and Sally had both been witness to so many of my sexual misadventures. They seemed like such unlikely confidants: straight African-Americans. Sally was even a Baptist. But they never seemed to judge me, even as Dave was shredding the many masks I had tried to put up to protect myself from discovery.

"Come on, who are you doing this time?"

"Can it possibly be worse than the other juicy stories you've told us?" Sally asked.

I blushed, feeling the heat from my face. "It's pretty icky."

"What's bothering you?"

"I am just a magnet for trouble."

"What happened this time?" Dave asked, lighting up a joint. He passed it to Sally.

"I think I'm doomed," I said evasively.

Sally passed the joint to me, and I took a deep hit. I needed to loosen up to say what I had to say.

"All right—remember Dwight?"

"The director of the play you're in?" Dave asked.

Sally added, "Yeah, the one who has the hots for you?"

"Come on, he never said that," Dave said.

"Oh, I could tell," Sally replied.

"Well, turns out you're right, Sally. He tried to put the moves on me. I wish you could see how oily and ugly this guy is."

"What happened?" she asked. "Come on, tell us the dirt."

"He said he wanted to help me rehearse—first, he said, in his dorm room."

"You didn't," Dave said.

"He did lure me into the tech room."

"And?"

"He pulled out his thing—"

"You're kidding! That's ballsy." Sally replied.

"Well, it turns out I may have done something with him during one of my Palmer Park episodes."

"May have?"

"I don't remember exactly, but I think I got the general idea of what we probably did in the park—I just didn't realize it was him. So, in the tech room, he more or less demanded that I suck him off."

"And what did you do?" Sally asked.

"I knelt down and started to do it—but when I tasted his pre-cum, it was so yucky it almost tasted like an ashtray." At this, Sally guffawed. "So I pulled away and told him I couldn't do it."

"Good for you, Jamie," Dave said.

"I ran out of the theater—and I told him I promised I'd never tell anyone about it because it would be bad for his résumé."

They both laughed, and I suddenly felt better about the whole incident.

"Brilliant," Dave said. "I ain't underestimating you any-more."

"Score one for Jamie," Sally added.

"But that was so gross—I still have the taste in my mouth," I said to elicit sympathy. All I got was more laughter.

"Jamie, we ain't laughing at you. We're proud of you," Sally said.

"You can't play 'Oh woe is me' if you really stuck it to the chump," Dave said. "I'm not worrying about you."

"Me neither. You're just fine, hon."

I didn't know I liked the sound of people not worrying about me. I was so used to my family worrying; I didn't know there was another option.

"What if Dwight tries to start rumors?"

"Chill out, he's not that stupid. And if he does, I can have a talk with him. No one has the right to fuck you over like that."

"You would?"

"Of course I would. Sounds like a real scumbag, but a real coward, too. You just stick up for yourself. You've shown you're no doormat anymore. Don't worry about him. Dwight sounds creepier than shit, man, but you handled it."

"I wish the past would just go away and leave me alone," I said, dizzy from the pot and emotionally exhausted from the confession.

"I hear you. There is no talking that will make this shit go away, Jamie. See it this way: You're still washing it off, but it's getting better. The worst thing you can do is wallow in regret."

"Regret? Ha! How many more Dwights am I going to meet? My past keeps catching up with me. How can I have a past? I'm only twenty."

"Twenty-one," Sally corrected and passed me the joint.

"Twenty-one. If it wasn't for this joint, I would be freaking out."

"Well, then take another hit. You *are* freaking out."

We fell silent again, letting the high seep into our brains.

"Then you think the dingus is worth a million? That's a lot of dough. *A lot of dough.* The minimum? What's the maximum? *You'd think me crazy. There's no telling how high it could go, sir, and that's the one and only—*"

"Jamie!"

"Huh?"

"You're acting out *The Maltese Falcon* again."

"I'm too high—Dammit! I was doing so well. I stopped these terrible binges, and then this Gary thing happens. He's the director. I have to see Gary every day. Fuck me!"

"Jamie, stop it. You mean Dwight, not Gary."

"Huh? I said Gary?"

"Jamie, don't go there."

"Sally's right. Dwight we can handle. That's what's here right now. Everything else is over."

"Wow, reality is now. Now ... that's the one and only truth," I said as the movie script drifted back into my head to avoid thinking. "Why did I let him get away with all that? What did I do to him? Why?"

"Are we talking about Gary now or Dwight?" asked Sally.

"Dwight. I don't know why I'm thinking about Gary. Did you know, for the longest time, I thought I loved him, but I let him ..."

Dave looked deadpan at me. "Jamie, you were a lonely kid, too young to know what you were doing. And an older kid took advantage of it. The guy belongs in jail, but you'd be better off just remembering the love part. You were innocent, and you were kind beyond your age."

"I was? Shit. Okay, you're right. All I know is I am screwed, royally screwed. Dwight ... You're both right. I've just got to let it all go. Okay. What do I do about him?"

"Dwight may be a predator, but you showed him you're no prey. Unless he's really stupid, he's going to be very chill onstage. My guess is he'll bend over backward to be nice to you. Relax. Come here."

I scooted over to Dave and faced him. He put his hands on my shoulders. "Learn your lines. If you just take care of business, no one is gonna say anything. You can't control what other people say or think. Just do your own thing. You've got friends on your side. No one's gonna mess with you. You're a cool guy and you're lovable."

"Huh?" Dave never ceased to amaze me.

"Yeah, maybe it's strange coming from a straight guy, but you are lovable, man."

"Really?" I didn't find Dave attractive, but I felt a strange affection overcome me.

"Of course. Here's something for free." Dave held my head and kissed me on the forehead, then let go. "There, that's proof."

"After everything I've done."

"After everything," said Sally, who then did the same. "You gotta get over that, man. It ain't what people think or say. It's what's in you, in your heart. And we're both telling you that you're okay." She caressed my arm. I began to feel overwhelmed with affection.

"I will be okay as long as no one kills me."

That was the strange thought I remember saying before I passed out in a three-way cuddle on the rug, a kind of platonic *ménage à trois*.

Chapter 4: Common Cause

I interpreted Dave and Sally's advice by deciding that instead of loving individuals, I would love causes. Martyring myself to a cause sounded more attractive than martyring myself to Dwight.

I went back to my mother's roots and decided to volunteer for community service. I wanted something to do with civil rights. By 1981, with the Reagan revolution in full swing, the civil rights movement was about as hopeless as my love life. So it seemed to need me the most, or at least it seemed the most familiar route forward.

But which civil rights community would I help? The LGBT community was invisible. There was no gay anything except dark, loud, and seedy bars. The hunt seemed impossible; there wasn't so much as a scent to go on. I don't know how much time I wasted until I finally gave up and looked under *G* in the telephone book. To my surprise, there it was: the Gay-Lesbian Hotline.

I wanted to call the number immediately. But Dave was home and I needed some privacy, so I waited until he left for dinner with Sally. After they left, I realized I needed to study my lines for the start of rehearsals. I picked up the script and looked at the cover: *Hamlet.* The irony of performing in this play during my present circumstances was suddenly painfully clear.

Do something! Call now, I encouraged myself.

I sat myself at the kitchen table. The phone was on the wall next to me. I decided I should have a nice cup of tea to go with this life-changing talk. All I could find was Dave's revolting herbal tea. I fished out a relatively clean cup from the sink, ran the hot water tap as hot as it would go, filled the cup with water, and dunked the tea bag. I put the cup with the putrid-smelling tea on the kitchen table and resolutely dialed the number.

"Hello, Lesbian-Gay Hotline. May I help you?" an effeminate voice asked.

Panic-stricken, I slammed down the phone. *Why the stereotype voice?* I wondered.

I dialed again.

"Hello, Lesbian-Gay Hotline. May I help you?" It was another voice that seemed even more effeminate than before, even lurid. I hung up immediately, then dialed again, hoping to get someone else.

"Hello, Lesbian-Gay Hotline—don't hang up," implored a rapid-firing acerbic, effeminate voice.

Are they all faggy? I thought and slammed down the phone. But then I felt stupid. I decided to wait a few minutes before dialing again. It's not that I disliked effeminate people. In fact, I found them very attractive. At that moment, I just disliked the stereotype. I dialed again.

"Hello, Lesbian-Gay Hotline. May I help you?"

"Well, you sound more kind than the last person I spoke with," I said, relieved.

"That's not possible. I am the only one manning the phones today. How can I help you? I understand it's nerve-racking to call the first time."

My fantasy of a Jerry Lewis telethon-style phone bank was destroyed.

"How are you feeling tonight?" he asked. I sensed he was being prompted.

"I thought you were alone."

"No, we always have at least one call-taker and one mentor."

"Oh."

"Please, you're calling for a reason, and that's why I'm here. May I help you?"

"I don't know if you can."

"What's on your mind?"

Having a rational gay person on the phone, there were so many things I wanted to talk about. At the same time, I couldn't think of anything to say.

"Are you still there?"

"I am … I'm just trying to figure out what to say."

"Just say whatever's on your mind. You must be feeling overwhelmed. I would—put the what? Put my hand over the transmitter? Oh now, wait a sec … how about this? Take a deep breath." He took an audibly deep breath. I copied him. He then exhaled and I followed suit. "Now just say what's on your mind."

"I hate myself."

I was horrified when it came out of my mouth. I slammed down the phone. I couldn't imagine why that had shot out. A few minutes later, I called back. But of course, the same person answered. I tried again an hour after that.

"Hello, Lesbian-Gay Hotline. May I help you?"

"Sorry, it's me again. I just thought I had come far enough not to say that ever again. I need to break out of this."

"Thank you for calling back, but what are you talking about?"

That was when I realized there was a woman on the phone and I was talking to someone else. "Oh, I'm sorry. I just meant, I'm scared. Alone."

"Sounds like you are feeling lonely."

"I have never felt so lonely in my life," I confessed.

"It must be awful feeling so isolated."

"It's frightening. I think I'm going to die. But what's worse is I think I'm going to die but no one cares." I surprised myself, unsure where I was going with this.

"You do? Why is that?" she asked.

"I think I have GRIDS," I said as if my mouth had a mind of its own.

"Really?" she asked, a bit surprised, her voice changing modes. "Do you have any symptoms—you know, out of the ordinary?"

"I think I have them all. I do. I have flu-like symptoms," I lied.

"Maybe you have the flu?"

"Well, I don't. I have strep throat, actually—had it."

"Oh. So maybe you're just feeling down from being sick?"

"I don't know. I fit the profile for GRIDS, anyway. I mean, not the bit about being in San Francisco or New York, but I just had sex with about forty-one people." My voice trailed off as the person on the other end gasped. "I probably shouldn't have said that. But actually, forty-three, depending on how you're counting. I mean, not all at once, but in bars and stuff. After a while, it adds up."

"I see. That's not so strange these days. So you know about gay bars."

"I really want some alternatives to the bars so I can be saved—safe."

"You know what GRID stands for?"

"Gay-related diseases?"

"No. It's gay-related immunodeficiency disease. That would cause some abnormal infections or symptoms."

"Oh."

"So first, let me ask you a few questions. Are you having any symptoms of GRID, aside from flu-like symptoms, like shortness of breath?"

"No."

"Unusual fatigue?"

"Nope."

"Dizziness?"

"Not more than usual—that's a joke."

"Lesions on your skin? Dark spots?"

"No."

"What other symptoms do you think you might have?"

"Guilt."

"I see."

"Herpes."

"I see. Been checked for VD?"

"How do you think I found out about the herpes and the ... other stuff? Never mind. I don't know where we're going with this line of questioning."

"We're not doctors, but I am not hearing any specific GRID symptoms. We just know so little about it; it could develop later. It still would be wise to play safely. If you're really concerned, I can give you some referrals."

"I've already been to the Lik Clinic."

"That's the best. They didn't find anything?"

"Well, not that."

"Then you shouldn't worry."

"You're not Jewish, then—sorry, that was a joke, too. My family has trained me for one single purpose: to worry. But I get it. Like playing safe with a condom," I said, recalling the clinic doctor's advice—not my behavior.

"And don't exchange body fluids."

"I guess that's why I really called. I don't want to exchange bodily fluids anymore. I just want to forget sex and do something else."

"It sounds like you're tired of just meeting people for sex."

"I want to find something I can do."

"What do you mean by 'something'? Some kind of activity?"

"Not hopscotch or croquet—okay, not funny either. I don't need to meet gay people at all, actually. But I am gay, and I want to do something ... well, gay. I want to do something gay without involving body fluids."

"Sounds like you're looking for some kind of volunteer work?."

"I really need some gay organizations to volunteer for. Something that isn't about sex, just about serving the community. I'm looking to meet other gay people … the ordinary gay people," I explained.

"I beg your pardon?"

"I have been in some … bad relationships at bars and parks—bad experiences. I want to meet gay people outside of sex; I don't want any more bad experiences. Does that make sense?"

"Yes, it absolutely makes sense."

"Good." I heaved a sigh of relief. "There must be some … organization?"

"Well, I like to think we do a lot to help people here at the hotline. We need volunteers."

"I don't think I'm ready for that. Is there a civil rights organization for gays?"

"It's great to get a caller who's looking to be involved in the community."

"Exactly, so I am actually doing something right for change. Great. Can you just tell me if there is an organization like that?"

"Right off the top of my head, there's the Detroit Organization for Human Rights."

"What! That's a gay rights group?" I was surprised. I had heard that name before.

"Yes, it is."

"No, I don't think so."

"It's the main local one aside from the Michigan Organization for Human Rights, which is in Lansing. I assume you're local to Detroit?"

"I am. But that can't be because my mother spoke to that organization—and she doesn't accept me. Are you sure it is specifically for *gay* rights?"

"That would be gays and lesbians—and bisexuals—and transsexuals. Maybe your mom is more accepting than you realize."

"That can't be." Anger welled up in my voice. "That doesn't make any sense. Do you know my mother? Never mind. Sorry. This is a gay community group, you're sure?"

"I promise. Interested?"

"They do public activities like demonstrate, support candidates—"

"Never knew. How do I join?"

"They meet on Thursday nights at the Pontiac Hotel. I can give you the organization's number. It's an answering machine, but someone will get back to you—usually it takes a while, maybe a week or so. When you call, leave a message for their membership chair, Ken. Do you want the number?"

"Sure." I felt thrilled, if a little squeamish. I had a possible new gay organization I could join—one that had nothing to do with bars, parks, or sex.

I got the organization's number. I couldn't believe my luck. At last, I could be gay without doing anything gay. My penance for my earlier debauchery was finally in sight. I already began to feel better: I could dedicate myself to helping my community, my people.

Chapter 5: The Birthday Party

It was my birthday and there was no cake. No cake, no friends, no family.

When I was a child, my birthday was the day I spent a whole year looking forward to. It meant nothing now. This made the loneliness in my bedroom even more oppressive and accusatory. It seemed all I had was my cleansing ritual. There I was, a belt in my trembling hand. Self-incriminations erased the fleeting feelings that I was getting better. Friends and family had rejected me when I had come out of the closet. Now I had rejected the gay bars that had offered me self-destructive sexuality instead of a gay friendship. So I was alone on my birthday evening with a belt in my hand.

Evenings were when I missed my family the most. And on that birthday in 1982, it hurt more than usual.

When I had lived at home, we used to talk almost every night. My parents would watch the news or documentaries almost nonstop. During that time, our voices would compete with Lou Gordon's, Walter Cronkite's, or Dick Cavett's as we discussed what was happening around the world. They were the most precious moments of being at home. I reliably had my parents' attention.

But now they were gone. And why were they gone? Because I had told them I was gay. It still made me feel very ashamed. I wanted to be proud of myself, yet their rejection shouted shame. No calls or cards on my birthday seemed to reinforce my bad feelings. And that was why there was a belt in my trembling hand.

Dave often wasn't around the apartment at night, and I had no television where Cavett's awkward monologues and comforting interviews of Groucho Marx or Katharine Hepburn could embrace me. I sat in my small room at my desk. The mattress on the floor seemed to beg me to kneel on it and whip myself in punishment for how I had screwed up my life.

Against the wall leading to my desk was a stack of milk cartons used as bookshelves. Whenever I felt these urges, I would usually grab a three-hour Wagner opera from the lower crates of records or a tome by Nietzsche to kill the time and let the impulses to hurt myself pass. My desk was a terrible mess—another thing I needed to be punished for. Belt still in hand, I slipped one of my closeted heavy metal albums on the stereo, this one by Quiet Riot, to deafen the noise I might make. This hellish, sexy music could urge me on to my primal need for absolution. I loosened my pants and let them fall to the floor.

Cum on, feel the noize.

I breathed deeply and raised my hand when I suddenly heard people outside, laughing hysterically. I was sure they could see my shadow against the curtains or that they had maybe even peeked through them somehow to see what I was doing.

Panicked, I shut off the stereo. In the silence, I had to find something to occupy myself—and quickly. Alone, the bad thoughts kept creeping in. During those moments, I felt very lonely. But I was determined not to go out. I knew that would only end in self-destructive sex.

I dropped my belt on the floor, pulled up my jeans, and walked into the cold living room. From a side table next to our dingy couch, I picked up the red rotary phone and took it, along with its long cord, into my room. I shut the door. I realized I was freezing cold and pulled on a bulky red sweater.

Since my parents kicked me out of the house, they didn't even know where I was. It was possible they were trying to contact me for my birthday. My fingers shook as I dialed my former home. I hesitated before I dialed the last number. A strong odor wafted from my armpits. I was dreading a new parental verbal assault. My urge just to hear their voices—to hear them tell me they still loved me—overrode my misgivings. I would talk to them in the spirit of love and forgiveness and win them over. I stiffened myself and dialed the last number.

"Hello, you have reached the home of—" droned the mechanical Midwestern voice.

"Ruth and Irving Goldberg," my mother's voice interrupted.

"When you hear the tone, say your name and leave a message. You have thirty seconds," finished the voice. Then came the beep.

I waited in silence until another tone sounded in what must have been thirty seconds later. I dropped the handset back on its cradle in defeat.

I sat. The room was now dark. I had no idea how much time passed before I found myself again holding the phone handset. The phone was beeping like haywire because I hadn't dialed a number. I hung up the phone and picked it up again to get a dial tone.

"I love you," I practiced. My fingers dug into the dial phone like it was going to slide away, and I drew my hand into the dialing motion as if the strength of my effort and the depth of my need would call my parents, would call them to the phone. The recording came on again. I waited for the cue.

"You have thirty seconds."

"Hi, Mom; hi, Dad. It's me, James." I used James, a more masculine-sounding name, as a branch of peace. "I was wondering how you are doing. I'm doing okay. I just want you to know … well, I just wanted to let you know that … I forgive you. I forgive you for throwing my stuff out, I forgive you for all the misery and pain you have caused me, and you don't even want to know what's happening with me—you won't even say, 'Happy birthday,' goddamn it!"

I slammed down the phone but caught my index finger between the handset and the cradle. I wanted to scream but stopped myself.

Sucking on my hurt finger, I wondered how I could erase the message I had just left. I quickly called back and added a meek, "Ignore that last message—kind of."

I wondered whom else I could talk to. I wondered who could possibly say, "I love you," or at least let me feel loved. I wanted to talk to Harold, my older cousin, but he was dead. Harold was the only other person in my entire family who was gay. He had died of a drug overdose when I was eleven. It was still a trauma in the family. Homosexuality remained largely unacknowledged except under hushed contemptuous breaths. No one had told me he was gay; I had figured it out myself. The fact that my Aunt Louise had thrown out a hysterical man dressed in female clothes from Harold's funeral had been a key piece to the puzzle. But at eleven years old, it had not registered. Only when I was struggling with coming out had the piece fallen into place. I hadn't known Harold so well, but with hindsight, I missed him. Harold could have been the confidant I needed on this twenty-second-birthday crisis.

Then there was my cousin, Rhonda; she had recently moved to Georgia. We had been good friends in childhood. Her father, my Uncle Max, had been in ill health and moved the family to warmer climes where, upon relocating, he had promptly died, leaving my Aunt Sylvia and Rhonda stranded in the Deep South. I hadn't spoken to her since last year when she had helped me find an analyst. That psychiatrist, Dr. Wire, had helped me come out of the closet, though Rhonda didn't know that. With some trepidation, I dialed her phone number.

"Hullo?" a distracted, familiar voice intoned.

"Rhonda?"

"Who the fuck?" She was annoyed.

"It's me ... Jamie."

"Jamie?"

"Jamie Goldberg, your cousin."

"Jamie! Oh my God, who died?"

"No one."

"Is your father okay?"

"Yes ... Well, I guess he is."

"What's wrong?"

"Nothing—well, something. I just wanted to talk." I wasn't sure whether this was still a good idea.

"Do you know what time it is?"

"I'm sorry, I didn't mean to wake you."

"Do you know what time it is?" she repeated.

"Sorry." I wanted to hang up.

"Well, you didn't wake me."

"Look, if I did wake you—"

"You didn't wake me up! But your timing is rotten. Please, just stop apologizing. Wait a sec. Brian—I mean Bill. It's my shithead cousin. I need to take this. Okay, Jamie boy, what is it? Is everything all right?"

"If this isn't the right time—"

"Thin ice, kiddo! You have my undivided attention now. Bill, just go in the other room for a sec—put on some pants, my mom might be up still … yeah, I know; it's my cousin, shithead. The coast is clear. Is everything all right?"

"Kind of all right." I wanted to say, *"Never mind."*

"What's up? And make it snappy."

"I'll call you another time—"

"Jamie, if you don't tell me what's up, I am going to fly back home and wring your motherfucking neck, so help me."

"I don't know where or how to begin this."

"What's the matter? You get someone pregnant?"

"No. Nothing like that."

"Hold on … Bill, I said one second. Cool off … wait a sec, Jamie …" She put the phone down.

I had sunk from my chair down to the cold floor, leaning uncomfortably against a milk crate filled with records. My ear felt sweaty. I realized I was clutching the phone too tightly. I eased up on the pressure.

"Okay, shithead, make it fast."

"I don't know where to begin. I just, well, you know how unhappy I've been?"

"Fine, don't make it fast," she moaned. "And?"

"You know I'm a loner and—"

"You're a weirdo; tell me something I don't know."

"I think I know why people don't understand me, why I am so … so … I'm a … what I am trying to say, Rhonda, is that I'm gay."

There was silence on the other line.

"Are you okay with that?"

"You're shittin' me. You gotta be fucking killin' shittin' me!" She was laughing.

"I am?"

"You're really gay?" she asked incredulously. "Mom!" she shouted.

What the hell is she calling my aunt for?

"Chrissakes, don't wake her up!" I heard a man's voice yell. "At least, not here!"

"Imagine that. She knew you were queerer than a three-dollar bill. Mom always knew that. Why didn't I put two and two together?"

"Is it that obvious?" I asked.

"What is it?" I heard my aunt's voice through the earpiece.

"Great!" the male voice said.

"Oh hi, Brian!" I heard my aunt say.

"Ma, his name is Bill."

"Oh yes. Brian was the nice one."

"Ma!"

"Okay! Okay, take it easy; it's not a secret or something."

"Ma!"

"Hello?" my aunt said into the phone.

"Hello? ... Hi, Aunt Sylvia."

"Who is this? You're keeping me from my program."

"Jamie."

"Jamie! I haven't heard from you in years."

Why am I talking to this woman?

"How is Irv doing?"

"My dad is fine ... I think. I haven't spoken to him for a while."

"That's great, dear," mumbled my aunt, who clearly was not paying attention. "Thanks for calling. Tell your father—oh, wait a second," she had started talking to Rhonda, "I am supposed to ... ask you—what? Gay? Oh, I knew that, Rhonda." Then she spoke into the phone. "You're gay, aren't you?" Then talking to Rhonda, "I told you, see. He says so—don't you, dear?"

"Sure." I felt lost.

"I'll ask ... starting when, dear?"

"Starting when, what?" This felt awkward having to admit how much later I had known than she had.

"Starting when were you gay?"

"I don't know. Some months ago."

"Oh, so it's recent for you."

Her surprise wisdom continued to be both unexpected and unappreciated. "How did you know, Aunt Syl?"

"Oh dear. Well, to be honest, I remember the time you came over when you were eleven and you went on and on about men's underwear—"

I felt a rush of embarrassment.

"Just a little boy and just obsessed with men's underwear, know what I mean?"

"I did?" Shame flashed through my body.

"Absolutely obsessed by it. You showed me a catalog of all these men in underwear. I told Max, 'I think that kid's a *faygeleh*.' I did. I really said that, Rhonda; yes, I did. You were just about drooling on that catalog of men's underwear. You know what I mean? You said, 'It's *so* interesting—'"

"All right—"

"'It's *soo* interesting!'" She let out a laugh. I was wishing I knew how to get her to stop talking. "I remember you saying, 'It's *soo* interesting.'"

"Okay," I said.

"After that, I mean, really, how could you not know, know what I mean?" She giggled again. "'It's *soo* interesting.'"

"I get it. Say, how are you doing?"

"I knew you weren't ready. I figured when it was time, you'd tell us, you know. I mean … I told your father and he just ignored it."

"My dad knew?" I switched from shame to anger.

"Of course he did … well, look, dear, I may have joked about it, you know what I mean? I didn't want him to be all upset. I knew it would be difficult. You know, he's so stubborn, that father of yours."

I was dizzy from her revelation. I wanted her to stop talking, but I had to know more.

"You knew before I did? Dad knew before I did? My dad—"

"You know your father. He didn't listen. So, how's he taking it, dear?"

"He hates me now."

"You need a hug, don't you, dear? Honey, just give him some time. I can talk to him. Maybe that will help, okay, sugar?" my aunt asked. Her kindness and surprising understanding melted my distress into love. "Anyway, good for you. That sort of thing still takes a lot of courage. We got the sweetest gay friends here, and the difficulties they put up with ... nobody really wants you to do it, know what I mean? At least your mom must be proud of you?"

"I wish she was."

"I'm sorry. I thought she'd be okay with it. But they'll come around; you'll see. They still love you. And I'm proud of you."

I was now dumbfounded. It was like she could read my mind.

"Of course, they need to adjust—and hate you?—No one can hate you, Jamie. You're too precious. They love you. You'll see." There was a long pause. She was waiting for me to say something, I suppose. "Jamie, I love you, too. You know that?"

"Thank you, God!—I mean, thank you, Aunt Sylvia." The words I desperately needed to hear gave me the strength I needed. I relaxed into my chair.

"Jamie, dear, many people love you, and have a happy birthday."

She remembered. I was too choked up to say anything.

"It's your birthday today, right? Well, then, I'll give you back to Rhonda ... you could at least put on a shirt, Brian ...

I'm not stupid but *honestly, deary.*"

"My name is Bill!" I heard the man bark.

"Don't bite my head off. I made a nice dinner, didn't I? Jamie, here's Rhonda. Last time I make kugel for you."

"Okay, shithead, happy birthday! Isn't that amazing? My mom told me umpteen years ago about you."

"You knew, too?" I was less amazed, but I wanted to milk the situation for all the love I could squeeze out of it.

"She did. My mom's very perceptive, kiddo."

"Do I look like a fag?"

"Of course not. No relative of mine is a *faygeleh*," she said, assuming that would be reassuring. "Anyway, I am so glad to hear it."

"You're glad to hear?" I hung on every word, no matter how flippantly it was said.

"Sure. That must be hard for you to … you know, to come out."

"You're the first person who seemed glad to hear of it. But how did you really know?" I asked.

"I didn't know. I suspected. Mom was sure. But I knew you never really dated, right? I mean, really; it should have been obvious. Once you get rid of all these stereotypes, I mean. I have gay friends, too, just like you."

"You do?"

"Yes, and they're just like everyone else—well, except for John. He's *so outrageous.* You have to meet him! And my mother was saying your father would have a heart attack if he found out."

"She did?"

"Your father can be so stubborn sometimes."

"Well, he knows now. I told him. He didn't die of a heart attack. But he stopped talking to me or supporting me. They threw all my stuff out."

"Oh shit. You're okay, aren't you?" she asked. "You got a place to stay?"

"Yeah and I got a job. I'm working at the Bagel Factory. It can just get … depressing sometimes."

"You're not thinking about committing suicide or anything, are you?"

"Suicide? Me? No, of course not—"

"Shithead, let's get this straight: You commit suicide and I am gonna beat the shit out of you." I desperately needed to hear that. "Anyway, answer me, 'I won't.'"

"I won't!"

"Good. Better not. And good for you. A job and a roof over your head? I'll come there myself if you ever need help getting a place to stay. I still have friends at Detroit State."

"I have a place to stay, a nice roommate. He took me in—"

"Good. It's late and I have things to do. Call me again later if you want. Is there anything else you want me to say?"

"I don't know."

"All right, all right. Shit. Dammit, let me say this: You're okay. You're a wonderful kid. This doesn't change how I feel about you. You're gonna be happy and meet the right man and raise dogs and live happily ever after, blah blah blah. Love you, kiddo—okay, Bria—Bill!" Click.

I felt great after I hung up. In the dark, I groped for my belt and put it back on my pants.

Chapter 6: Rough Run-Through

"I pray thee, do not mock me, fellow student. I think—"

"Dwight, make Jamie stop! He's crowding me again."

Ben straight-armed me out of his way. I almost fell over. Hank Garvey playing Bernardo even gave me a push but Billy Thompson, who was playing Marcellus, grabbed my shoulder to steady me. That didn't stop the others from laughing. We were rehearsing act 1, scene 2 of *Hamlet* when Horatio tells Hamlet he saw his father's ghost.

"Ben, it's an intimate scene," said Dwight, standing up from his seat in the front row. Just as Dave had predicted, Dwight had been very helpful to me ever since the tech room debacle.

"What?" Ben whined.

"It's an intimate scene. You need to be gentler."

"Gentler! So you agree with this twerp?" Ben asked. The rest of the cast, seated in the front rows of the small theater, were still laughing at me.

Ben and Dwight continued to argue, but I lost the thread when I saw, at the back of the theater, my beloved—or former beloved—Casper. His sweet smile and lips still made me hope we had a chance to be together. Despite our rough sexual encounter, there was something about his gentle voice and kind demeanor in school that made me think we had some chance of having a relationship, even if it was platonic.

"Ben, listen to Dwight. He's the director, not you," said Mr. Nathan, who was seated next to Dwight. "But Jamie, let's be mindful of Ben's space. Closeness is good, but don't block his line of sight."

"You agree with him? That's not what I mean. He's playing Horatio like a fag," Ben whined. The word *fag* drew some giggles from the room.

"I'm not doing anything but standing close," I said. "Hamlet is emotional. I should be there to support him—"

"I am not emotional! What am I, a girl?"

Mr. Nathan glanced at an impassive Dwight, then got up from his seat and walked onstage. "Is this distance intimidating?" asked Mr. Nathan, standing about five feet away from Ben.

Ben shook his head no.

"Jamie, this distance will do. And Ben, no one doubts your masculinity, which is why you should be comfortable accepting support from your best friend."

"But *he* isn't my best friend."

"Offstage has nothing to do with acting. On *this stage*, this Horatio is your best friend. If he doesn't stick with you, you are really lost—*and you, Hamlet, know it*. Lucky for you, there is little on earth more dependable than your friend Horatio. Understood?" Satisfied, Mr. Nathan returned to his seat in the front row.

"Then have him stop being so—"

"Ben, who's being emotional here? Calm down. Read the text. Hamlet is completely spooked and suicidal. Jamie has a point," Dwight said.

"Right, and I'm Hamlet's best friend."

"We don't know that!" said Ben, walking upstage to appeal to Mr. Nathan.

"Ben, have you heard anything Arthur said? Horatio is his only true friend in the entire play," Dwight said.

"But Mr. Nathan—"

"Direct your comments to Dwight, not me."

"Dwight, he's going to try to make me out as a ... you know."

"It's not like Hamlet is Mr. Macho Man either," I added. "He only sarcastically compares himself to Hercules, doesn't he?"

"See! He thinks Hamlet is—"

"Gay!" I shouted. "But that isn't what I said. I just think he's less macho."

"We're all entitled to our opinions," Dwight said. "Just keep going with the scene. I see nothing wrong."

Because Ben was still pouting, I said, "Look, I'll stand farther away, okay?"

"Wait a second, Jamie," said Mr. Nathan, standing up. "Let's get another opinion. Casper, do you think there is a problem with how close Jamie was?"

Casper looked right at me and smiled. My heart leaped.

"I think everything's just fine. Just looking at the blocking from here, I think Horatio should be closer because he's a close friend. Bernardo and Marcellus are loyal soldiers, but not his friends," Casper said. "I also just want to say, Ben, divorce what you know about Jamie offstage from the performance. All I see onstage is a very concerned friend."

I couldn't stop the fantasy that Casper had forgiven me for—well, whatever I had done—and we could be friends again.

"Let's get back to 'I pray thee'?" Mr. Nathan softly asked Dwight.

"All right everyone," Dwight announced, "let's pick up at 'I pray thee, do not mock me.' Ben?"

"Stop that," Ben complained. "He's doing it again."

"Now what?" Mr. Nathan asked.

"He's looking at me."

"That's called acting, Ben. You're taking this too personally. That's not like you."

"I have to look at my *friend*," I said.

"You're not looking. You're leering at me, you ..."

"Stop!" Mr. Nathan turned to Dwight, "Go on, say what you were going to say."

This seemed to take Dwight by surprise. "Enough. Ben, this is an ensemble. Jamie is giving you focus, and I want you to communicate back your friendship," he directed with Mr. Nathan nodding his endorsement. "Remember what I said: A good actor is a generous actor. You both should be playing off each other. Jamie, stay close to Ben, but don't block his view from the audience. I like you being engaged with his eyes. Ben, I want you to do the same. Actually, I want all of you making eye contact like Jamie. Go on, Ben."

Ben turned to me and hissed, "Don't be a you-know-what."

"Look," I whispered back, "you are meeting your best friend at a very tender moment. I am concerned because I love you."

"Just tone it down."

"Ben, back up a little and start from 'But what is your affair'!" Dwight yelled.

"All right already." He turned back to me. "But what is your affair in Elsinore? We'll teach you to drink deep ere you depart."

I pretended Ben was Casper and looked him right in the eyes. It was the only way to feel friendship, not hatred. Mindlessly, I put my hand very softly on Ben's shoulder. He winced at the touch.

"Sorry," I whispered and withdrew it. Then I said, "My lord, I came to see your father's funeral."

"I pray thee, do not mock me, fellow student. I think it was to see my mother's wedding."

Interpersonally, it was very tense. I stepped back, though now I was as far away as Marcellus and Bernardo. When I stepped closer, Ben glared at me. At first, I thought of retreating, but then I realized the tension helped the scene move.

"Indeed, my lord, it followed hard upon."

"Thrift, thrift, Horatio. The funeral baked meats did coldly furnish forth the marriage tables. Would I had met my dearest—stop it!"

"Stop what?" I asked.

"What is it this time?" Mr. Nathan asked. "Ben aside, this was really great—all four of you."

"I hate the way he's looking at me!" Ben shouted.

"You have to have some interaction, Ben. Otherwise, it will look like you don't care about Horatio. And Horatio's arm on your shoulder was perfectly fine, though, actually, it's *you* who should put your arm on Horatio's when you're inviting him to drinks. I can buy you don't like Jamie, but Hamlet and Horatio are best friends," Mr. Nathan lectured. "You told me you thought Hamlet was a piece of cake. Well, the cake seems to be eating you."

"It's Jamie—"

"Look, if it is so much trouble handling eye contact with Jamie, then pretend you're looking at Barb. We can have Barb here for the scene if that helps."

"Come on, Arthur, he's about to kiss me."

"Jamie, were you about to kiss him?"

"No. I am three miles from him," I said. "But I think Horatio is more than just a friend. He loves Hamlet—very deeply. Hamlet loves him back. The text even says so."

"We're not a couple of queers—or, sorry, *I'm not*."

This time, no one laughed. Dwight looked at Mr. Nathan.

"All right, Ben, cool it!" Mr. Nathan shouted. "Go ahead, Dwight."

"I can accept that there is an element of desire here, Jamie, okay?" Dwight said stoically. "But it isn't, what d'ya call it? Bi ... directional. Don't *pressure* it."

"Bi-directional?" Ben asked. "He's not bi—"

"Bi-directional, Ben, not bisexual. I am taking your side here."

"Oh. But there's no way these guys are queers like Jamie—said they are."

"Okay, that's it. Stop that. I won't tolerate that, Ben." Mr. Nathan said. "Everyone here, listen to this announcement: You are going to have respect for one another. I don't want any slurs—racial, sexual, ethnic, or otherwise. Ben, in the confines of this play, you like Horatio and I want to see that, dammit. It's perfectly okay if Horatio is in love with Hamlet and Hamlet is his closest friend. It helps the conflict onstage, not the conflict here in rehearsal. Stand closer, Jamie—Ben's not going to hit you."

"But I will," he whispered.

"Ben," I said, "let's be friends. I want us both to look good."

"No, you don't. You want to be a ham."

"Ben, we play as a team. Would you prefer to see how your understudy can do the scene?" Mr. Nathan asked.

"No!"

Mr. Nathan sat down, gesturing to Dwight, who said, "Sheesh. Let's get back to the play."

"Dwight, you can't agree with that bullshit," Ben whined. "Just because Jamie's a perv doesn't mean he can do this to the entire cast."

"Perv, Ben?" Mr. Nathan said calmly.

"Sorry, Mr. Nathan, but I'm not making a fool of myself onstage—"

"That is exactly what you are doing, and I want it to stop."

"Hamlet passionately loves Ophelia. Horatio is just a friend. Period."

"I think it is safe to say that Dwight and I both agree your Hamlet is not homosexual," Mr. Nathan said.

"I told you!" Ben shouted triumphantly.

"So you are both right. But I won't tolerate you calling names like fag or queer to intimidate Jamie," Mr. Nathan announced. "He is quite right to show love and affection for Hamlet. And Hamlet is emotionally upset about the queen's remarriage—the only thing he cares about right now is Horatio's support. Maybe the affection even enchants him."

"That's right," Dwight piped up. "Hamlet has bigger fish to fry. Horatio is offering him the comradeship he needs."

"It's just like when I have a girlfriend who needs emotional support," Billy said. "I may feel attracted to her, but I don't take advantage of it. She accepts the support."

"Who asked you anything?" Ben complained.

"That's enough of that. Billy, that was beautifully put," Mr. Nathan said. I couldn't help but smile. I was standing up for myself and even getting some support.

"But Shakespeare never intended this," Ben whined.

"I am sorry, Ben. I didn't realize you had communicated with Mr. Shakespeare," Mr. Nathan said.

"Who apparently had boyfriends, according to his sonnets," I added.

"Being that way is never in any of his works—"

"Anyone remember what I teach in my Shakespeare class? What do we know about Shakespeare or any playwright?"

"We can't be sure of anything," Dwight said. I was relieved. The embarrassing situation in the tech room would be forgotten. Dwight and I were on the same page. Ben was going to lose this argument.

"Look," I said, "I'm not doing anything to you. I am just playing my role. I'm not crowding you. I touched your shoulder. You said no and I respected that, so respect me and let me play my role. I've done nothing to you. Let's just be friends."

"Oh, come on! Mr. Nathan?"

"Jamie's reaching out to you. He made you an offer. Are you going to accept it?" Mr. Nathan asked.

Ben sighed, "Faggot," under his breath.

I reached out my hand. "You can't convince me of your view," I said, "and I won't try to convince you of mine. Can we call it a truce?"

Ben looked miserable and cornered. Suddenly vulnerable, he looked oddly attractive. I thought he could finally feel the shoe on the other foot.

"He's going to show me up with this f—gay thing."

I don't know what came over me, but I gave a quick peck on his cheek. Ben reflexively slapped my face.

We stared at each other. It wasn't hatred; I felt something else. My face tingled from the slap.

"Okay, let's take a break!" Mr. Nathan called. "Ben, I want to have a word with you in private."

"Are you going to need me anymore today?" Casper asked from his seat in the back.

"Nope. We're good. Everyone else back in ten minutes. Ben, come with me. Let's get some fresh air."

Mr. Nathan and Ben walked out. I saw Casper getting up to leave. Everything seemed to be going my way, so I thought,

Why not try and reconnect with him? His beautiful blond hair and penetrating blue eyes gazed toward me. I waved to grab his attention before he left.

"Casper! Casper!" I ran after him.

At first, he tried to ignore me, but then he stopped just outside the theater.

"Okay, kid. What do you want?" His look of exasperation was so far from what I wanted.

"Thank you, Casper, for chiming in for me."

"You were doing a good job—until the end."

"I know, I kind of snapped."

"I wouldn't say that. It was pretty ballsy, what you did in front of everyone. I've never seen you do anything like this before."

"Thank you, Casper. I was wondering, if you weren't busy, maybe we could grab coffee?"

Casper suddenly looked distracted. He looked around to see whether anyone was looking.

"Please," I said. "I need to talk to you."

"I'm meeting someone."

"Who is it?"

"Why do you care? It's one of my friends."

"Can I join?"

"I don't think that's a good idea."

"Can I see you some other time?"

"Jamie ..."

"Casper, I'm ... I've learned a lot. I want you to know I still love you, if you're willing to give me a chance."

"Oh, stop this charade, will you? Look, we're working together and it's going well. Let's keep it that way. After rehearsals, keep away from me. And they need you back inside." He walked away.

"What have I done that's so horrible?" I asked, but his slim, sexy body kept on walking. I couldn't look away.

He paused and turned around. "Jamie, get real. You're not exactly the marrying kind, so drop it. I'll talk to you later."

"'Not the marrying kind'? What's that supposed to mean?" But I knew full well. The innocent image I still had of myself hadn't quite caught up with what I had been. "I've changed," I added half-heartedly. "I'll talk to you later," I said as he walked away.

I wanted the chance to explain that I knew how far I had descended. I just wanted him to know I was trying to climb back.

Variation: Etudes Good and Bad

February 1982

Chapter 7: Doors Open

I was afraid to call the number that the Lesbian-Gay Hotline had given me. I was worried because I thought they would ask embarrassing questions and might even know about my reputation. The gay world felt so small. Still, I just took a deep breath and dialed the number. As I expected, there was an answering machine.

"Hello, you have reached the number of DOHR, the Detroit Organization for Human Rights. At the sound of the tone, please leave your name and number." Then, fainter, "I know—I am pressing the right button now." Beep.

"Hello, my name is Jamie Goldberg, and I am interested in joining your organization and making a difference. You can call me at Lincoln five-eight-two-three."

I hung up the phone, expecting a call back in a few days. I had no sooner stepped out of the kitchen when the phone rang.

"Hello?"

"Hi, may I speak to Jamie Goldberg?" an older, effeminate voice asked.

"That's me."

"My name is Ken Finocchio from DOHR."

I was a little surprised. I wasn't quite prepared for such a quick call back. But his voice was very welcoming.

"I understand you are interested in joining us? Or, as we like to say, opening doors—get it? DOHR is our acronym."

"Ah, how nice." I forced a laugh. A bad sense of humor was more welcome than none at all, so I thought I would offer some peevish humor of my own. "This is a lesbian-gay rights organization or something like that, right?"

"Yes, of course."

"I just was asking because the words *gay* or *lesbian* don't appear in your name."

"Uh-huh. Yes, I can see it might appear to be a closeted organization. But if we did have the words *gay* or *lesbian* or, for that matter, *bisexual* or *trans* in our name, I would be inundated with so many crackpot calls and threats—phew! I get enough of those already."

"But that's what happens when you're on the front lines."

"I guess DOHR is not on the front lines. But as of this moment, it's the line there is, and I think we are effective."

"Well, I'd like to help."

"We need people like you." Such kindness. I wished I had thought of this before I had submerged myself in gay bars and dark rooms. "But tell me, why would you like to join our group?"

"To fight the good fight," I said. "Get our rights and teach others that we are … who we are. I don't want to have sex at all."

"I beg your pardon?"

"I mean, I want to join because you fight discrimination … it's not a pickup place, right?"

"Mmm …"

"I really want to do something where I can contribute to the community. Perform a service."

"Good. We do have some open positions in our group for students. Before I get into that, do you mind a couple of questions? Just a formality, but it's protocol."

"Sure."

"So to begin, DOHR stands for the Detroit Organization for Human Rights."

"You know, for a gay pride organization, you don't have much pride in the name."

"All right already! I get it. I like the enthusiasm. One more question: Can you name a gay politician?"

I finally understood I was being quizzed on my gay credentials. "Oscar Wilde," I shot back.

"Not a politician, but I'll accept it."

"I'm ready for the next one if the answer is Leonardo da Vinci or Michelangelo."

That worked. Ken chortled on the phone. "Sorry, Jamie, if I sounded suspicious. I get all kinds of wacko calls." The way he said "Jamie" made it feel like he knew me.

"Who's a gay politician? I don't know of any."

"Well, the most obvious one is Harvey Milk."

"Harvey Milk? He was gay?"

"Of course."

"The guy who was shot along with a mayor?"

"Yes."

"You wouldn't know from the news coverage."

"He was openly gay—that's what got him assassinated."

"Incredible! This is what I want to fight. You know I would never have found you if it wasn't for the gay-lesbian hotline listings in the telephone book."

"We definitely need someone with your passion and focus. I assume you're familiar with the group?"

"Just what I heard from the hotline."

"Really? And nothing else?"

"I came out recently and I want to get involved, know what I mean?"

"Sure, I was just wondering if you knew about us from some *other avenue.*"

"I come from a family of political activists."

"Exactly! I knew it." I could swear there was a sigh of relief on the other end of the phone. "Membership is a bit expensive, but we have a free membership for students like you."

"How do you know I'm a student?"

"Oh—uh—your voice." This conversation started to sound surreal.

"I'm a student at Detroit State."

"See, I was right. Your voice. Like I said, we have a free student membership. We're trying to do more outreach to the universities. And maybe you can help us with—well, it'd be especially helpful if you don't mind putting your name out there. Being out seems very important to you. Why don't I take your number? I can have a membership form ready for you at our next meeting. Your name's Jamie Goldberg?"

"Mmm … yes," I said.

"Goldberg? … Goo-lld-berg. Just wondering, not that it matters at all, but by any chance, are you any relationship to Ruth Goldberg?"

I had thought I was ready for just about any question except that one. "You're kidding?"

"Okay, I take it back. Never mind, it was just a guess. She's in the Democratic Party. She's a head honcho of the Wayne County Democratic Central Committee."

"Head honcho!" I couldn't help myself. "'Head honcho' is a bit of a stretch—all right, if you must know, I'm related. She's my … mother."

"I beg your pardon? I didn't hear you. Did you say she's your mother?" His voice suddenly sounded ecstatic. "Hold on a second. Wait right here; don't hang up."

It sounded like he dropped the phone on the ground. I heard animated talking in the background.

"James, you still there?"

"Yes, it's Jamie."

"Jamie, right. I'm sorry. I have it written down right here. Ha ha. Which college did you say you go to? U of D?"

"I said Detroit State … I'm a political science major."

"Oh, excellent. Prelaw?"

"Of course," I lied in case this conversation was getting back to my mother.

"Our meetings are the second Thursday of the month at seven. We'd love to have you at our next meeting, which is this Thursday. Do you think you can make it?"

The welcome was at once overwhelming but transparent: I was being loved for my lineage. "Yes, I can make it." I didn't want to dampen his enthusiasm with the fact that my mother and I hadn't spoken since I had come out of the closet.

"That would be great. Oh, but the meetings are held Downtown at the Pontiac Hotel. Maybe you need a ride?"

"Sure. That would be helpful. I'm in the New Center area near the D State campus."

"Good. Give me your address, and we'll find someone to pick you up and take you back home. In fact, we have another student who also comes to our meetings—his name is Brian. You two will get along great. He'll pick you up before the meeting, like around six-thirty, okay?"

"Thanks. I live at 231 Seward, near Woodward. I'm looking forward to this. I want to help bring us into the light of day so we don't have to keep crawling around at night."

"I beg your pardon?"

"It seems that except for the hotline, everything in this community is clandestine. I want us to be easy to find. I want it to be easy to help those like us. I could have used that help."

"Right on. We all could have. That's the world we all want to live in. Welcome to the fight, James."

"Jamie. Only my mother calls me James."

"We'll see you Thursday."

Chapter 8: Kumbaya

One morning during an African Studies lecture, I was learning about the under-appreciated Menilek II of Ethiopia from one of my favorite professors, Dr. Harold Gulden. At the end of the lecture, I planned to talk to the professor about Menilek's victory over the Italian army. But before I had a chance, Queen Gertrude showed up. Dr. Gulden looked up in surprise.

"Wrong history class, you want readings on the French Revolution down the hall." The class laughed hysterically.

Barbie Jackson, who was both playing Queen Gertrude and dating my archenemy, Ben, showed up at the classroom door in full dress waving to me with an urgent gesture.

"Mr. Goldberg, it seems you are wanted by royalty. I'll remember this when I greet you next time in class,"

Dr. Gulden chuckled.

Fearing the worst, I rushed over to her.

"Hey, Barbie, what are you doing here?"

"I want to talk to you."

"What's happened?"

"Let's go somewhere to talk."

"Okay, but at least take off the wig."

"Oh shit, I forgot! No wonder everyone was looking at me." She quickly took off the wig and the royal gown and folded it over her arm as we walked.

Abandoning my thoughts on Menilek II, we went to the cafeteria and spoke over a lunch of something they called Swedish meatloaf and large glasses of Coca-Cola.

"Barbie, please tell me, what's this about? Is something wrong with the play?" I asked.

"Let's just get one thing clear," she said. "Stop calling me Barbie."

"Oh, but I thought everyone called you that."

"Everyone except my friends."

"Barb?"

"Yes."

"Then it's Barb. Does that make me your friend?"

"Not really. Ben wants to see you."

"He does?"

"Yes."

"He wants me to be there, too."

"I'd appreciate that. Last time we spoke, he slapped me."

"I think that's what he wants to talk to you about. Think of me as a kind of shuttle diplomat."

"You don't look like Henry Kissinger."

"Huh?"

"You put him up to this?"

"Okay, fine. He doesn't even know I'm here. But this play is my big chance. I worked hard for this part. I don't want you two screwing this up for me."

"What do you want from me?"

"Ben is very worried about you upstaging him. He doesn't

like you as it is. He thinks he holds the ace. He told me you couldn't go onstage with a black eye."

"He's threatening me?"

"Of course not! It's just talk. He's freaking out. He doesn't want any hint that he might be gay because he feels that will ruin his career."

"I don't want to upstage anyone, but I do want to be *onstage*, if you know what I mean. What about *my* career?"

"Oh, he thinks you've sunk your own ship there. Look, this isn't really about you or Ben. Everyone in the cast needs this thing to work."

"I'm doing my best."

"Yeah, I know. Casper thinks so."

"Casper!"

"But he thinks you're trying to get revenge for how Ben bullied you this past year."

"Why didn't Casper tell me himself?"

"He says you're impossible to talk to. That you keep trying to hit on him. He's straight, you know."

"Terrific." I started to suspect this Casper conversation never really took place.

"Casper hinted that one of you may be removed. I don't know who. Ben's most accomplished; you're a newbie. But it's clear you were the better actor in the rehearsal—or at least smarter."

"Thanks."

"You little shit."

"Oh. So what are you really getting at?"

"Huh?"

"Come on, everyone thinks I'm Mr. Doormat. What does

Ben–I mean *Casper* think I have to do to make this work for everyone?”

"Can you drop the gay bit about Horatio?”

"What?”

"Okay, that not what he said.”

"Who's *he?*”

"Listen to me. Don't change anything. Do exactly what you're doing. The audience—well, part of it—will understand. Just don't make it an issue during rehearsals.”

"Okay. Mr. Nathan told you to do this? Not Casper?”

"They both did.”

"Fuck!”

"Jamie!”

"I can't say that?”

"I've never heard you say any swear words.”

"That's because I have never been this screwed—oh yes. I have. What about Dwight?”

"Oh, come on. You must know by now that he's Mr. Nathan's puppet.”

"Well, that's not charitable,” I said, completely disingenuous. "But I get it. Here's the deal: A more professional rehearsal. I get that. That has to mean you respect me and Dwight and everyone else, and so does Ben. No more fag stuff. Ben stops taking center stage except for the soliloquies.”

"You think that will work? I'll tell him what you said. I just can't promise anything.”

"I see. Casper and Arthur had nothing do to with this. That's why you ran over here. Is Ben really going to hit me?”

"He already did, huh?”

I looked at my plate. My Horatio was beginning to look like the meatloaf.

◆◆◆◆

The next day, I was alone in the same cafeteria, this time with one of their famous British burgers. What was British about them, I never knew, except they tasted bland.

"You want to see me?"

I looked up to see Ben holding a cafeteria tray.

"That was quick. I wanted Barb or Casper here, though."

"I'm not going to do anything. I'm sorry I hit you. I felt provoked." He spoke like it was a script he had been told to deliver.

"I did provoke you, but I can't apologize. I will continue to provoke you. But I promise to do it professionally."

"Then there won't be any of … you know, that. You're dropping the fag thing?"

"Still that?"

"What?"

"*You* drop the *fag thing* and I will, too. Never call me that again. Be respectful, and I will return the favor. In rehearsal," I said, determined not to change a thing as Barbie had recommended.

"In the rehearsals?" Ben asked, a bit surprised.

"And you promise you're not going to hit me? I've heard about threats."

"Who told you that? I'm not going to hit you. But you better not hit on me."

"Really? What do you know about anything?" I had no idea where I was going with this until I sang a few bars of the song "Hurts So Good." My heart started to pound. Self-hatred flooded my brain as I sang it—quietly, but loud enough.

"You're a sickee, know that? Fine. In rehearsals, we're the best of friends. Outside of rehearsals, stay the fuck away from me." He got up to leave.

"I was just joking!" I shouted as he left.

I sat there alone with my British burger and Coke. *Why did I do that? I was doing so good until then.* I put extra mustard and hot sauce on the bland burger, hoping for some taste and comfort.

◆◆◆◆◆

The next day, I was alone with chicken á la king and two anonymous typewritten notes that were stuffed in my jacket.

One read *Faggot, keep this up and you'll get a lot of trouble. Don't walk alone if I were you. There's a knife with your name on it.* The second one read *Keep up the good work. More than one person is cheering you on.*

Empty threats and empty praise; I could do nothing with either. I recognized these things from the time my own mother had received death threats and anonymous letters because of her civil rights work, especially ever since she had worked to desegregate the Oakland County jails. She had just carried on, and now I realized just what courage she had. *She must have felt scared,* I thought. *But that must be what real courage is: going forward despite fear.* I lost my appetite for the chicken.

◆◆◆◆◆

The next day, it was Mr. Nathan's turn at the cafeteria. All I had was a hotdog, Mr. Nathan just a cup of coffee.

"Jamie, mind if I join you?"

"Please do, Mr. Nathan. Let me guess: You want the play to succeed and I'm screwing up and you want me to stop being gay—I mean, Horatio to stop."

"I beg your pardon?"

"Isn't that what you and everyone wants from me?"

"No, it's not. The director, who is in charge of the vision, is Dwight. You've convinced Dwight that his vision is the tension between a homosexual Horatio and a straight Hamlet. Both love each other, albeit in different ways. That makes you the one sticking up for Dwight's vision and Ben as trying to tear it down. I am also here defending that vision, and I think everyone has been spoken to."

"Oh, thank you, God! You know, everyone's been trying to intimidate me."

"Let's clear that up, too. What I want from you is clarity on showing due respect for Ben and the other cast members. Kissing Ben like that was not helpful and, more importantly, not professional. I want a public apology to him. He will also apologize for slapping you and calling you derogatory names. From that moment onward, I want a generosity of spirit and team-playing. Ensemble acting."

"Thank God. And I don't have to shut up about my interpretation?"

"No, who told you so?"

"Well, Casper did—at least that's what Barb said he said. And there's an anonymous note I received."

"Hmmm, if he did say it, he's just concerned about you."

"He doesn't show it."

"Well, I hear that's because you two aren't personally on the same page. Fair enough?"

"Yeah, I guess so."

"But I don't agree with Casper. I am seeing something I never saw in you before."

"Me?"

"You seem to be handling yourself very well."

"I am?"

"I probably should have handled it differently, but I was hesitant the other day to intercede because I was wondering where you were going with it. You were quite forceful—you have Dwight completely intimidated."

"I had no idea. I guess it feels safe playing a gay character and knowing you're there."

"But that's not the issue here. About your decision to play Horatio as a gay character: You made your intentions very clear, so we don't need to discuss this anymore. Just do it."

"What if Ben objects?"

"He'll do so politely and respectfully. He may challenge you. If you don't have any answer for that, then maybe you should listen to what he has to say. When you two leave your personal issues outside the door, then inside the rehearsal, everything will go well. You're both very talented actors. You will find a way to accommodate each other; that's what we do. We act as an ensemble. Luckily for Ben, he has plenty of soliloquies to feed his tender ego. To change the subject, what do you think of Alec?"

"He's amazing. He's helped me a lot and he's very generous onstage."

"And Barbie?"

"She's doing her best. She's very dedicated."

"Are you doing those things?"

"I'll try harder."

"You are easily the most prepared. No one has to feed you a line—that's clear."

"I hate being blindsided, but I feel I am right now."

"Am I being unfair?"

"No. I just thought I was doing so well. And I didn't realize I was being a jerk."

"You like to do that, don't you?"

"What?"

"To head off criticism, you like to criticize yourself and much more extremely than what the other person was going to say. Jamie, we talked about your past. But you do use it as a weapon when needed. It's a way of escaping from me."

"Escaping what?"

"Escaping the fact that—"

"I'd never use a weapon against you."

"Escaping the fact that you fucked up. Acknowledge the screw-up, own it, and learn from it. Then keep the good stuff and try to turn down the volume of the bad."

"I clearly screwed up and I want to learn. And I'm not ..."

"A Detroit Red Wings fan."

I laughed. "No, I am not. I'm also not a bad person."

"Wow, what an admission. It almost sounds like you're confessing to a crime, but I'll take it. At our last rehearsal, it seemed like you were out for revenge. No matter how deserved, revenge never works. Anyway, you made your point. You humiliated Ben just as he tried to do that to you. It's a stalemate and now it stops. Besides, great acting is a much better vehicle for your vindication than one-upmanship. No one likes a prima donna or a ham unless you are truly an experienced virtuoso. Ben needs to control his temper. You need to control your impulses."

"I don't think I understand, Mr. Nathan. I thought I was supposed to trust my instincts."

"Impulses are different than instincts, and please, just call me Arthur. I don't do well on a pedestal.

"Jamie, when you were out of control, you impulsively kissed Ben as a provocation—not as an act of love. *Your* Horatio wouldn't do that, would he? Even though he lies awake at night dreaming of doing exactly that. He wouldn't kiss Hamlet without Hamlet's consent; he loves him too much. Though he would give anything to have him, he will never get what he wants—until the end. And that brings me to my other point. In this production, just before he dies, Hamlet will give you a sign—the consent, if you will. You and Ben will agree on it beforehand what it is, and on that sign, Hamlet dies, and then you can kiss him and say, 'Now cracks a noble heart. Goodnight, sweet prince.'"

"Really?"

"Yes. Everyone—Ben, Dwight, and myself—have agreed to that. And going forward, relax that aggression and lean into Horatio as best you can. If it helps, I will be there for you, so charge ahead by keeping your instincts truly Horatio's instincts, not Jamie's impulses. Are we good?"

"We're good, Mr. Na—Arthur."

"Good. I'll see you at rehearsal."

"Thanks. I'm so hungry, I'm getting another hotdog."

Chapter 9: The One and Only

DOHR meeting night: Thursday, 6:45 p.m. A fashionably late student drove up to my apartment in a vehicle that resembled a motorcycle wrapped in a yellow tin can.

The window on the driver's side rolled down to reveal a dark, mousy, and devilishly handsome boy. It was love at first sight—until he opened his mouth and said acidly, "You Jamie?"

"I love you, too," I said, trying to be cheery and spritely.

"Get in," he said, "I'm Brian. *The* Brian Kitson," as if I should recognize his unknown name.

"Okay. You're the person giving me a ride to the DOHR meeting? I'm Jamie," I replied, doing my best to refrain from calling myself *the* Jamie Goldberg.

"Right, come on, get in already." He sounded a tad hostile. "We're late."

I ran around to the passenger side, opened the tiny door, and squeezed in.

"I'm the *student representative* for DOHR," he said.

"Nice to meet you, student representative."

"Yeah, well, fuck you. I heard all about the great Goldberg," he quipped.

We drove off into the vacant city streets, heading toward the freeway.

"Look, I don't even know you. What's the matter?"

"You want my job, don't you?"

"I didn't even know your job existed until just now." I was taken aback by the blatant hostility from a complete stranger. That was all it took to spark my self-hatred again. I immediately suspected that he knew everything: my reputation, my sexual self-destruction. For all I knew, he might even have been one of my sexual escapades. His look of contempt was almost a guarantee. I swallowed my feelings and decided to fight this.

"You know me?" I asked tentatively.

He sneered back at me.

"Watch the road!" I yelled.

He looked back at traffic and veered away from an oncoming car. "I *know* how to drive," he snapped defensively. "But you must have heard of *me*."

"I'm sorry, just—light! Light!" My consternation was interrupted by Brian running a red light. "Do you know where we're going?"

"Of course I know. *I* have been there *many* times," he said with the nerdy emphasis of a poor actor.

"Good, because I don't have a map."

"I don't need a *map*, deary."

"Okay, but please keep your eyes on the road—and shouldn't you use your turn signal to change—"

"Got it!"

We sat in silence while we drove down the concrete caverns of the sunken Lodge Freeway toward Downtown. He was driving way too slowly for the left lane, and horns were honking all around us.

"Can we try this again? My name is Jamie."

"I know, you already told me." Again, hostility flashed on his face.

"Yes." I heaved a sigh. "What? You hate Jews?"

"Not all of them."

"Forget it. I don't know you. I don't want your job, whatever it is, but stop talking. You need to concentrate on your driving!"

As he drove recklessly down the freeway in his tin can, it was becoming clearer to me that, from a sexual cesspool, I was now walking into a political minefield. I decided I would try and calm this kid's fears.

"So, you're the student representative. Of course I should have heard of you. It's great you're doing a job *nobody* wants … what does a student representative do anyway?"

He just winced and muttered, "I'm Brian Kitson," and didn't say anything else for a while. He reluctantly added, "I act as the spokesperson for DOHR to the universities. To State, U of D, Marygrove, all of them—an occasional high school. I've even met with your provost."

"Oh wow."

"I delivered a big presentation on gay rights for him with our proposed nondiscrimination policies."

"Wow, that's impressive," I pandered. "Been with the organization for a long time?"

"Yes, I have … over three months."

I wanted to burst out laughing. He made it sound like he had been a member for years. "Well, if there is anything I can do to help out, you let me know, I'd love to volunteer—"

"I'm the volunteer."

"They only need one volunteer? Look, maybe I can just help you out—"

"I'm doing a good job."

"I'm sure, that's why you feel so secure." I wondered what it would take for him to loosen up. "I don't want to be a student representative."

"I bet you don't."

"No, I'd rather tear your clothes off."

That silenced him for a while, so I didn't bother to add, "Just kidding."

"What's the organization like?" I asked.

He remained silent.

"Come on, how can I step all over you on my way to the top if you don't tell me about the organization?"

Finally, a smile. "Well, they can be a bit ... prickly."

Gossip worked. "Picky?"

"*Prickly.* There's a lot of talk of bylaws, and they use Robert's Rules of Order—so it can be a bit stiff. You'll get the hang of it. I am sure you know all about it with your background and all."

"Kindly leave my background out of this. And I don't think I've ever heard of Robert's Rules," I lied. But I did wonder what about my reputation included Robert's Rules of Order. Certainly not the bushes in Palmer Park. "What's the leadership like?"

"I bet you'd like to know them."

"Look, I told you I don't want your precious position. I want to help this organization, so can we just be friends?"

Brian grimaced at first and then looked at me out of the corner of his eyes.

"I am just here to help—we're on the same side, you know. Fighting discrimination. Gay rights."

"Don't be pathetic. Okay, let me tell you some ground rules: No one goes near Phil. I know Ken has the hots for you, but stay away from Phil, get it?"

"I don't know who Phil is. Ken can't have the hots for me because I've never met him."

"You never met Ken?"

"No, and believe me, there is one thing I am not interested in and that's sex. With anyone. You're hot, but the tearing-off-clothes comment was just a … icebreaker."

"*An* icebreaker."

"I beg your pardon?"

"*An* icebreaker, not *a* icebreaker."

"As I said, I only want to help out the community—and improve my grammar."

That got a laugh out of him. "That's what they all say."

"Let's just say I've made a few mistakes in my past and I am not eager to repeat them, so I am just playing it celibate for now. I just want to—"

"Help out and fight the good fight," he shot back sarcastically. But then he added softly, "You're not fooling me. You're the young chick. They'll fawn all over you."

"I can handle myself. I don't want to be fawned over."

"They're chicken hawks, and they know the rules better than you. All right, if you're as innocent as you say you are, then if you need any help, then just let me know. They'll have you doing things you never thought you'd do." That seemed over the top.

"Good. Thank you. I've had a hard time. I don't want to cause anyone any grief—and I am not innocent ... so, what's your story? You said earlier I should have heard of you."

"Wait, you really never heard of me? Brian Kitson?"

I shook my head.

"Phi Gamma Delta?"

"Oh wait a sec, you were kicked out of a fraternity or something like that?"

"More than kicked out. I was the president, and they caught me with someone—"

"Wow, you were having sex in the fraternity with a guy? I think that made the school papers."

"Oh, I did that all the time. In fact, I made it part of the hazing." He grinned.

I laughed along, though it sounded to me like an abuse of power.

"Anyway, there was this guy I liked, and we were kissing in my room and got caught. Somehow kissing was more offensive than fucking. After I got caught, the fraternity went out of their way to say I was being thrown out because I was gay, which was against university rules."

"It isn't at Detroit State."

"Not yet. We're working on it. You can probably help."

After my little anti-sex spiel, I was a little surprised to feel a hand on my thigh.

"I'll give you some advice: Ken and Phil have the upper hand, but everyone wants the power from them. You just stick with us and everything will be fine. And Phil has the power—not Ken. That queen is just in it for the sex, if you ask me. Screw around with him and the next thing you know, you're screwing around with Phil."

"Is that what happened to you?"

"No, Phil and I are lovers now, and I don't—I don't want anyone else to get … hurt."

"Oh, I thought for a second they lived together."

"Don't be dense. Of course they do."

I was completely confused. "Who's Phil anyway?"

"Phil is *the president* of DOHR. Ken is the membership chair. They live together, but *I'm* Phil's lover—get it? Keep away from my Phil, understand?"

"I thought you just told me to stick with you guys? Look, I just told you I don't want him or anyone else. I just want to fight discrimination and for gay rights."

"Right, you just come to these meetings for the fun of it."

I wondered what kind of sexual bombshell this Phil guy must be to inspire this kind of jealousy. I looked carefully at Brian. He looked about the same age as I was. He was handsome with sharp features, mousiness notwithstanding. I wondered what he was so paranoid about.

"Stop the charades. You got connections."

"No charades. Look—no, don't look at me! Look at the road!"

He almost hit a car as we exited the freeway.

"You just happen to be joining a political organization you know nothing about. Phil and Ken run the organization, so of course, you'll ..." His voice just trailed off.

"Of course I'll what? Look, can you lighten up? Unless he looks like Humphrey Bogart, your Phil is safe ... besides, I can't help being who I am. I just want to—oh, forget it."

"Okay, just be careful. Friendly advice, that's all." He looked down and saw I had an erection. How it had gotten there, I don't know. "You are going to be very popular. Especially watch out for Casey Winograd."

"Casey Winograd?" The name sounded vaguely familiar.

"Yes, he's the vice president. Just ignore him. Casey and his creepy boyfriend, Neil, are major-league losers." Before his hand returned to the wheel, he checked to see whether I still had an erection. I did.

"I don't control these things," I said. "The stiffy, I mean. I know politics. But I just want to—"

"Don't be a jerk, James."

"It's Jamie. Only my mom—"

The quarter dropped. My background he was referring to was not based in Palmer Park but rather in the Wayne County Democratic Central Committee.

"What I mean is, of course I know politics, but I don't know this organization at all. At the end of the day, we're all connected somehow in getting gay rights passed, aren't we?"

"Of course."

"I'll focus on that."

"Clueless," he sighed under his breath.

In icy silence, we drove down to the monumental Pontiac Hotel. At first glance, the hotel was an art deco beauty. On the second glance, it was a dirty, unkempt eyesore: a tawdry monument to the forgotten glory of Detroit.

We parked the car on a street near the hotel. Brian wanted to avoid paying for parking. Getting out, I noticed someone had keyed the side of his car with a barely legible slogan: *Hungry? Eat your foreign car.*

We walked up to the door of the hotel where two men were smoking. One of them, a roly-poly guy with a jovial mustache, looked vaguely familiar to me.

"Hey, Brian!" one shouted.

Brian didn't answer.

"Is that James Goldberg with you? Hi, Jamie, remember me? Casey's the name, and this is my friend Neil. Go on inside. I'll see you in a moment. We're just getting started."

Neil yelled, "Welcome to our new student rep!"

Chapter 10: Ensemble Entanglements

The lobby of the Pontiac Hotel was just like the outside: a tattered old relic. The faded art deco interior was compromised by a smoky haze hanging over the lobby. It smelled like grime, bleach, and cigarettes. There was a handwritten gray cardboard sign attached to an old art easel:

Cadillac Room:	The Glory to God Singers
Pontiac Room:	CANELLED
Penobscot Room:	Private Meeting (members only)

I looked at the sign. "There's no DOHR meeting. Are you sure it's today?"

"Don't act stupid," a smoldering Brian Kitson said.

"Maybe we're canelled?" I asked. Brian looked morally offended. "It was a joke."

"We're the private meeting. Come on."

"Private? Are we ashamed of the group?"

"No, the hotel is. Will you come on, let's go."

He walked on ahead. I had to go the bathroom, so I took a detour.

The men's room was dirty and smelly. Someone stood in the middle of the three urinals. I walked up to the urinal to his right, and, as I was peeing, I noticed he was stroking his cock.

He nodded over to a bathroom stall. I just knew it. This was the real purpose of DOHR.

"Are you with the … private meeting?" I asked. "DOHR?"

At which the guy rapidly zipped up his pants and left.

"Wait, I just wanna know—"

When I walked out of the men's room, I saw the man disappear into the door marked *Cadillac Room*. I mindlessly followed. I walked in, there was a chorus singing energetic gospel music. The music was joyous and no one seemed to mind I was the only white face in the crowd. Swaying to the music, I abruptly remembered I needed to be in the Penobscot Room and quickly left. I felt just a little ashamed: DOHR was a political organization, not a sexual one like, apparently, a church. I was sure I needn't be afraid of sex interfering with my work.

The Penobscot Room was a surprisingly soulless and generic hotel conference room; any old charm had been replaced by whitewash and dim lighting. Just like the lobby, the small, dank room had an acrid, smoky cloud hanging over it. Classroom-style folding chairs stood in rows leading up to a large podium up front. The chairs were peppered with people, mostly sitting along the aisles, leaving huge swaths of empty space in the middle of the rows. Red, glowing cigarette tips moved like fireflies. The room could fit over a hundred, but there couldn't have been more than fifteen to twenty people there.

I stood off to the side. At the front of the room, I could see a brightly lit dais. Behind it stood a tall, pencil-like man with jet-black hair and a mustache. He must have been in his thirties. Casey, the man from outside, was beside him. Casey wore the clothes of a much younger man, including ill-advised tight blue jeans. Brian, who was seated in the front row, had his eyes glued on Mr. Pencil, whom I took to be the magical Phil. He was reciting in a completely lifeless intonation, the polar opposite of the music I just heard.

"This section, point three-subsection-a of the article under consideration, will allow us to form a united front, a real community by reaching out to new organizations and affiliate groups of all varieties. Widening our reach–"

"Speak up!" yelled someone. I was impressed someone was paying attention.

"Widening our reach," he almost shouted before immediately going back to his soft monotone, "will, in effect, make this an umbrella organization of many like-minded groups if they meet the certain criteria we will now outline below under point three a, sub b. We are looking at groups with common goals and different membership profiles …"

The lack of energy in the crowd perhaps had something to do with Phil's monotonous voice. He was just as much of a mousy man as Brian was a mousy boy. Clearly, they were meant for each other. Brian had nothing to worry about. Neither sex nor politics nor money could get me involved with Phil.

Phil continued to drone on about acceptable and unacceptable partner organizations. Casey sat at a table next to him. They were an odd couple: tall, skinny Phil and the roly-poly

Casey—kind of like a gay Laurel and Hardy. I was a little unnerved when Casey stared at me and smiled. My face blushed. I hoped he wasn't someone I had tricked with in Palmer Park.

Brian got up and looked around. Seeing me, he walked in my direction and ushered me to the front row to sit beside someone on the aisle seat. Brian whispered to him: a balding, tall, older man, though definitely boyish, with a cute John Waters mustache and smooth, shiny, white skin. Brian patted the chair and indicated for me to sit there, then returned to ogling his personal rock star.

"How all this can affect the subject organization is clearer under subsection f. We see there the mention of the extension of voting terms under certain circumstances, which are outlined in the next article under sub-subchapter one ..." Phil droned.

The middle-aged boy leaned over to me and spoke in a loud whisper. "Hi, Jamie, glad to see you. I'm Ken. Ken Finocchio. We spoke on the phone."

The effeminate voice was familiar. Sitting this closely, I noticed his little bulbous nose. It made him look quite cute, like a little puppy-dog man. I suppressed the urge to pat his head and scratch under his chin.

"Hi, Ken." I offered my hand, feeling like that was a stiff, distancing thing to do. He looked at the offered hand and then shook it long and softly.

"Brian should have brought you here earlier. I am afraid we've already started. This will go on for a while. Come outside with me."

I was relieved to find kindness after Brian's caustic personality. As we walked to the back of the room, Casey stood up. He seemed perturbed. "Why under only certain circumstances? And what's this about voting for removal from office? This sounds very irregular, Phil. What—"

"Case, as I try to point out in article six—it's on page forty-three, so you can follow along—it states that under the provisions outlined herein and not otherwise to be amended except as provided for in the bylaws ..." The droning continued.

Out in the hall, the air was comparatively fresh.

"Hi, again, James. It's great to have you here."

"Jamie."

Ken was touchy-feely. His arms were all over me in a second with a hug hello. Then his hand rested on my shoulders. I understood now what Brian meant by chicken hawks. Feeling put off by his aggressive friendliness, I didn't register much of what he said until he came to his last sentence: "We just think the world of your mother."

"You do?" I asked incredulously, "You know my mother?"

"I know what you're thinking. We're officially nonpartisan, but we're mostly all Democrats here. There's a few self-hating Republicans, but we're mostly—"

"Hey, Ken! Sweetie!" Neil bounded toward us. He was an effeminate man, husky and young, and had a very thick head of dark-blond hair.

"Oh God, here comes one of them," Ken whispered to me. He did not look happy to see him. "Hello, Neil," he intoned. I assumed Neil was one of the losers Brian had mentioned.

"Say, that is really good," Neil said, eyeing Ken's head. "You just have to tell me who your barber is. I must see him sometime."

"Hilarious, Neil. In ten years, we'll be seeing the same one. Now, if you don't mind, I'm busy."

"Busy with this week's conquest?"

"Do you mind? He's a new member and a very special one."

"I bet he is, ha ha. But I have to talk to you." He had an annoying singsong voice. You couldn't help but think he was hiding how he really felt. "About this *community* amendment you guys are pushing. You didn't have anything to do with it, *did you?*"

"It's all Phil's work. It's legalese I don't understand or care about. Now, please, if you'll excuse me, I am talking to someone right now."

"I'm on to you—both of you. Droning legalese is how you hide everything."

"Neil?"

"Yes, yes, excuse me. Now, who is this cute young thing? You didn't introduce us." Neil looked at me with an unabashed lascivious expression.

"Please, this is our newest member, James Goldberg," he said proudly.

"Jamie," I corrected.

"Jamie? That's a *gorgeous* name—but I already know you," Neil squealed. Immediately, I thought again of some possible drunken encounter.

"You know me?"

"Well, not personally, but Casey is my lover … you know, Casey? He knows your mother quite well."

"Really, does everyone here know my mother?"

"Oh yes, Kenny boy told us." They exchanged evil glances for a split second, and then Neil faced me with a broad smile. "And yes, of course we know who your mother is. Like I said, Casey knows her quite well."

"Oh, she does?" Ken asked.

"Yes, *he* does, sweetie."

"Well, excuse us, now, Neil. Jamie and I have business to attend to."

"Go ahead. Can I watch? I mean it. I'd like to hear what you tell our new members. You know, in case I take over as membership chair someday."

"You know already—*sweetie*."

"That's my line, and I am just fascinated with how you work. You know—these new members."

Ken rolled his eyes. Judging from Neil's glee, this seemed to be exactly the effect he was after.

"We can do this afterward, but here are just some forms to fill out," Ken muttered as he pulled some papers from an open briefcase on the floor. "Besides, we're missing the meeting. It usually starts with introductions, and we were hoping to introduce you. Maybe we can squeeze it in toward the end."

"Looks like you're squeezing him already," Neil said.

Ken took his hand away from my shoulder, and we walked back toward the door. But Neil paused at the door and tapped my shoulder. I bristled, expecting another grope, but it was just a tap.

He motioned for me to follow him, then glanced at Ken, who also stopped before going inside. "Please, after you, Ken. Jamie, let me just speak with you for a moment. You don't mind, do you?" Neil asked me.

"Not at all."

"He's missing the meeting," Ken protested.

"I know that must be killing you, but I'm going to speak with Jamie for just a minute. I hope you don't mind, Ken?"

Ken clearly minded. "Okay, if you must. Jamie, come sit by me afterward. We'll go over your membership application."

"Don't worry, he wouldn't miss it for the world."

Neil stared after him as Ken walked back into the Penobscot Room. He stood extremely close to me. "It's so nice to meet Ruth's son." He was touchy-feely, too, but more daring. He put his arm around my shoulder, then caressed my back.

"You know my mother, too?" I asked.

"Not exactly. Let me introduce myself properly." He shot a glance toward where Ken had stood. He then let his arm drop, allowing it to casually graze against my ass. "My name is Neil, Neil Bradley—I know: two first names, ugh. I am the secretary for DOHR. It's an honor to have you as a member."

"It is?"

"Certainly. Your mother is well-respected in the Democratic Party. I'm Casey Winograd's better half. Case used to be on the Wayne County Democratic Central Committee with her. You must know him from way back. He's changed a bit—used to be skinnier than Phil back in the day."

"The name does sound familiar." I was beginning to feel a sense of relief that the recognition of the fat man at the podium may have had nothing to do with Palmer Park. I relaxed so that even the random pat on my ass made me feel welcomed.

"Yes, now you remember. Your mother is very supportive of us."

"Of who?" I asked incredulously. This could not possibly be my homophobic mother.

"Of who? DOHR, silly."

"She is … supportive? Are you sure? Did she say so?" I wondered why she would be so supportive of a gay political group but not her own gay son.

"And not just DOHR, but Casey in particular. You look surprised. Casey had an anti-discrimination suit against the bank where he worked. They fired him for being gay."

"My mom helped?"

"She was very supportive. There was really nothing to be done, the damn banks."

"Yeah, banks are terrible. I hate them. Especially the Detroit National Bank. Republican monsters," I echoed.

"You said it. That was the bank he worked for. Anyway, Case did get her to speak here once."

"*My* mother?"

"Yes."

"What did she talk about? I remember her mentioning a group called the Detroit Organization for Human Rights, but she never said it was a gay rights organization. Was it always a gay rights group?"

"Please, *lesbian and* gay rights. We're a *community* now." He looked around as if to see if anyone heard us. "By membership, it should be gay and lesbian, but who's counting."

"When did my mom actually speak here?"

"Not so long ago. Maybe a year and a half ago."

"What, you mean after I came out?"

"I guess so. Anyway, before you leave tonight, see Casey. He's *dying* to talk to you. I think you will get along famously." Neil couldn't help himself giving me another hello hug—this time without the nonchalant brush against my butt.

"Thanks. Shouldn't we go inside? This is my first meeting. I might be missing something," I said nervously.

"Oh, there's no worry about that. Phil's still talking. Well, perhaps you are missing *something*." We turned to walk back into the room. "Anyway, all I can say is welcome; we need young energy to revitalize the group. Maybe you can be our student liaison or something like that?"

I stopped in my tracks before the door. "Isn't Brian Kitson the student representative? He gave me a ride here."

"Brian? Brian *Kitson?*" he asked as if completely surprised. "Is he still here? He's the university liaison. That's busy work. You're going to have an important job." Neil put on a smile. I was flattered, and it helped explain Brian's less-than-thrilled reaction when he had met me. I was falling right into the middle of things, whether I liked it or not.

"Neil, I'm sure Brian is doing a great job."

"*Great* doesn't even begin to describe it, dear."

"Look, it's just that I don't want to get involved in any internal fights. I'm here to fight discrimination and help the community, not to get caught up in internal politics, okay?"

"Sorry, Jamie, politics is politics. Idealism is great. Hold on to it as long as you can, but reality is inevitable. To get what you want done, you have to fight for it both inside and out." Then, with a drag queen-like flourish, he added, "Welcome to the club."

"Well, I'd like to get a nondiscrimination clause passed at DSU—especially for the housing policy. Whatever I can do to help that cause, sign me up," I said, recalling how my homophobic resident assistant had thrown me out of the dorms.

"With all due respect, that's chicken feed. Don't talk to a provost. Talk to the mayor if you want to get things done."

I was duly shocked by what he said. He stared at me for a moment.

"Okay, you're definitely the type for us. We need new blood in the organization. It's actually got nothing to do with internal politics. Little Bri, dreary boy, slighted the women's community when he gave a recent presentation at Marygrove College. I said he was too young. But Phil and Ken were all for it. Brian gave the talk on gay rights and never mentioned lesbians, not a single time—to a historically women's college. Stupid, thoughtless, exclusionary. And—believe me—did we hear about it. So now we fight internally to get the right person in front of the right audience."

"We all make mistakes. I'm sure he won't repeat that," I said, trying to sound objective.

"You can say that again!" Staying neutral was going to be very difficult indeed. "It was definitely *not* astute. How can you be in politics and *not* be *astute*? Slips like that cost us real big. I mean, look in that smoky backroom we have in there. Not a single woman, sweetie. You get it, don't you? No community, despite what Pencil Boy—I mean Phil—is trying to do to Case.

The largest feminist group in Michigan are lesbian separatists. I am very sympathetic to their cause because men treat women like shit. And we can't come across anything like the way straight men are: Any insensitivity and we're judged very harshly."

"I see. I suppose any effort we make to get female members could make us look like we're in competition with feminist organizations for women volunteers."

"*Astute*. That's what I mean. You get it."

"It's disempowering women," I added, hoping I was on a roll of astuteness. "How do we get out of this mess?"

"Exactly. You get it. How refreshing. That Bri—what a ditzy queen and his puppy-dog attentions to Phil are *embarrassing*. You know they sleep together. I can't imagine what Ken makes of them—Ken and Phil live together—but those two … shoot, I am a gossip. That doesn't matter. What matters is Ken and Phil are supposed to be lovers—or at least, you'd think they were, except for the way Bri fawns over Phil. I normally wouldn't mind, but it sets a bad example of thinking with your dick, putting a little prick like that in charge of important matters."

"Yes, I see. I'll go back in now."

"I'm not fighting Phil. His idea to make partner organizations is spot-on," Then with a slight pat on my butt, "And before you leave, sweetie, remember to stop by and see Case."

"Okay." I said, wondering how I could completely sneak out of the building.

"Promise?" Neil asked.

"Sure." *Who are you, my mother?*

"How sweet, And, if you need me, I'll be in the back."

Inside the room, onstage, they were discussing the same bylaw change, supposedly the amendment Neil had been talking about. Contrary to what he said, Neil followed me and sat in the second row right behind Ken and me. Ken was listening intently to the arcane proceedings.

Neil leaned over and handed me a green sheet of cardboard. "Use it for voting," he whispered. "The front is green for yes, and the back is red for no."

"Voting?" I asked. "I'm not even a member yet."

Ken then leaned over. "You are now." He handed me a clipboard. "Use this to fill in the forms. It's really just a formality. Fill it out and give it to me before you leave."

"That goes for Casey and me, too," Neil said in a loud whisper.

"Thank you, Neil, you're *so helpful*. Jamie, just make sure you cross the box for a student membership; they're free. I see Neil gave you a card to vote. When they vote for the amendment, just raise the green card to support it so we can have a quorum."

"I'll wait until I'm officially a member," I said.

"Oh, but you practically are," Ken enthused.

"Do you have a pen?" I asked him.

Before he could answer, one appeared from behind, offered by Neil. "You can keep it, dear," he answered proudly.

I looked at it. The pen read *Hotel Pontiac*. I dutifully filled in the forms and handed it back to Neil. It seemed like I had to find a way to walk the tightrope of getting to know Ken and Phil on one side and Neil and Casey on the other.

Neil began to message my shoulder. "You need to relax, sweetie." He then waved his hand to the podium. Casey was slow on the uptake. When Casey finally looked up, Neil pointed to me and then gave a thumbs-up. Casey waved back. The funny way he waved his hand triggered my memory. I did remember Casey. Many years ago, when he had been younger, he used to visit our house. He often volunteered to help with mailings, which meant we were often at the same table folding political literature and stuffing them into envelopes. I even remember him having a younger man in tow. I looked at Neil; it had not been him.

Neil leaned closely to my ear. "Come over to our house after the meeting. We can tell you more about the group and being our liaison."

My internal political and sexual alerts sounded off. I also remembered what Brian had warned me about.

"I can't. I need a ride home," I said.

"Don't worry about that," he assured me. I was unsure if he meant he was going to seduce me or drive me home.

After a while, it started to become clear that this amendment discussion would eat up the entire meeting. Reluctantly, I listened. When all was said and done, nit-picky details aside, there seemed to be no controversy. The bylaws amendment removed term limits on officers so Casey could run for vice president again since no one else wanted the job. But more important was a new amendment that added a kind of affiliate membership: people who could vote and run for office by being a member of another lesbian-gay rights organization whose political positions and fee structure were at parity with the host organization. A complex web of checks and balances was being added to this provision to assure DOHR wouldn't be taken over. It all seemed hopelessly convoluted so that anyone could interpret the rules however they wanted.

I reviewed my mom's political decision-making process. First, I liked the proposal. It allowed new groups, like—as Neil had pointed out—a lesbian separatist organization—to be voting members without actually joining. As far as I understood, there was a specific lesbian separatist organization that wanted to ally themselves with DOHR. This approach seemed like a way of including them. Second, the amendment was a politically viable decision: They needed Casey to run for a third term, and he was practically a friend of the family. Moreover, the addition of related groups would give the LGBT movement more clout than working separately. Finally, there was no objection to it from neither the Casey/Neil camp nor the Phil/Ken camp. There was some objection, but it seemed more emotional than rational.

At one moment, Neil got up and walked over to the podium; Phil sat down next to Casey onstage.

"Okay, we have a motion on the floor," Neil announced, "to amend the nomination rules and allow a new voting membership category called affiliate members. Do I have a second?"

There was a second in the crowd.

"If you vote aye, please raise the green side of the cards now." Neil spoke in a formal way with no trace of his more playful effeminate voice.

About two-thirds of the room raised their cards. I waited until the last minute to raise the green card. It was a trick my mother had taught me, so that you can vote for something without encouraging others to follow you. Nevertheless, as the votes were being counted, I noticed heads turn to look at me. A new kind of reputation was preceding me.

"If you vote nay, please raise the red side of your cards now," Neil added listlessly.

A few scattered cards went up.

"The ayes have it, sixteen to five. That does qualify as a quorum and the measure passes." Neil said to a peppering of boos. Then at once, like a switch was flipped, his voice regained its playfulness. "That concludes the agenda today, boys and girls. See you all same time, same station, for another frolicking episode. We'll have a special presentation by the Episcopal archdiocese from Lansing. Oh, and we might even get lucky and not discuss any more bylaws. I even heard a rumor we might move into the Cadillac Room. Stay tuned darlings." He banged a gavel on the podium, and everyone got up to leave.

Neil descended the podium and approached me. "You coming with us?" he asked. "Don't worry, I can see you get home. I promise we're not going to bite."

I had to laugh. "Okay. Yes, sure, I'll go," I said. Ken shot a glance at me when I said that. Then Neil walked over to Casey at the podium.

Ken got up and turned to face me, "Good luck, kiddo, with Neil and Casey," he said with a trace of sarcasm. "Be careful, Jamie. Remember, you're a valuable member of the team. Phil and I would love for you to come over to our house for dinner sometime. We can have Brian bring you over, okay?"

"Thank you," I said. "I'd like that."

"We'll give you a call later." He walked away toward Phil. They hugged and kissed perfunctorily.

I noticed Brian had stayed in his seat the entire time. Brian's eyes furtively looked away, but clearly he was waiting for some sign to approach. At one moment, Phil beckoned him, not unlike a puppy, with a kind of come-here gesture. Brian rushed up to Phil tail wagging. Ken looked perturbed but forced a smile.

"Brian wants to come over," Phil said.

"That's sweet," Ken whispered acidly. They huddled together, talking. Luckily, that took the pressure off me for going to Casey's.

I walked over to Brian after their huddle. "I don't need a ride home, Brian, I am going to see—"

"Yes, I know all about it! Thanks a lot," the peeved little brat said. "You ruined my entire night."

"I did?"

"Yes, Phil wants me to go with you to Neil and Casey's. To make sure nothing ... happens."

"Well, maybe that's not a bad idea? After all, we get along so well. I hope this night never ends."

"Ha ha. I'm just trying to help. Why does everyone think you know politics? You're as naive as they come. I'll protect you."

"Thank God for that," I added sarcastically.

"Right. Listen up: Neil seems as nice as can be; he probably asked you to be a student rep, right?"

"No, he didn't."

"Good. So we're going together to their house." Now it was clear for whose sake he really wanted to tag along. "Let's you and I just pretend we're together."

"What?"

"Humor me."

I did not want to humor him. I had known Casey. The trust level with him was suddenly shooting higher than with the little brat. I didn't need to replace Brian as a student representative, but I was damned if I was going to sell out to the likes of him.

"It will never work. They must know you're with Phil."

"They don't—just humor me. I know what I'm doing. And don't talk about Phil and me to anyone."

"You're kidding; you practically kissed him in front of the entire audience. Forget it. I don't want your help: I am going alone."

"Look, we got off on the wrong foot. I'm sorry. I just want to make sure we don't lose you. You're a valuable new member. Okay?" Brian said unconvincingly. Before I could respond, he then walked over to Neil and said, "We'll meet you at your house, Neil!"

"Oh really? You joining us?"

"Yes, I am. I'll drive Jamie." He put his arm around me awkwardly.

"Oh, just *love* to see you, sweeties," Neil quipped.

"Well, I guess we're going together." I said, unsure how this all had happened as we all left the Pontiac Hotel.

Chapter 11: Intimacy and Interference

We arrived about the same time as Neil at his house in Royal Oak. While my apartment was in a grimy but characterful neighborhood in Detroit, this place reeked of a lush kind of safety and sanitary boredom as virginal white snow and evergreen trees adorned the large front yard.

"Wow, this place is beautiful," said Brian.

"You like this?" I asked.

"Better than that junk heap you stay at." Brian clearly preferring the boring suburbs for 'real life' in the city. Neil bounded up to us.

"Welcome to *chez moi!*"

"You have a big house," I said.

"This? Well, its our little bordello, haha. Come right in."

He opened the large white door and inside it looked predictably sterile. It was the kind of place you walked in and felt like you couldn't touch a thing because the slightest move could cause untold damage to property and the sense of order.

Neil gathered our coats and put them into a closet almost the size of my bedroom.

Neil's large suburban house was decorated in cold modernity. It was brightly adorned and upper-middle-class ordinary.

The walls were lined with lit shelves loaded with fancy glass-ware and shiny knickknacks. The living room had sparse furni-ture, with two plush couches flanking a glass coffee table and a faux fireplace. The couches were all-white cushions with chrome trim. The white pile carpet was sparkly clean compared with the dingy blue one in my house.

Brian and I sat together on one couch. He had his arm uncomfortably around my shoulders. I found this a quite dis-tasteful and dishonest display. Moreover, I felt my personal no-sex, no-touching, no-nothing vow was being compromised.

"Brian, please—don't."

Reluctantly, Brian removed his unwanted arm. I pressed myself into the opposite corner of the couch.

Neil was bringing us glasses of wine when the door opened. Casey walked in. He flashed a sharp glance at Brian, and Brian sent one back at him. I felt I was in the crossfire of a political ambush.

"Case, we have company already," Neil said as he gave us glasses of white wine. Neil went over and collected Casey's jacket and hung it up, which struck me odd that Casey wouldn't do this himself.

"Hey, boys. Glad you could make it," Casey said, taking a seat on the couch opposite us.

"Let me get you a glass of wine, Case." Neil flashed a smile at him and walked back toward the kitchen. Casey looked approvingly at me. To everyone's surprise, including mine, I stood up and sat next to him.

"Glad to see you again," I said.

"Now you remember me?" he asked.

"I remember you used to come over and stuff envelopes in

our living room. You brought a friend of yours ... er, Robbie was his name?"

"You have a memory. Don't say his name too loudly around here, though." Casey shot a glance toward the kitchen. Brian squirmed uncomfortably.

"He was very funny, I recall."

"Yes, he was. But that was a long time ago—at least in gay years. Anyway, it is so good to see you again. Congratulations on coming out. I would never have guessed. When was the happy event?"

"Not quite two years now."

"That's wonderful. Welcome to the team. Brian, we have you to thank for bringing in a real valuable volunteer."

"Oh no. He just gave me a ride," I said loudly. "I found out about DOHR all by myself through the Lesbian-Gay Hotline."

This made Casey stare at Brian with a quizzical look. Brian then looked down toward the floor.

"Oh really? Well, the hotline is an excellent group. We're big contributors. It certainly is great you want to be a part of DOHR. It's a natural with your mother also potentially involved. You know, I worked with her years ago on the Oakland County jail desegregation and, for a while, on the Wayne County Democratic Central Committee. She's an amazing woman, you know."

"'Amazing' is the word, all right," I quipped. "Always full of surprises."

"And yet very constant," Brian said. "We should get *her* to join DOHR."

"I don't think that's such a good idea," I said.

"No, it's not," Neil said, returning with a glass of wine.

"Because she's already a member." He handed Casey the glass and then sat next to Brian. Brian, just as I had done before, slid to the opposite edge of the couch. Neil sighed and flipped his wrist. "Oh, you need some more wine, Jamie?"

"Not at the moment. Neil, did you say my mom had joined DOHR?" I asked, trying to contain my disbelief.

"Not exactly. She became an honorary member about a year ago," Neil said. "But she's always been very ... supportive." He went back into the kitchen.

"You're surprised?" Casey asked.

"She isn't active in the group?" I asked.

"No, not really. But she did speak and does let us know when the Central Committee considers anything important to us."

"How often is that?"

"You'd be surprised. You'll see, we have a broad scope in our charter. Not just human rights, but also access to government."

"I got some goodies," said Neil, who came back with the bottle of wine and a plate of cheese and cucumbers. Without asking, he refilled my glass. "Just adding her name to our group is very important."

Brian was upset, which seemed to please Neil. He plopped down beside him.

"A toast." Casey raised his glass. "To Ruth Goldberg and the heir apparent." Brian turned red.

Having downed the first glass out of pure anxiety, this time I sipped the wine. Its taste was different from the soda pop wines we drank in the dorms, this had a strange combination of sweetness and acidity.

"Now, we'll need to find you a position, Jamie ... let's see—" Casey then turned to me and winked.

"Student rep?" Neil offered.

Brian was about to say something, but Casey quickly cut in. "Our friend Brian here has that job already, don't you?"

"Yes, I do; you know that."

"And you do such good work. You like that job, don't you?"

"You know I do."

"Oh, good, that's excellent. Yes, I seem to recall hearing about an interesting conversation you had with the Cass Tech provost." Casey smiled and Brian blushed.

"It was Marygrove," Neil corrected. Brian winced.

Casey looked at Brian with a wry grin and then looked at me decisively. He was clearly about to play a trump card of some kind. "Jamie, I know: You should be our Central Committee liaison. It's not really a student position, but with your experience and connections, it would be a natural fit."

"Wow, that's an important job," Brian said.

"All the more reason to entrust it to your friend Jamie, " Neil asked looking Brian straight in the eyes, "don't you think, Brian?

After an awkward pause, everyone was looking at me.

"What do you think, Jamie?" Casey prompted.

I had no idea how to answer. The last thing I wanted was to be a liaison on my mother's home political turf. It was getting thick not telling them that she and I were not speaking. "That would be awesome, Casey," I lied. I shuddered, pondering her embarrassment when my appearance would advertise she had a gay son.

"Good. When Phil told me you were coming to the meeting, I was delighted." Casey chuckled. "Say, do you remember we were on television together?"

"We were on television—oh, you mean the schoolyard thing?"

"Let me see, you must have been six years old or so. It was a television ad for Zolton Ferency when he ran for governor—"

"That's it," I remembered.

"Yes, your mother was good friends with Harriet—Harriet what's-her-name, you know, Ferency's campaign manager—you remember, Neil?"

"Welton something?"

"No, that's not it. The one who was pretty tight with Representative Joe Forbes—and, uh ... Sam Hauptman of the UAW? Anyway, in the commercial, I was pretending to be a teacher. You and a bunch of kids were running out of school."

"I remember seeing it when it aired during the eleven o'clock news!" I cried. "It was the latest I was ever allowed to stay up. That broadcast was one of my prouder moments as a child, even though none of my friends saw it."

"Now, how can we get your mother more active on our team? I can't think of any better way than making you our liaison to the County Central Committee."

"But I can do that. I have lots of experience now as the university rep," Brian said.

"Oh, come on," Neil said. "James's—Jamie's mother is on the committee. You should be proud of your little friend. This will be perfect for him."

"Or maybe not so perfect," I muttered.

"Why not?" Casey asked. I was quiet, then Casey and Neil

exchanged glances. They both looked at Brian, then at me. "Something private?" I nodded yes. "Say, Brian, why don't you go on home?" Then, turning to me, he said, "I'll give you a ride home. We won't be long."

Much to his astonishment, Brian was summarily dismissed. Neil happily showed Boy Wonder the door.

Casey looked at me softly. My hyper sex alert was calmed, realizing this was a family friend. I felt safe.

"Now that our friend is gone, I want you to know I think this is a very important position for you to take. But I have picked up on the fact that perhaps things are not so good between you and your mother."

"No, they're not."

"Politics is one thing. When it's in your own backyard, it's another. How bad is it?"

"We don't speak ... because I'm gay. She kicked me out of the house. They threw away my stuff."

"Really?" Neil asked.

"That's very surprising," Casey added.

"I think she would be ashamed if I showed up at her committee meeting. I don't think that's the way to endear yourselves to her."

"Oh dear, that is bad! I had no idea. I am so sorry; that must be tough, sweetie," Neil said.

"But it can't be as bad as all that. I know her, Jamie. It's just ignorance about the community. That's all it is. Once she knows us better, she'll come around; she will, you'll see. I know she will. It may be a little awkward at first—"

"Awkward and complicated," I added.

"Listen, she's already a member of our organization,

though I know the not-in-my-backyard routine. Still, she's old school. Remember: They never had a class on gays and lesbians, never read about us, and never met us except through our enemies. She is exactly one of those we have to win over. If we can't do that, then we don't have a prayer, do we?" It was odd hearing my family life reduced to a political strategy.

"It's pointless. She hates me," I said.

"She signed up as an honorary member," Casey said. "She didn't do that because she hates you. She's spoken up in committee meetings for us. She just had other ideas about who you were."

"Yeah, but knowing Ruth," Neil said, "she may have done it for political reasons. She isn't the only politician who's an honorary member just to give some token support."

"Maybe. But she certainly didn't do it for fun and prizes either. She didn't have to." Casey made eye contact with me. "Look, Jamie, I noticed you voted for the amendment. Why?"

"Let's see. First, not because you told me to. Second, the inclusion of other groups appealed to me. I am a lefty by nature. Third, it was a simple case of reality. The group needed a vice president, and no one was stepping up but you. You were at your term limit, and in order to run again, the rules needed to change. I didn't see any organized opposition to the measure, and you needed a quorum. It seemed like the right thing to do."

They both were nodding their heads. "Can you do it?" Neil asked.

"Can you be our liaison to the County Central Committee?" Casey repeated. "To some extent, we're using your relationship to get a deeper commitment from Ruth, but I think that can also heal your relationship. Either way, Neil and I have got your back. And she wouldn't dare embarrass you at the committee meeting. She's too savvy for that."

"Look, it will be awkward at first. If you want, one of us can go to the first meeting," Neil offered.

I immediately felt afraid, so their offer to go with me sounded like a blessing. But then I saw something new inside myself. It was a picture of a little boy being led into school by his mother. I just wasn't a little boy anymore.

"I have to just do this alone. You know what my mom feels about you, this organization, and myself. If you can live with the consequences, I'll do it."

"Good, we'll back you up. You can't predict what happens despite your best efforts."

"And I suppose the meeting's better than hearing nothing from her," I said. Neil and Casey laughed.

"I will tell you plainly: I know her. I think it's more likely that she will come to our defense. At any rate, we stand a better chance with you up there than with anyone else."

"I want to do something to help the gay community. That's why I joined."

"And this is your chance," Neil added.

On the quiet ride home, I thought about what I had just consented to. Was I really going to confront my mother on her own playing field, the Democratic Party? Where had this courage come from?

I hated baseball. But I felt like I had just hit a grand slam.

Chapter 12: Relentless Ritual

I came home from my political triumph ready to brag to Dave, but he wasn't home. Then I remembered I had told him what sellouts the Democrats were while I was trying to out-left wing him during some political debates. We would politically commiserate against the Republicans and the big banks financing them, like the infamous Detroit National Bank. But we also railed against the Democrats for not standing up for the socialist agenda like in Europe. I may have overplayed my hand.

When Dave had taken me in, I had been warned by an ex-girlfriend of his that he was quite homophobic, so I had tried to hide who I really was. I'd attempted to ingratiate myself with his way of thinking to avoid being homeless. It later turned out that he didn't care whether I was gay or not. Nevertheless, he didn't forget my diatribe against the sellout Democrats. So it was probably better not to tell him about DOHR.

With the apartment all to myself, I decided to listen to an old favorite opera, Wagner's *Tannhauser*. I remembered, when I was younger, how I had related to Tännhauser's yearning for redemption. I thought playing it would encourage me on my path to community service.

I was wrong. Tannhauser's hopeless search for forgiveness on account of his sexual depravity only brought to mind my own. His impossible journey for acceptance and repentance only brought him rejection, humiliation, and hatred. I started to fear it would be the same for me.

During Tannhauser's ill-fated journey to find absolution in Rome, the haunting memories of my own sexual depravity vividly came back to me in a flash. The nights of letting myself be preyed upon—and then Gary. Gary, who I had thought had loved me, yet had taken advantage of me. I couldn't shake the guilt. I uncontrollably obsessed over these lurid flashbacks of bended knees, hiding in shrubs, or tensing my prostate as tightly as possible to maintain an erection so I could finish off some slimy guy. Suddenly, I felt an uncontrollable rush of anger at myself.

"You asshole! How could you do this to yourself!" I howled. At first, I recoiled from what I had just yelled. I was certain someone had heard me. I peeked through the blinds, but there was no one outside. Then I wasn't even sure whether I had really said it out loud or if the sheer vehemence in my own head had forced my thoughts to leak out for all to see.

With a flash of shame, I turned off the opera. Impulsively, I switched the stereo to a radio station blaring heavy metal music. Why had the self-hatred returned? Had I not resolved it all? I had come out of the closet. I had admitted I was gay. I had confronted Gary's memory. What more did I want from myself? Where did this vehemence come from?

Before I could answer that question, I was kneeling on the blue carpet in the living room and taking the leather belt from my pants. A song from the radio even seemed to be egging me on: *Do me a dance, you're a dancer/Harm yourself, you doer of evil.*

I already knew what was going to happen. "Please don't," I whispered to myself. I didn't want to do it, but I felt powerless not to: With the aggressive beat in the music and the accusation from the opera, I felt compelled to show my remorse and prove my regret with my own aggressive beat.

I was already caught in the circle of self-loathing: first hating myself, then stopping only to hate myself for hating myself. There was no escape except one. Lowering my pants, leather belt in hand, I submitted to it, all the while thinking, *Why?*

My hand reared back with the belt and swiped downward. Crack! A shiver of pain penetrated my body as I struck my ass. The pain flooded me, again and again. Searching for absolution, I continued. Searching for the feeling of too much, too much in order to prove my atonement. Again, another crack on my back. The pain throbbed with warmth. Another lash across my back, and the pain forced me to focus on the pain and the pain alone. Again. And again. I buckled under its force.

Then came the beginning of a sense of release. *Harder,* I urged myself. *Atonement.* I demanded more penance. *Why!* I screamed again inside my head as I whipped myself—harder.

I whipped myself as hard as I could. It wasn't enough to chase this searing hatred away. Before, when I had done this to myself, I may have been lost in it, but now I was horrified as I watched myself. I was powerless to stop, but equally revolted and ashamed. Eventually, frustrated that I could not achieve enough pain to satisfy this burning need to atone, I turned the belt around so the buckle would hit my ass as I lashed out at myself. The sick thud it made still wasn't enough. I reared back again, but I went too far and the belt buckle wrapped around my head and struck my cheek. I howled in pain.

"Ow! That really hurts!" I cried.

I caught myself actually yelling this out loud. And suddenly, something inside me snapped. I became conscious of what I was so compelled to do. The compulsion melted away, and I felt stupid, morbidly stupid, and immediately ashamed for what I had just done.

The brutal pain in my face didn't stop. It still throbbed to confront me with what I had been doing to myself. I crouched down into a ball, and pain quivered through me. I quickly became paranoid that I had knocked out a tooth. I grabbed at one that hurt, but it seemed solid. I tried wiggling it again and again and again. Then I remembered I was in the living room. Dave could come home at any time. The radio caught my attention. It was blaring another song with lyrics about being pushed to the limits until you drop.

I turned off the stereo. I even turned the dial of the receiver to cover up the heavy metal radio station from Dave. After that, with paranoid frenzy, I slithered into my room and shut the door. Once there, I grabbed at my teeth again to see if I had knocked them loose. The spot where the buckle had landed on my face still stung when I touched it.

Slowly, I began to calm down. My teeth were okay. My face would be bruised, of that I was sure. But I had already made up the excuse I would tell Dave and anyone else: I fell. I fell on the floor when I tripped over the rug in the living room.

My back ached and I felt exhausted. I crept onto my mattress and fell asleep.

I awoke in the middle of the night. My face burned with pain. I padded into the bathroom. When I looked in the mirror, as I feared, I had a deep bruise and a scratch on my face. Guiltily, I practiced my excuse, reciting it in my head: *I fell tripping over the rug. I have to pay attention more to what I'm doing.*

As I left the bathroom, I saw one compromising detail in the living room: My belt was neatly curled up on the sofa. I must have left it on the living room floor and Dave had found it there. I felt humiliated that there wasn't even a chance to cover it up now. I thought maybe I could sneak to the drugstore and buy some makeup and cover the bruise—I'd have to do that at school anyway. I couldn't play Horatio with a bruise on my face.

At once, my panic dissolved. I felt calm and surprisingly compassionate. *You fell. You just fell.* Then, with the raw lyrics from the heavy metal music still pulsing through my brain, I asked myself, *Why did you have to do this? Can't we just stop hating myself?* I had to laugh at myself, thinking *we* when there was just me. How I wanted to distance myself from my own behavior. Where did this terrible voice come from that was so critical of everything I did? It seemed to thrive on a sense of guilt. But my problem was not knowing if there was any amount of remorse, apology, or regret that could expiate this guilt. What would it take to stop hating myself, once and for all?

I thought about that: the end. What would end this? Could someone love me? Could I see a psychiatrist? Suicide was too simplistic a gut reaction. I just knew that was the coward's way out. I knew that firsthand by feeling the coward when I had attempted it before I came-out when I was sixteen. Suicide could not be the answer: There had to be something life-affirming.

Almost on cue, I felt a draft in the room. It was uncomfortably cold, but it was also refreshing. I covered myself with a warm blanket. And slowly awakening in my body was something milder ... I felt it. An inexplicable yet welcomed throbbing between my legs. It beckoned me as if it was some kind of answer. I thought I had sworn off listening to this desire, yet it tempted me with sweet, ethereal longings. Then, amid whispers of Casper and the possibilities of love, I came. Afterward, I fell asleep and the painful assault became a distant dream. The ritual had never happened. I really had fallen down.

Variation: Four Voices

March 1982

Chapter 13: Sea of Troubles

I was walking the halls of the Theater Department when a familiar sharp and angry voice resounded from one of the empty classrooms. I peaked in: it was Ben standing at the lecture podium and rehearsing to himself.

Studying his script so seriously, he looked very pretty. He was wearing tight clothes that showed off his slim features. I would call it a swimmer's build. *How perverse for me to spy on him practicing his lines,* I thought. I felt both the urge to yell at him and to lie down at his feet. Looks aside, he seemed to be mauling Shakespeare. I could imagine hearing Mr. Nathan saying, "Come on, go deeper."

"To die: to sleep; no more; and by a sleep to end the heartache and the thousand natural shocks that flesh is heir to; it is a consummation—" Ben looked up and saw me at the doorway. "Do you mind? Beat it, faggot. You don't have Dwight or any other theater fags to hide behind. I'll beat the shit out of you, so help me."

He went to slam the door, but I stuck my foot in the doorway.

"Bastard!"

"I can help you," I meekly offered.

"I don't need it, especially from you, of all people." Surprisingly, rather than try and slam the door again, Ben stared at me for a moment and then walked back to the dais. I followed even though he turned and flashed angry eyes at me.

"Please?" I couldn't quite understand it, but I felt this sudden compulsion to help him. I didn't care what he thought or did to me. Though we were easily twenty feet apart, I could almost feel his breath. My heart beat very hard. Ben's presence started to become larger than life; the idea of being angry at him felt ridiculous. I forgot all the bullying and humiliation. His tightly packed body just dared me to touch it.

"Look," he said, "keep away. I don't want you coming on to me." The insult felt like a challenge. I wanted to help him. "I am not playing Hamlet like a fag."

"I'm not asking you to play him like anything but yourself." I stepped toward him. Maybe I was coming on to him after all. "I want the whole production to look good—including you."

"Why? We hate each other."

"I don't hate you."

"Since when ..." He glanced down, I assumed at my crotch. "You are coming on to me, you faggot."

"Sorry," was all I could think to say. I could feel my erection against my pants.

"I don't understand you. Last rehearsal, you tried to fucking humiliate me in front of everyone."

"That was a mistake. Look, I'm sorry. Can I make it up to you?"

"You're trying to put the moves on me."

"I am not." I stepped closer, right by the dais. He backed away. "Casper told me to reach out to you—it was also Mr. Nathan's idea."

"Yeah, I spoke to Casper about it." Ben's eyes looked as if they would slice me in half. "Don't come closer."

I stepped back. Feeling the threat of violence, I noticed how strong and muscular he really was. What was going on in my brain, I couldn't understand.

"What can you know about this, huh? Look, Jamie, I'm serious. I am going to kick the shit out of you." He took another step back, but I hadn't moved closer. He was almost against the wall. "You remember last semester when I elbowed you in the stomach? That was no accident. I will gladly do it again *onstage* if you so much as embarrass me. Get it? And no professor, no director will be there to protect your faggot ass in back of the theater, shithead."

He was extremely intimidating. I was close to shaking until he said "shithead." I laughed because it reminded me of my birthday call with Rhonda.

"What's so fucking funny? Don't believe me?"

"I think I know something you don't."

"Huh? Fuck you—what?" Ben was finally disarmed. I had managed to distract him from the elephant in the room: my erection, which I couldn't seem to will away even as I pictured Richard Nixon instead of Ben.

"You're right," I said. "You don't need any help from me. You're blowing it all by yourself."

I don't remember how it happened. Ben had backed up against the wall and I was right up next to him.

"I am?"

"You'll embarrass yourself with no help from me." In spite of myself, I couldn't stop wishing I could touch him.

"Fuck you!"

I shivered. Realizing I was so close to him. He returned to his script at the dais.

"I'm trying to help you."

Ben made eye contact with me. "Don't fuck with me."

"That's better." I stepped back.

"What is?"

"Less anger and more uncertainty. You're playing Hamlet with too much anger."

"Because he's angry at fate."

"Maybe. But more importantly, he's suicidal. He's deadly serious but also uncertain if killing himself is worth it or even the right thing. I know something about that."

"If you tried to commit suicide, then go back and do a better job—Jesus."

"Don't use anger. Hamlet's not angry. Maybe he's frustrated. You shouldn't be angry at me either. We're in this together. I'm your best friend, your closest ally—onstage. We're gonna be onstage four hours a night staring at each other, pretending we're friends. Can't we be real friends?"

"You're coming on to me."

"In this speech, instead of just funneling your anger at me, think how much better it would be if you also funneled friendship. Anger and friendship together. The uncertainty will add depth. He doesn't commit suicide, after all, even though he thinks about it so much."

Ben stood there, speechless. He looked down again at my crotch. Thank goodness it had retreated.

"Suit the action to the word," I said. "The word to the action, as it were. The mirror up to nature."

"Ha ha, aren't you clever. What are you driving at?"

"Read your lines like they're a meditation on death. You're alone, and you think no one is listening—ever been there? A moment when you think no one is around. When you can finally think, meditate on a subject you can't solve. Meditate as if there's nothing more important in the world than to solve the riddle: 'To be or not to be.' Ever dared to put a razor blade close to your wrist? Maybe you know what it's like. Maybe you've thought about it before, like I have. Life might be so worthless, the only choice is to end it all. A moment when you feel every-one hates you and can't understand you, all because of who you love or who you are."

Ben stared at me intensely. I didn't know if he was going to shout at me, hit me, or cry on my shoulder. I braced myself for all three. At one moment, I could see Ben was about to yell.

"I don't know your pain. I'm sorry if I sounded like I did. I'm just sharing some of mine. All I'm saying is to put your pain into Hamlet." Ben had such power over me as a bully. But being so vulnerable to him, he suddenly seemed powerless. I just couldn't help starting to feel extreme sympathy, if not love, for him. "I'm just saying I do know what it's like when people judge me, hate me, and throw me out of my house based on what I am—something I cannot change. I know what it's like when Hamlet thinks the only escape possible is death."

"You tried to do it?" he asked.

I nodded my head.

"Well that's not *my* Hamlet."

I couldn't help but feel I was making love to Ben with my words. "Fair enough, but even your Hamlet, just for a moment, thinks that the only answer to the darkness is dragging a razor blade across his wrist. He just about says so. For me, that's the moment when the soliloquy takes place."

"You're a real piece, Jamie. I get it. Sometimes I swear I don't know whether to beat the shit out of you or shake your—" He looked down at my pants again and then looked away. I could feel there was nothing to see. More than anything, I wanted to ask, *"Can we be friends?"* or maybe, *"Can I kiss you?,"* but the words wouldn't come out.

"To be or not to be, that is the question." His voice quivered. I held my gaze, and he looked into my eyes. It was clear to me he knew that meditation.

"Whether 'tis nobler in the mind to suffer the slings and arrows of outrageous fortune." His anger crescendoed into doubt. "Or to take arms against a sea of troubles, and by opposing—end them."

A tear ran down my cheek.

"To die: to sleep; no more ..." He was choked up and couldn't finish the line. "All right, Jamie, get out. You're not getting to me, you hear, faggot?"

"That was powerful, Ben." I turned to leave and walked to the door but then turned around. "I am afraid of you. I admit that. And I think you are used to me backing down, but I am not doing that anymore. I am either calling your bluff or you're going to do whatever you do, but it doesn't scare me anymore. In the past, you slapped me, you've elbowed me, spit on me, and I survived. Hit me whenever you want. I am not backing down—but I am also not hitting on you, even if I want to—and I just realized that's exactly how I am playing Horatio. So plan your beatings now, *sweet prince*."

For once, Ben was speechless and his mouth agape.

"All right, I'm going. I hope I helped with something. That's all I want to do now. I promise you, I'll never try to humiliate you again. That was when I was feeling vindictive and self-righteous. I didn't like that feeling."

"Okay," he said. "I get it. I'm sorry I slapped you. Now get out of here and leave me alone. We can both tell Arthur we made nice."

Exit Horatio.

Chapter 14: Grunt and Sweat

Thanks to DOHR, I had an important cause again: human rights. I also had a calling: the theater. Both politics and the theater felt like the right future for me. Politics let me use my skills as an activist I had learned from my mother. For the stage, I could process my own emotional issues, critically and insightfully, thanks to Mr. Nathan's inspiration. Finally, I had a gay outlet that was sexless and consequential. The next stage would be to find some way to pay for college.

Bereft of my parents' support, I needed a job that paid good money. The one I had at the Bagel Factory, while fun, was not earning enough for my tuition and books. This would be the pinnacle of my development: actually holding a normal job and making enough money to be self-sufficient. A fresh start in a professional environment. A new job with a chance for a clean slate, to work where no one knew anything about me or to what depths I had once descended.

I went to a temporary employment agency called The Quick Girls. They assured me I didn't need to be a girl as long as I was quick. My quip about being a "quick boy" was not received with the intended levity. Nevertheless, they found a job for me right away. I didn't really care what it was, as long as I could make what they called the Quick Girls minimum wage of $5.50 an hour. Almost double what the Bagel Factory paid. Plus, I could prove to myself that I was capable of fitting in at a regular job. An august professional institution seemed just the ticket to this sought-after normalcy.

My first assignment didn't seem like the best one in the world, but I assumed these jobs didn't last long, so I didn't mind being a receptionist. Plus, I was working for a trust division of the Detroit National Bank. When the woman from Quick Girls first told me to report to the Veterans Trust Division, I was very excited. I imagined some marbly place with gold bullion, silver-encrusted certificates, bonds, and the other trappings of ill-gotten wealth.

Banks were so American and mainstream: the reticent tricklers of Reagan's trickle-down theory. Dave would be upset if he found out, but there was no reason he ever should. I imagined the job would only last a week or so. Besides, as a receptionist, I might even help break up trusts or decide which ones should be broken up. I might even be a whistleblower. I would get lauded by Hugh McDiarmid in the *Detroit Free Press* and cursed by *The Detroit News*.

On my first day, I dressed in a suit that barely fit me. I had grown taller since I had last worn it. I got off the bus in downtown Detroit. All my desires for this job seemed to be coming true. Well-dressed people walked about in suits and ties, carrying briefcases. I saw big cars, taxis, lots of pedestrian traffic: This was the bustling, hard-boiled city of Detroit.

The Detroit National Bank—"The DNB, the DNB, that's you and me, for me and you," went the famous jingle—was impressively situated in one of the largest and grandest buildings in the city: the Pontchartrain Towers.

I pushed the tall revolving door and *behold*: There it was—marble, marble, marble. Ceilings so high even Goliath did not need to worry about bumping his head as he was being rejected for his car loan. There were gilded counters and desks. Even the elevators were beautiful with old brass gates.

This is it! I thought. *I've made it to legitimacy.*

I reported first to the personnel director, Mrs. Battle. Her large oval black-frame glasses ornately adorned her austere face. Her cherrywood desk was very bank-like, formal and neat. She held a thick folder of papers as if she had an entire dossier on me.

"So, are you ready to work for the Detroit National Bank? I will tell you, this is quite an honor for a young man such as yourself."

I loved the sound of it already.

"This is a job with responsibilities, and you will need a special financial clearance. The bank will do you the favor of putting up the bond for you as long as you work through Quick Girls, but when you convert to full time—if you can—you will have to provide that yourself. Do you have any questions?"

I had no idea what she was even talking about. "Am I starting today?"

"Of course, but first, you have to fill out some papers. And then we have to process your documents." She shoved a thick packet of documents in my hand. "I will call you when your desk is ready. I see you will be paid by the Quick Girls at a rate of four dollars and fifty cents an hour. They will raise that to five dollars and fifty cents on your thirty-day anniversary. That is not a calendar anniversary but a work-hours anniversary."

This is the real world of finance! Very sophisticated, I thought.

"Since you are part time, it will take three months for you to reach that rate. Nevertheless, we decided you shall qualify immediately for a free lunch at our bank cafeteria, so you don't have to roam about the city."

Free lunch! Who ever said there wasn't any such thing?

"That means you are entitled to two dollars and fifty cents off whatever you buy at the cafeteria during lunch hours. If you go out to lunch, that will be entirely at your own cost. I can't recommend the cafeteria, quite frankly." Then she glanced at me over her glasses. "But for you, I imagine the two-fifty will be worth it and probably superior to whatever you are used to eating. Sit outside and fill out your forms. Hand them in and then sit. I will call you in when I've had a chance to process these papers. After, you will report to Vice President Tobias Washington of the Veterans Trust Division on the mezzanine floor. That's all I have, and since you have no questions, welcome aboard. Now go fill out your paperwork—quickly."

"Where do I go?"

"You see the chairs outside my office?"

"Yes."

"Perhaps you can draw some conclusion from that? And take this pen, which I expect returned without needing to prompt you."

"But you just did."

"Mmm. I assume you're too young to have a driver's license?"

"No, I have one."

"You do? Well, how good for you. I need it, and I will return it to you when you finish this paperwork."

It took about an hour and a half and several rounds of Mrs. Battle rolling her eyes at me to get my clearance. Finally, I was on my way to a job reporting to a vice president. I could hardly wait to work on those trusts.

Vice President Tobias Washington's office was on the mezzanine floor, I was told. But I was not told how to get there. I thought it had to be an important floor: a floor with a name instead of a number. Everyone knows the best seats at a concert are in the mezzanine. I went to take the gilded elevator, but there was no button for the floor.

"Where is the mezzanine?"

"Use the back elevator," a chic, well-dressed woman snapped. "You're holding everyone up."

"Sally, can't you see he's new?" another woman came to my defense. "Just go out to the left, to the back of the lobby. There's a small elevator there. Press two. Go out, and you'll see a sign for the mezzanine."

In a dark corner at the back of the lobby, there was indeed a small nondescript elevator, carved out of a chunk of bank. I decided the stairs would be better, but the stairway smelled moldy and the concrete steps were dank. The stairway was killing my first-day buzz, so I went back to the elevator. Its doors squeaked open, and after I pushed the faded button, it creaked and lurched to the second floor.

The second floor itself did not disappoint: It was palatial. There was a small but very neatly written sign that read *Mezzanine* with a downward arrow pointing toward a small staircase. The small staircase was dark, but at least it was lined with red carpet.

The mezzanine ceilings were considerably lower. On one door was a gold plaque that read *Detroit National Bank, Trust Division*. I opened the door and beheld plush green carpet and fancy wooden paneling. On the floor, next to several formal cherrywood desks, were stacks of colored certificates with gold fringe. I knew I had made it.

A middle-aged woman rushed to greet me. "May I *help* you, young man?" She said the word *help* as if it was absolutely repugnant to her.

"Yes, I'm looking for a Vice President Tobias Washington," I said proudly.

"Oh," she said, relieved. "You want the *Veterans* Trust Division—they're next door." She turned to another woman sitting at a desk. "You forgot to put the combo lock on the door again. See what happens?" She turned back to me. "Don't dawdle young man. Shoo."

Chapter 15: Natural Shocks

Back in the hallway, I opened the Veterans Trust door to reveal a water-stained beige carpet and dingy off-white walls. To the right, a hallway led into a compact room. To the left of the compact room, I saw a door with a small plastic sign: *Vice President Tobias Washington.* I walked into the compact room.

There were four desks and chairs. Old and mismatched, they were crammed together in the center of the small room, forming an oblong diamond shape. In front of me stood a small, scratched gray metal desk with a large phone console and a manual typewriter. To the left sat a frumpy-looking woman. She was poring over little bits of paper like she was doing a jigsaw puzzle. There were stacks and stacks of thick powder-blue folders piled up on all of the desks except the one in front of me. In the back of the diamond was a desk with mountainous stacks of blue folders. To the right of me, across from the puzzling woman, sat a huge burly man talking on the telephone. Despite being on a phone call, he seemed to be very bored.

"He has to stay there, ma'am ... yes, he does." Despite the urgent content of the conversation, the man's voice was completely disengaged. "That being the case, you shouldn't have cashed the rent check … If he smells so bad, tell him to take a shower … He did what? … Oh, I am sorry … I am sure it ruined the carpet … I am not laughing." He took a folder off the pile on his desk and started writing in it. "Uh-huh … Great … I mean, terrible … Really terrible. Keep me posted. I am really interested, and I assure you I am calling about it immediately … good bye Mrs. Feather." After he hung up the phone, he continued writing in the folder.

I noticed that against the wall behind the man was an opening leading into a little booth; it looked like a teller's window, except for the extremely thick plastic that covered it. I waited, but no one acknowledged me. Feeling awkward, I cleared my throat. "Ah, hello?"

"Who the hell are you?" the man asked softly.

The frumpy woman looked up at me. "Oh. Hi there. Can I help yuh?" she asked in a Southern drawl.

"Yes, I am … from the agency."

"*You're* Jamie." She got up and walked to me.

"Yes."

"I told you it wasn't a woman," the man said without looking up.

"I can see that, Eli." She looked at me. "Don't mind him; we all get used to him."

"You do?" Eli continued without looking up from his folder. "Why thank you, ma'am."

"Soon-ah or late-ah," she added. "You're Jamie Goldberg?"

"Yes, I am not a woman. Is that okay?" I wondered whether this was a job specifically for a woman."

"It's fine, but Jamie can also be a woman's name, and we have had mostly women filling the receptionist role. It's good to have you aboard. Okay, well, this here's your desk ... hey! Eli! Who's gonna show him what to do?"

"Not my job." Eli kept his nose buried in his folder.

"Not your job? I'm just the bookkeeper. What do I know about it?"

"I'm sure I don't know," Eli said.

"You're one of the trust officers," the bookkeeper said.

"I don't know anything about it."

"Ha, I bet! Great, you're a big help."

"You know me, Judy. Any way and any time."

"Except when I really do need your help ... like right now. Well, hi. I'm Judy Walker. I'm the bookkeeper." She motioned to the man's desk. "That is Elijah Pepper."

"Don't give him no Elijah crap, Judy." He got up and reached out his hand to me. I leaned over and shook it. He almost broke my hand squeezing it. "Call me Eli, please. Good to have you around, James—don't use Jamie; it's a girl's name."

I could feel the heat rising from my face.

"Eli! What do *you* prefer?" Judy asked. "James or Jamie?"

"Well, after that—James."

"Good for you, son."

"Enough now, Elijah."

"I told you to cut that Elijah crap out."

"*Elijah's* the assistant trust officer." They exchanged mock angry grins. She looked around. "Caroline isn't in yet, and I don't see Toby either. Did you see Toby?"

"Ain't seen 'em all day," Eli said, "and don't worry, James; I thought Toby was a woman's name, too—still do."

"Hush with that!"

"Just sayin' 'cause that's how it is … wasn't anything particular, know what I mean?"

Judy rolled her eyes.

I decided to play my cards close to my closet. I would not talk about being gay, studying theater, or volunteering for the Democratic Party. I was in a conservative mainstream bank, and all they wanted to see were results.

Judy presented my beat-up metal desk with a Vanna White flourish. "Where to begin? It's really simple. You just have to answer the phones and talk to people. Right, Eli?"

"Sure thing."

"Talk to them and route the call to the right people, right? That's what a receptionist does, isn't it?" I asked.

"Well, actually, just answer it. Eli and Caroline get overloaded. Toby is too busy, and no one wants to talk to me—or at least, they shouldn't. So you have to take care of the calls yourself. It's nothing difficult. Just pretend you're them."

"Just pretend I'm who?"

"You'll see. It's easier than I'm making it sound. You also need to keep an eye on that doorway there." She pointed to the thick-glassed teller window. "That's where our vets come in to pick up their checks. We usually mail them, but some like to pick them up and cash them with a teller downstairs. They may not have ID, so the teller will often call you to confirm you gave them the check. Got that?"

I peered at the vacant booth. "Got it."

"And I promise, the glass is pretty thick. It's more than bulletproof."

"Bulletproof?" I shot back.

"Yeah, we found out last week, didn't we?" Eli chuckled.

"You did? Did someone try to hold you up?"

"One of our vets came looking for the millions of dollars he was sure we were hiding from him—don't laugh, Eli. It ain't funny. That's how we lost Melissa."

"We weren't in no danger. It was barely more than a BB gun," Eli said. "He's back in jail now. So we don't have to worry about him for a few months or so."

"We don't?" I asked.

"Do you know what we do?" Judy asked.

"No idea at all."

"Terrific. I must thank Mrs. Battle again." Judy heaved a deep sigh. "We take care of vets. Veterans. They all went into the military normal, but didn't come out that way. They can't take care of their own affairs. So a court appointed us their fiduciary, meaning we kinda look after 'em."

"We take care of their finances and things," Elijah added. "Caroline, who sits over there, handles the finances. I handle the things."

"Oh. Then what do I do?"

"Just have a seat. Wait until Caroline arrives. She can explain it better than we can."

I sat at my desk. Their phone system was hopelessly complex. It had a whole console of cryptic buttons with four extensions: *Judy*, *Toby*, *Eli*, and *Frank*. Judy turned to go but then quickly turned around.

"Oh yes, the phones. When you see one light up, you just pick up the phone like a normal phone. You've been a receptionist before, right?"

"No. Not really."

"Well, how hard can it be? You'll be fine. The phone rings and you answer, 'Good morning, Veterans Trust Division, how may I help you?' They're usually calling for Caroline. So if she's in, it's really simple. You just press *PCT* to pick up and then this *GPD* button and press the pound sign and the star and *Two* together and then press *Frank*."

"Why Frank?"

"Caroline replaced Frank, but no one knows how to change the labels. If you can figure it out, you'll be the town hero. Anyway, taped there to the desk is a little cheat sheet of how to work the phones. See that? Just study it and you'll be fine."

"I get a call; I say, 'Good morning, Veterans Trust, can I help you?' and find out who they want to talk to; and then transfer the call."

She smiled and said loudly, "Yeah, though Eli usually takes them—"

"What was that?" Eli yelled.

"Oh, so you're listening."

"Ha ha ha, very funny. James, you make sure it's not a vet on the phone. If it isn't a vet, those calls you can route."

"How will I know if it's a vet?"

"Believe me, that won't be hard," Judy quipped. "And for the vets, just take a message."

"That doesn't really work," Eli said.

"I write down that they called, right?"

"Not exactly," Eli said. "*You* talk to them. Maybe you gotta, you know, talk with them a bit. Pretend to be friendly, see how they're doing, and then *persuade* them to hang up."

"What?"

"That didn't come out right. Find out who they are. If they're a vet, you talk to them. You know—wear them out a bit, and then if you have to, if it makes you feel better, you can write down what they want. Then reassure them the check is in the mail or everything is okay, et cetera. If it's anything too hairy, then pass it along to me."

I said, "Oh my God," under my breath.

"But if it's anyone else besides a vet," Judy continued, "just transfer the call to whoever they want to speak to or take down a message and place it on the person's desk."

"Unless it's Toby's wife," Eli interjected.

"Oh yeah, unless it's Toby's ex-wife. If it's her, just take a message. Never forward that call to him; he'll get upset. That's really all there is to it. Any questions?"

"What's that dull buzzing noise?"

"Oh, that ..." Judy tried to listen for it. "I think that's the lights, ain't it, Eli?"

"The lights and the generator above us, that gives off a buzz from time to time. Nothin' to worry about. You'll get used to it. On Thursdays you may see a cockroach or two 'cause that's when they spray the floor above us," Eli said, who noticed Judy was giving him a dirty look. "Whatcha' lookin' at me for? Think he won't notice."

"I don't think he needed to hear that on day one."

"*Excuuuse* me."

"That's about it, James—oh yes, also, if anyone shows up at the booth, you just see what they want. In the gray strongbox on the ledge next to the booth, there's a stack of checks. Just find their check and give it to them. If there isn't one, just say, 'Sorry, there's nothing for you today. Come back tomorrow.'

That's very important. Don't say, 'Come back later.' Say, 'Come back tomorrow.'"

"All right. What's the combination?"

"What combination?"

"Of the strongbox."

Judy laughed. "That's broke. Hasn't worked since I can remember. Just open it."

"Aren't you afraid someone might steal the checks?"

Judy just laughed and started back to her desk.

"That's it?" I asked.

"It will be enough," Eli and Judy said together. They laughed.

"What goes up the chimney?" Eli asked.

"Smoke!" Judy said. And they reached over and linked pinkies. "May your wish and my wish come true," they said in unison and laughed.

I sat down at my desk. It was nice to have a desk. I had never had one before. It wasn't quite what I had expected. But it would be an important challenge: strange machines, strange people, and stranger customers.

I looked down at my desk. It was covered with little taped-down slips of paper with strange directions like *Use the LTD button to park a call.* I checked the drawers. The bottom one had a box of feminine napkins in it and a small radio. I heard a strange zipping noise and looked at Judy's desk. I noticed it had an old mechanical calculator with a perpetually long stream of paper dangling down to the floor.

That's when Vice President Tobias Washington walked in.

Chapter 16: Outrageous Fortune

You knew Tobias Washington was a vice president: three-piece suit, tie, handsome but in a no-nonsense financial way. Slim and sleek, even sexy from the right angle. A short-cut Afro meticulously framed his face, which was adorned with an elegant mustache. He caught me staring at him, and I looked away. Knowing what I knew about Detroit National Bank, I couldn't help but wonder if he was the only Black vice president there and whether they had given him what was clearly the lowest totem-pole department.

"Oh … you must be *Jamie*?" he greeted me as he stuck out his hand to me. I shook it. His grip was strong and firm. He looked me in the eyes with a searching expression. It made me wonder if he wasn't part of the tribe.

"I told you it wasn't a woman," Eli said.

"I can see that, Eli," Toby said.

"It's James," Judy said. Out of the corner of my eye, I saw her shake her head no to the vice president behind me. This was a bad sign: I was being judged already.

"Oh, right, James Goldberg. Everyone! Staff meeting! In the back," Toby announced.

I hadn't even noticed, but on the back wall behind the

desks was a narrow door with a keypad on it. Toby walked back and typed something on the keypad.

The door opened, and we entered the glory of the Trust Division on the other side: a deluxe meeting room with the green plush carpet. The room was lined with storage cabinets. Coffee, tea, water, and some cookies were laid out but not meant for us since no one dared go near them. Toby stood there at the head of the room, debonair yet firm.

"Okay, let's get the ball rolling ... oh, where's *Miss* Caroline?" Toby asked.

"I'm here!" a sleek blonde cried, running in on her high heels and carrying an armful of the familiar blue folders.

"Great. I hope everyone had a great weekend. First, good news today: We have a new receptionist for the summer, a temp from the Quick—err, Girls, Mr. *James* Goldberg. James, we'd like to welcome you aboard. James's main tasks, as I am sure you've been told, will be answering the telephones and helping you all as your assistant.

Did I just get a promotion? I thought to myself.

"James? What happened to Jamie?" Caroline asked.

"Name change. I told you it wasn't a woman," Eli said.

"I can see that, Eli," Caroline said.

"James, first you should know something about our department. We are the Veterans Trust Division. That means we take care of former veterans whom the court appointed us as their fiduciary. This department is a little unusual in that all our trustees are mentally incompetent. Many of our trustees are even cared for against their will."

"Can you blame them?" Judy interjected. "Who wants to be taken care of by a bank?"

"Judy, please. For various reasons, these people cannot handle their own finances anymore. So it is up to us, including you, James, to take care of our trustees' fiduciary responsibilities—"

Judy interrupted again. "'Fiduciary' means we're like their parents."

"No, Judy, we are not their parents. They are free to do anything they want; we only control how they spend their money. They control how they spend their time, where they live."

Caroline forced a cough.

Toby sharply glanced up at her. "They do determine where they live, Caroline. But they can't always financially afford where they want to go. That's when we have to step in. Some of them have trouble functioning, so Mr. Pepper here is our field guy. He does all the heavy lifting."

"I *am* their parents," Eli said.

Toby sighed. "Our primary responsibility is managing their basic expenses. We make sure their food, clothing, and housing are paid for. What they do with the rest of the money is their own business."

"If they got any," said Eli dismissively.

"Our primary responsibility is to get promoted out of here in six months, or we end up like Frank," Caroline quipped.

"Caroline! This is serious work. Important work. Now, I must admit, very few of our trustees have much money left. Okay, Judy, don't look at me like that. The VA isn't very generous, and the bank fees have to be paid, but we have no control over that either, and we don't concern ourselves with it. Now, you, Mr. Goldberg ... Judy, don't pout."

"She's not pouting, Toby. These guys are dirt poor and you know it," Eli said.

"Lower than dirt," Caroline added.

"Okay, okay, they're treated like animals by the government. Happy? Does that change anything? Anyway, you, Mr. Goldberg, have a taxing job. You are to answer the phones. Remember one important rule: Don't forward any calls from vets. You handle all of those yourself, except in a real emergency."

"How do I *handle* them?"

"You'll see; it will be easy once you get the hang of it. Mostly it's checking to see if they have a check waiting for them and, if they do, give it to them when they show up at the counter. There will be occasional requests for money. Those you write down and hand to Caroline. Otherwise, you handle the vets by talking with them. Talking with them frees up our time to do our work. It also makes the vets feel there is someone who cares."

"Whether you do or not."

"Not funny, Caroline. Caroline is our trust officer. Mount Pepper does all our field work. Judy here is our bookkeeper—hey, what's so funny?"

Everyone was snickering.

"That's mighty cold, Toby," Eli said. The snickering grew louder. "That's terrible. Mount Pepper ..."

"Shoot, did I say that again?"

"Mount Pepper," Judy and Eli said together and roared with laughter.

"What goes up the chumney!" Judy blurted out.

"Ch-ch-chumney!" Eli sputtered between laughs.

"I am sorry, Eli," Toby declared. "Come on. Focus, people. Everyone knows I didn't mean that."

"Chumney! Mount Pepper!" Judy exclaimed. "Oh, Elijah, that's terrible."

Toby tried to continue as if nothing had happened. "Rarely, you'll be forwarding calls …"

No one had stopped laughing.

"Come on, people …"

"Mount Pepper." Eli shook his head.

"Chumney!" Caroline cried.

"If someone calls, and they …" Now even Toby was laughing, "need help, tell *Mr.* Pepper or call his pager …"

"Mount Pager," Judy said.

"We're finished now?" Toby asked. "I am going to continue. Any arguments over money that you can't handle, you give to Caroline … okay, get it out of your systems; I am not going on until you all stop."

The door opened, and someone stuck their head in the doorway and looked around. Finally, the laughter subsided. The person then closed the door.

"Any arguments over money that you can't handle, you give to Caroline. Also, it's no secret that I get quite a few calls from my … ex-wife. If you can please just take a message when she calls, I will call her back. If the phone rings while you are busy with something, Judy will back you up. Any questions?"

"Are these people crazy?" I asked.

"Crazy isn't the proper term," Toby demurred.

"Oh no! No way. Our trustees weren't born with mental illness," Eli said. "You won't hear me talking too nicely about some of these guys; they won't bathe or have basic hygiene. But they can't help it. Some of them went into battle and saw horrible things, things you and I can't imagine."

"But some of these guys never saw combat," Judy explained. "They were—"

"All right, Judy," Toby broke in. "I agree with you, you know that … but that's not going to get us anywhere. We have a minimum of resources, but we still have a job and an obligation to discharge."

"Are these people dangerous?" I asked.

"We've had no fatalities yet, right, Eli?"

"A few broken bones, but so far, no fatalities, Toby."

"Eli, please."

"James, you may hear some shocking things on the other end of that line," Judy said, "but don't you mind none. These fellas are as harmless as anything. And if you run into them on the street, you'll see they are often as nice as can be."

"If any situation gets too … heavy—you know, too involved for you," Eli added, "you can always pass the call to me or Judy. Caroline handles the legal things."

"Thanks, Eli," Caroline said.

"You're welcome, *Miss* Caroline." Eli flashed a smile.

"Okay, I really mean it, drop the 'Miss Caroline' shit now!" Caroline shouted. Judy stifled a snicker, but Eli didn't stifle his.

"All right, I think that's about it for this meeting. Well, I think we can all get back to work now," Toby said. "Welcome aboard, James."

Chapter 17: Sea of Troubles II

We all walked back to our dingy desks. This was not turning out to be the bank job I had expected, but no matter. I had finally made it: I was about to be accepted into normal society. They had welcomed me, even if I wasn't a girl. And I even had my own desk.

I was confident until I sat down at my desk. The chair wobbled and squeaked. Suddenly afraid, I looked at the phone console like it was a monster.

Then the phone rang.

"It won't bite you," Judy said.

I picked up the phone. "Hello?"

The phone was still ringing.

"You have to press the flashing button."

I realized one of the four lines was flashing. I pushed it.

"Hello? I mean, good morning. Veterans Trust. This is …"

"You're not Sheila. What happened to Sheila?" a fey-sounding voice asked.

"I'm sorry, I guess she doesn't work here."

"Oh, no matter; any minor peon like you will do. I need a new pair of shirts, really nice shirts. I like the *Gah-vin-chee* much better than the Ralph Lauren they make me buy, and I know a great bargain at the Shirt Box. You've been there, of course?"

"Uh … no, I actually never shopped there."

"You are kidding me. Where do you buy your shirts?"

"Me?"

"Yeah, you!"

"Oh, I go to Hudson's or, for something special, to Jacobson's … hello? Hello?"

"Who was that?' Judy asked.

"I don't know."

"Well, remember to ask their name."

"What do I do with my half-written memo?"

"Just throw it out."

"Throw it—hey, what's that smell?" I asked. Some horrible odor wafted into the room, emanating from the booth.

"That's General Grant," Judy whispered.

I got out of my chair and looked. An absolutely filthy person stood behind the booth. I walked toward him with great trepidation.

The phone rang.

"Phone!" Judy yelled.

"One minute, sir!" I yelled to the booth and ran back to the desk. "Hello, Veterans Trust. May I help you?"

"Yes, this is Herbert Peacock. I need to speak with Judy. I want to know if my check is going to be ready tonight?" I put the call on hold.

"It's a call for you, Judy."

"Who is it?"

"Oh, uh, a guy named Herbert Peacock."

"That's for you."

"But he asked for you by name," I said.

"Tell him the check will be in on Wednesday, as usual, and he does not need to call again."

"Oh, okay." I picked the phone back up. "Hi, Herbert?"

"Herbert? I don't know you, young man. You better call me Mr. Peacock."

"Oh. Yes, Mr. Peacock."

"That's better. Say, what happened to Linda?"

"You mean Sheila," I said.

"Now if I mean Sheila, I will say Sheila, young man. I never liked Sheila. I prefer Linda."

"Linda?"

"Call back Tuesday," Judy whispered.

"Linda is here tomorrow. I am here on a Mon—hello?"

He had hung up. I was batting a thousand. I walked back over to the booth, trying my best to withstand the smell. He was perhaps the saddest man I had ever seen: the misery on his face, the filth, the madness. It broke my heart.

"Oh, hello, sir." I softened my tone as much as possible.

"Give me my fucking check, you fucking thief!"

"General, that's not how we behave!" Caroline yelled without even looking up from her paperwork. "You promised me."

"Come on, Miss Caroline; I don't know this asshole liar."

"Better be nice to him; he's got your check. Ask nice!" she shouted.

"You're a fucking thief," he whispered, "but *may I please* have my check?"

"W-w-why ... y-y-yes, of c-c-course," I stuttered.

I looked through the checks in the strongbox. I wondered what real name would be on the check. I was looking for a first name or last name of Grant. After thumbing through half of them, I was about to ask Caroline, but then I spotted it: a check for General Grant. On the stub: first name *General*, last name *Grant*. Amount: $1.50.

"I found it."

"You did? You must be a fucking genius."

"No more checks if you swear one more time!" Caroline yelled. I walked over to hand him his check.

"Stupid, piss-drinking bitch," he whispered, then added a little louder, "This bank is lucky to have people like you." He then muttered something I couldn't hear.

I slid the check under the window.

The phone started ringing. General Grant took his check. "Fucking thief," he said under his breath again and walked away.

"Phone," Judy said.

"I hear it. I was just giving the general his check." I scampered back to the desk. "Good morning. Veterans Trust!"

"Oh, Eli was right. You must be the new *young man*," came an elegant-sounding voice.

I sighed in relief and immediately regretted my short-tempered greeting. "Yes, I am, ma'am. How can I help you?" I replied, trying to regain my receptionist bearings.

"Is Mr. Tobias Washington in?"

"Why, yes, he is in, ma'am."

"Good, you are such a polite young man. Please put him on."

"Right away. Who may I say is calling?"

"This is Mona, his ex-wife," the voice on the phone said.

Fuck!

"He's in a meeting."

"Oh, I bet he is; just transfer the call, dear."

I looked for the transfer button, which I had long forgotten.

"What are you looking for?" Judy said, trying her best not to sound exasperated.

"The transfer call button."

"Who is it?"

"It's Mona, Tobias's ex-wife."

"He told you not to forward the call to him. Tell her he's out."

I picked the phone back up.

"I am sorry—"

"This is the last straw! This is a lack of respect! Do you hear me, young man?"

Putting my hand over the mouthpiece, I said, "I think she's really angry; you shouldn't have said that so loud."

"You didn't put her on hold?" Judy was furious. She got up from her desk. "Gimme that," she said, grabbing the phone, "Mona, this is ... Mona—She hung up."

Judy put the phone down. Anger flared in her eyes. "It's really quite easy to remember. All those codes there on the table don't mean much, just those three there in the middle. *P-C-T* will transfer them. *L-T-D* will put them on hold. Hold! Remember hold. Jesus."

"Oh, *L-T-D*—hold?—why is that? What's it stand for?" I asked.

"It stands for *hold*." She smiled stiffly.

"Thank you."

"No sweat. You're new. It takes getting used to. Now, where was I?" she said, going back to her desk. "Oh yes, the monthly account for Dean Pendleton. I lost track here after I was interrupted for no reason, so I guess I will just have to start all over again!"

"Can't you read the tape?" I asked.

She gave a small, forced laugh.

The phone rang.

"Good morning, Veterans Trust. How can I help you?" I asked, wincing in anticipation of a new verbal assault.

"Good morning. May I speak with Caroline, please?"

Finally, a normal person.

"Who may I say is calling?"

"Donald Pepper."

I dutifully put the call on hold. "Caroline, a Donald Pepper is on the line."

"Find out what Pitt wants," she replied, nose still in her paperwork.

"Hello, Mr. Pep—"

"Please, it's 'doctor.'"

"What? I'm not a doctor," I said.

"No, no, no, *I* am a doctor. I have a PhD."

"Oh, Dr. Pep—Dr. Pepper—"

The man laughed hysterically. "I gotcha! My real name is Pitt."

Everyone else in the office giggled or tittered, too, apparently knowing what joke I had fallen for.

"What do you want to talk to Caroline about, Donald?"

"Oh, good; that's good, too." He chuckled. "Tell Miss Caroline I wish to buy a record."

"Miss Caroline?"

Caroline flashed me an evil look.

"I mean Caroline—I was just repeating him. He wants to buy a record," I repeated loudly.

"Yes, he can. Tell him to keep the receipt. It can't be more than ten dollars an album."

"She said, you can buy the rec—"

"You haven't even heard what I wanted yet."

"It doesn't matter as long as it's un—"

"Doesn't matter!"

I switched gears. "Of course it matters. Sorry, what was I thinking? I'm new. Please, tell me what it is; which album you want to buy."

"Well, I don't know yet. Maybe I'm going to buy a new album of mariachi music."

"That sounds interesting. Do you like Mexican music?"

"Mariachi music, not Mexican. Take that cotton out of your ears."

"Of course. But you like music."

"Oh yes, I like all music, so I am trying to sample one of everything."

"And you're on the *M*'s now."

"No. Latin America. By region, alphabetic order makes no sense with music."

"That's great, Dr. Pep ... Donald, that's great. Just make sure it's not more than ten dollars an album—and keep the receipts."

"I will. Tell Miss Caroline thank you. And a good day to you. I haven't talked to you before; you're very nice. You can tell everyone I said so." Click.

"Donald Pepper—I mean—Pitt says thank you, Caroline."

"That's what I live for," she said, still deep in her work. She then got up with a stack of paper and walked toward me. "Here you go," she said, dropping the stack and a thick computer printout roll on my desk. "These are trustee receipts you have to file. The receipts have the name on the back. You just look up their case number on this printout, write the case number on the receipt, add the total of all the receipts next to their name on the printout, and then give the printout back to me and file the receipts in their folder. Got it?"

"Of course. Where are the folders?"

"The filing cabinets in the back."

"How will I know which goes where?"

"I know one thing is for sure, *Jamie*." She smiled. "We pay you to find out."

Calling the pile of arbitrary scraps of paper *receipts* was a stretch. The scrap paper had some amount scribbled on them along with a name and a date, usually illegible. They were taped to little ticket-like things that had Caroline's typed explanation and an initial for her approval. Some were approved by Eli.

Some tickets read:
Pocket Kleenex for R. Bruson.
Bail for Brandon Williams.
Ice cream cone for Bryan O'Ryan.
Emergency underwear for Jack Prach.

Lice cream for Willie Balmoral.

Slowly, a predictable pattern emerged from the receipts. Most of them read like this: *Birthday money for Bryan O'Ryan. Mother's Day money for Bryan O'Ryan. Valentine's Day money for Bryan O'Ryan. General Marat Day money for Bryan O'Ryan.* The slightest hint of a holiday had dozens of requests for money from almost every trustee in amounts that varied from $100 to fifty cents.

Another batch of receipts read like this: *Bus trip home from Flint for Mr. Wiler. Bus trip home from Ypsilanti for Mr. Wiler. Bus trip home from Kalamazoo for Mr. Wiler. Bus trip home from London, Ontario, for Mr. Wiler.* One even read *Bus trip home from Boise, Idaho, for Mr. Wiler.* I wondered why Mr. Wiler always needed a ride home but never a bus ride to anywhere.

I was into the zen of reading these receipts when the phone rang again.

"Hello, Veterans Trust. Can I help ..."

"Yes, you can help me, you fucking son of a bitch. This is Maximilian Schell, you bastard." His voice was loud, angry, and violent. His voice hit the letter *B* like a drum. "Give me my goddam money, you bastard. I know you got my five million dollars while you hole me up in this stinking hole, you motherfucking bastard. I heard that you and Toby go to the ballgame on my fucking millions."

I was sweating. "Sir, would you like to talk to someone? Caroline perhaps?"

"I don't want to talk to no fucking chiselin' bastard. You all gonna die. Die! You think they can hold me in here forever, you motherfucking chiseler? You can just kiss that ass of yours to hell and goodbye and, wait a sec … Okay … Yeah … All right." Then his voice changed abruptly. It went soft and friendly. "I gotta go. Someone else is gonna use the phone. Bye now. We'll talk later …"

It suddenly occurred to me he was waiting for me to say something. "Goodbye?"

"Goodbye." Click.

Judy looked at me. "Child, you are white as a ghost."

"I'm dead. We're all dead. My life, our lives, were just threatened. That guy said he's gonna kill us."

"Oh, was that Bert?"

"No, he said he was Maximilian Sch—oh, right," I said, remembering the actor's name, Maximilian Schell.

"Yeah, that was Bert Thomas. That's his real name. He's in the Northville Psychiatric Hospital. He's allowed to make a phone call every once in a while. Are you okay? He's not going to harm us."

"Yeah, I'm okay. That's just shocking to hear, you know. Why is he like that?"

"Frank, the guy here before Caroline, he told me that the army enrolled him in some experimental program." Judy hesitated and glanced at Toby's closed door. "They were putting LSD in his food to see what would happen to him. They didn't even tell him. He was already in prison. They said he'd get out early if he took part in a secret test." She shook her head.

"It worked," Eli piped up. "He got out early—from that prison."

"Lord help us if he ever gets out of the psych ward and comes here looking for his millions. But after what they did, can you blame him?"

"That sounds so completely illegal," I said. "Didn't he take them to court?"

"Honestly, James, use your head. How's he gonna take anyone to court?" Eli asked.

"Can't we get a lawyer?"

"No, James." Eli also looked at Toby's closed door. "We co-op-er-ate with Veterans Affairs, not fight with 'em. We're just the fiduciary. One vet did sue and lost his VA benefits. If we did something like that for one of our guys—lose a man his benefits—well, he wouldn't thank us for that, now, would he? Being a fiduciary means you save his money, not lose it."

"We're all God's children, Eli," Judy said.

"Maybe not according to Uncle Sam," he said. "You just wait, boy. This place will change you."

"But there must be something we can do for them?"

"Take care of them like we're supposed to. There ain't nothin' else you can do. Look," Eli looked at his watch, "they are the way they are because they are the way they are. Get it?"

"Not really."

"Eli," Judy said, "no one understands that line but you, so just give up on it already."

"No one appreciates a turn of phrase around here. I'll put it this way: It is so much bigger than all of us put together. It ain't funny. Don't get personally involved. You hear me?"

"I hear you," I said.

"Good. You just answer the phones. Put on a shell. Be nice. Be polite. But let it alone. You follow me, Jimmy? You let it alone. I am gonna go help move Ronald Ritchit." Eli got up, putting on his coat.

"Again?" Judy asked.

"They say he stole from the kitchen … but they just usin' that as an excuse to get rid of him. I'll be back later."

The phone rang again. My heart sank. I picked up the phone.

"Good morning, Veterans Trust. This is James Goldberg. May I—"

"Hello, hello, Caroline? Is that you? I am so glad to hear from you, yes, really glad, aww, this is Bryan O'Ryan," came the rapid onslaught of words. "I am here on the ground floor of the Veterans, aww, Trust Division at Detroit National Bank, Caroline. How are you, James Goldberg? You aren't wearing a helmet, are you? It's a beautiful morning. I got up and had a cup of coffee, no helmet. It's going to get even hotter—sparks, if you don't talk about it. Just even hotter … sparks, aww, don't talk. This is just twenty-three days after General Marat's birthday. That's right, just one hundred and seventy-five months ago, the good general came to the rescue during the Civil Brain War, 1789 to 1799, so we have a special day—a parade down in Hamtramck. I saw the mayor there with his pretty wife, Mrs. Roman Gribbs. Roman, aww, marching in the tent, shock—in the tent—shock—how do you rate? The sergeant in Fort Raleigh in North Carolina, he salutes me, 1789 to 1799, a fine man, yes, aww, a fine young man from Tennessee and I salute him back. Our own people were marching up to the lines and we were going to war and General Marat saves the—how do you rate? I went on this truck, this special emergency medical leave truck shock—on the bus to go back to Detroit, back to this wonderful city, my hometown, the town I love—shock—the town where I was born and never seen before, well, this morning we went to the lines of the state and the good general was leading his troops but I liked him, aww, down to the city county building at nine this morning 1789 to 1799 a nice corporal—I liked him, aww, I liked, I liked, I liked him, a lot. But he had to go on emergency medical leave—how did we rate? We were discussing parking lots we should build Downtown, a new parking structure across the street and I met a fellow from Tennessee, a nice fellow, both on emergency medical leave there. How do you rate? Aww, 1789 to 1799, he says to me and I salute him back there. How do you rate, boy? A chaplain asked me what went wrong when I met this guy—shock—from Tennessee and the chaplain tells me I am going and I can be saved, aww, on emergency medical leave along with my friend from Tennessee, General Marat was meeting his troops and he asked, 'How do you rate?' 1789 to 1799 all we had to do was put the helmet on, aww, that's all … we were saved … we were fixed with the helmet on, aww, a chaplain. I was going to be a chaplain, that's the profession best suited to you, sir, aww, and we were just going to see my friend from Tennessee, aww, loved like a brother that's okay loved like a brother, that's okay, like a brother … this guy from Tennessee, on the bus, friendly man. What, do I need a helmet? For 1789 to 1799, loved like a brother, and I thought, 'What do I need a helmet for?' A metal helmet, 1789 to 1799, they had just shaved my head—why put a helmet on me? I am going home shock, shock, shock, shock. I don't need a helmet so I want to take the helmet off, and one side was prepared to fight the other, this was war Civil Brain War and our president, aww, love me, shock, love, shock, and my friend, aww, 1789 to 1799, he's a friendly guy, I liked, I thought—I thought loved like a brother no more 1789 to 1799, how do you rate? 1789 to 1799, loved like a brother 1789 to 1799, loved like a brother. 1789 to 1799 ... well, goodbye."

Click.

Chapter 18: Grunt and Sweat II

"My lord his Majesty commended him to you by young Osric who brings back–to him that you ... that can't be right ..." Alec lost his place. He was offstage reciting a part for a missing actor.

"He sends ..." Dwight prompted.

"He sends to know if your pleasure hold to play with Laertes, or that you will take longer time."

I was onstage close to Ben as if to protect him from the approaching threat. I stood closer than he wanted, but I felt I needed to show the connection between Horatio and Hamlet. My Horatio sensed danger for his beloved Hamlet.

Ben was visibly annoyed and turned his shoulder away from me.

Stepping forward, his chin jutting arrogantly, Ben announced gruffly—and, I felt, inappropriately, "I am constant to my purposes, they follow the King's pleasure. If his fitness speaks, mine is ready; now or whensoever, provided I be so able as now." He ended with an operatic flourish with his hands. I couldn't help rolling my eyes.

"The King and Queen all are coming down," Alec announced.

"In happy time." Ben's one-dimensional machismo still spouting, he walked away from me.

I approached him. With a broad step, he moved away and began waving his hands randomly in the air.

Alec said, "The Queen desires you to use some gentle entertainment to Laertes before you fall to play."

"She instructs me," Ben pronounced.

I came closer to him and put my arm on his shoulder. He moved away but I stayed close.

"You will lose this wager, my lord," I warned in his ear.

"I do not think so. Since he went into France, I have been in continual practice. I shall win at—stop it! Jesus! Will you get this guy off my back?"

"What's the trouble now?" Dwight folded his hands. "Everything was going smoothly."

"What's the trouble? He's always crowding me, touching me, and spitting in my ear."

"Nay, good my lord—" I tried to continue when Ben shoved me backward. "I did not spit in your ear!"

"Ben, chill out, everything's fine!" Casper yelled from the back of the theater. Having Casper there was such a relief. I felt like a real comrade in arms with him during these rehearsals.

"Nay, good my lord!" Dwight yelled, trying to force a restart of the rehearsal.

"Nay, good my lord—"

"It is but foolery," Ben said. "But it is such a kind of gain-giving as would perhaps trouble a woman—stop looking at me like that! I hate you, Jamie!"

"If your mind dislike anything, obey it—"

"Make him stop!"

"Okay, everyone cool down," Mr. Nathan said calmly from the front row.

"Arthur, he's not going to be happy until he has us all playing queers."

"Language!"

"Sorry, Mr. Nathan, but—"

"I get it. Horatio plainly sees the danger that Hamlet does not. This is logical, Ben. You're getting out of line. From here, he's not looking at you with anything except concern. But it seems to me you are both too confrontational to be friends."

"Oh, come on, you know that's not true. I could tell you— never mind."

I looked over to Dwight, hoping he would back me. He stood silently and resentful in front of Mr. Nathan.

"You're letting him get away with this?" I asked Dwight.

"Say something, Dwight. Are you the director, or did Jamie get promoted?" barked Ben.

"Really?" I paused, expecting someone to come to my defense. Instead it was complete silence. I began to feel very insecure.

"We've been over this," I protested, walking upstage to Dwight. "It's Hamlet's own words—"

"Stop it. Everyone relax!" Mr. Nathan demanded. Then, looking around at the entire ensemble gathered for this reading rehearsal, he added, "Okay, everyone take a pause. Dwight, continue without Horatio. I'm taking Jamie outside to have a chat. Excuse us."

I could feel my face on fire from blushing. Humiliated, I walked with Mr. Nathan just outside the theater door. I took a huge breath of fresh air. I hadn't realized how hot I was. The breeze from the door sent chills as it cooled the sweat around my forehead and neck.

"Why are they being so difficult?" I sighed again, trying to subvert what I thought was coming. I plopped down onto a bench in the hallway.

"Excuse me, Jamie, but who's being difficult?" He towered over me with an uncharacteristic glower. Then, lightening up, he sat next to me. That familiar smile made feel completely self-conscious. I straightened up, sitting stiffly upright on the bench while he stared directly at my eyes as if he could see right through me.

"You're angry at me? I don't think I've seen you angry before. It's because of me, right?"

"Jamie, you are marvelous and sometimes marvelously infuriating."

"Me? I thought Ben—why me?"

Mr. Nathan looked held into gaze. "Jamie, what are you doing?"

"What do you mean?" I sunk back against the wall again. The pressure of being so humiliated in front of everyone. No one had come to my defense. And now someone I truly respected and revered didn't like me. "Why did you humiliate me like that? Everyone seemed to be ganging up—" I couldn't finish the sentence. I feared I would lose control.

"I wasn't the one doing the humiliating, Jamie—come on, this isn't Ben or Dwight you're talking to; it's me. Just think. What do you think you're doing?"

I was suddenly unsure of everything. What had happened had seemed so clear and now so confusing. "Rehearsing? Playing my role?"

"Rehearsing or needling?"

"Me? I'm just trying to get some emotion out of Ben."

"Well, you did that. But not the kind that makes good theater. Let's just be clear: Everyone knows what you are trying to do. You've made little secret that you're trying to make Horatio an openly gay character. That's brave and you're doing well. But that's not the problem. The effect you're having on your fellow actors is going to have consequences that you need to handle. Ben is going to be very sensitive to how you play the role. Let me ask you a question, and I need an honest answer: Are you needling Ben?"

"No, we promised to stop that, and I thought I had."

"If Ben is giving you negative feedback—or anyone, for that matter—you need to respect that and modify what you're doing. You don't cave in for someone else, but you do need to show some sensitivity and some reaction to their feedback. The characters communicate onstage—a give-and-take—and neither of you are doing that right now. You are bullying him, whether you intend to or not."

"You think *I* was the bully?"

Mr. Nathan nodded his head in a damning assent. I hated being blindsided like this, even when it was the truth I was ignoring.

"I am? How? ... I don't see it ... I trust you. You wouldn't say this if it wasn't ... true. I was just playing my role as I see it—was that so bad?"

"Jamie, you know better, don't you? What if Ben did that to you? I think—"

"He called me a queer!"

"I think, in the past, he has needled you, even bullied you. You didn't like it, did you? Besides, bullying in a classroom is a lot different than doing it onstage."

I remembered Ben spitting at me in class. Just thinking about it, a burst of hatred convulsed through my muscles. "I hated being bullied. And now after one bad rehearsal, I'm no better than he is?"

Mr. Nathan didn't take the bait.

"I'm trying to act."

"I don't think so," he said. "At least, not in my book. Remember my description of bad acting?"

"I'm being a sponge?"

"No, that's one kind of bad acting. You're acting one play while Ben is acting another. Look at me, Jamie. It's not working. Good actors are generous and reflect back the energy to others and share the stage."

"I know, I know. I was just trying to get Ben to show some emotion, some ... energy." I looked at Mr. Nathan. He just kindly stared back, not buying anything I was saying. "Strange. I think I'm wrong most of the time, and when I finally think I'm right, I'm still wrong."

"I will venture to say you aren't looking at it from the correct perspective."

"Isn't that the same as saying I'm wrong?"

Mr. Nathan chuckled and I laughed, too. The chuckle cleared my throat, my eyes, and my mind.

"When you think you are wrong, it seems to me you're just being open-minded. You know you don't have the answers, because nine times out of ten, there are no answers. Thinking that way leaves things open. Onstage, that lets others in and able to play off you. I admire that about you.

"You are correct: I think you are wrong about being wrong. But this, whatever you were doing onstage just now—that was forcing your interpretation down our throats."

I was already beginning to feel the self-hatred creep back. I slid down even farther on the bench.

"You act as a team or it isn't acting. Otherwise, it's just *mental masturbation*. Don't look down like that, Jamie, I know what you're thinking. Remember who you're talking to—you're not worthless. Your vision for Horatio is one of the hardest possible things to do here. You just can't make your problem everyone else's."

"My problem?"

"You have to play Horatio together with Ben. You two have incompatible visions of who Hamlet and Horatio are. But you can't, nor do I want you to, control what Ben does. Just respect his limits and his interpretation. I'm a little surprised you don't see the effort he's putting in. Yes, I know what he said—the queer thing. But I do see the energy between you two. There is something going on and I won't venture to guess. But yes, I see what's in store for you, and it will not be pleasant. It will be great acting, if you allow it, but it will be a difficult road ahead. The sooner you let these things roll off your back, the easier it will be for you."

"Wait a sec. If it's incompatible, why doesn't Dwight do something about it? He's the director, in charge of the vision."

"Maybe this is his vision."

"Can't you tell him?"

"Have you been listening?"

"Yes, but I thought I might try not to." I forced a laugh.

"I see you're feeling better. Anyway, I certainly don't want to change anything in your interpretation, only your behavior. I cast you two to begin with, and I like it just fine. If you'll calm down and let Ben be Ben and Jamie be Jamie, we're all good."

"All right. You think I was … getting back at Ben? I'll even admit I'm angry at him for what he did in the past. But I like him now."

"Then show kindness onstage. Act in the way I taught you both, and you will be fine."

"Why is the road so hard for me?"

"Who told you acting—or love—was easy?"

"I think I'm in love with him."

"Fine, but this Hamlet is not in love with you. He's making moves you weren't expecting. He's not giving into you and he doesn't have to. You're still stuck loving him. To Ben's Hamlet, you are a friend, and not a particularly close one. It forces you to humble yourself. You show love, he returns it cooly—or maybe worse, maybe he uses you for it, though I haven't seen that so far. You show vulnerability, but he gets to shrug it off or even ignore it. That is what unrequited love does to people."

"Of course, I know about that."

"But there will also be an immense amount of tension and dramatic possibility between you two. Ben will have you on edge because he doesn't know if he can trust you. You just have to trust him."

"That sounds one-sided."

"Lead by example. That's the part you've chosen to play. Or at least that is the position you find yourself in."

"How do I get myself out of this?"

"Please listen, Jamie: Don't get *out* of it. Go *with* it. You'll learn more than anyone else in the cast about real acting. Just take Ben along for the ride and make it easy for him to be his Hamlet while you be your Horatio. Communicate your love without shame or shaming. That's what I recommend."

"And we never quite meet except when Hamlet's near death."

"Bravo. Perhaps. Perhaps not. That is something you need to negotiate with Ben. And maybe, just maybe, you and Ben in that last act can meet together. That might be nice, Horatio forgetting his passion and Hamlet his aloofness. All that's left are the dying words of innocent affection. Then you get to have the last line. I would pay to see that."

"That's what I want to do. But why did I have to be humiliated in front of everyone, Mr. Nathan?" I was no longer slouching but leaning on the edge of the bench.

"Can you get this into your head? You were humiliating yourself and it had to be stopped. I believe I was doing you a favor. Look, Jamie, unless you are completely blind—"

"I am!"

Mr. Nathan laughed.

"Jamie, precious few want you to succeed. Most in the department are uncomfortable with this, even the dean. By playing Horatio gay, you're taking on a red-hot potato because it suits you; just don't be surprised when others don't want to get burned if you throw the potato at them. Do you see? You're really pissing everyone off, even people who want to be on your side. Now, how do you propose to get yourself out of that mess?"

I sat up erect on the bench.

"I'm in a mess? Okay, okay. I get it." I looked at Mr. Nathan. He was completely calm. Without a trace of blame. "Should I apologize?"

"No! Jesus, I expect that from the old Jamie." Mr. Nathan smiled and stood up. He went to the stage door and peeked into the theater.

I stood up and followed. I thought we were going in. Mr. Nathan backed away from the door without looking, and we collided. His glasses fell to the ground.

"Sorry, Mr. Nathan, I thought we were going back in."

Mr. Nathan first looked perturbed, then chuckled. "The old Jamie." He bent over and picked up his glasses.

"The old Jamie? I didn't even realize there was a new Jamie. Okay; I get it. Acting 101: I know Hamlet is the hero and the focus. I'll do my part. Horatio will do everything to support his beloved no matter the personal cost—that's what Horatio is for. That's my function—my backbone, as you call it. Okay? That's who I'll be up there. And I will just accept Ben for who he is. If I get too close, I'll back off. I'd like to go back in there, and shake Ben's hand."

"That's a great idea. I can't predict how Ben will react. But I know it will send a message to the team. Over time, I think you can win over everyone, even Ben, but only if you make it easy for everyone. Start with a better rehearsal. People will slowly realize who you really are. I'll tell you confidentially, there are about a half a dozen gay and lesbian members of the crew that are secretly cheering you on. But no one owes you anything. You took this one on yourself. So to them, you're a leader. Don't look to Dwight or anyone else. Your head is extended so far over the guillotine block on this one that I can't imagine an easier victim. Tread carefully."

"So I can play Horatio as a gay man?"

"No censorship here. Nor from Ben."

"I better prepare for the fallout."

"I can't tell you what that would be."

"All right, Mr. Nathan."

"I told you, call me Arthur."

"Okay, Arthur, but I'll just say that I think Ben's bravado is not a real Hamlet. Are you happy with his performance?"

"My opinion of his performance is actually none of your business. But I will tell you this: Ben has a raw side. You touch it the wrong way, and this is what you get. But if you touch it the right way ... maybe you'll be surprised."

Mr. Nathan put his glasses back on and looked at me kindly, which made me suddenly feel confident. "You two will have a natural tension—no Stanislavsky method needed here. Trust yourself: It will work. Ben's trying to be a good actor, too. If I may quote our Polonius, 'Give every man thy ear, but few thy voice; take each man's censure, but reserve thy judgment.'"

"Alec is hilarious, he plays that so fatuously. Okay, I better get back in there."

"I just checked; everyone left. They all must have used the other door. I think they wanted to give us some time. We're working with a good team: good crew, good cast. We all pull for one another. That means both of you. I root for Ben, too."

He'll eventually be rooting for me, it occurred to me. I was going to have to act at loving someone who I knew didn't love me. I decided to treat Ben as if he was Casper.

"But before you leave, I need to talk to you about something else—something personal," Mr. Nathan said.

"Okay," I said, unsure what would follow.

"Jamie, Jamie, I want to tell you this. Gary isn't in that room. You've already grown so much since you came to talk to me before rehearsal started—but you have a lot of work left to do. Gary's not a member of the cast. He's not onstage or even in the audience. Ben isn't Gary. Dwight isn't and I'm not. No one wants to victimize you. Not even Ben, okay? We're all going to cheer one another on. It will be hard work, Jamie. But you can do it. You won't fail me and neither will Ben. Can you trust me on that?"

I couldn't talk. This time it wasn't because of tears, but astonishment. Finally, I spit out, "I swear I never think about him anymore." But as soon as I said it, I realized I was wrong. "I only see him—Gary—in everything I'm doing. That's why it's all wrong. He's destroying me."

"Instead of seeing Gary, see Ben as your savior—see Hamlet, the one you love as your ticket out of Garyville. The man who abused you as a child, he isn't here anymore. Only those who want you to succeed."

"I am so ashamed. Does everyone know?"

The silence felt like total damnation. Then Mr. Nathan put his hand on my shoulder.

"Jamie, no one knows anything about him." He shook my shoulder. I nodded okay and he let go. "Good."

"Must it always come down to this? 'O, that this too too sullied flesh would melt?' Oh God, that it should come to this!" I looked up at Mr. Nathan. "'I thought I had come so far, and I am still in this.'"

"Well, you're quoting Hamlet, so you're already channeling the bad into the good. I'm satisfied now. Are you?"

"How do I face them tomorrow?"

"Your intuition is good. Shake Ben's hand if that feels right. I personally think it's unnecessary. This little cooling-off will do the trick. Let me give you one final piece of advice … you want to influence Ben?"

"Yes."

"You'll have to do that offstage and alone so he feels no threat. Understand?"

"Let him get angry at me?"

"Courage," Mr. Nathan said and left.

Courage? Did I have enough courage to make peace with Ben? And did I have enough courage to make peace with my own mother? Little did I know she was my next challenge.

Chapter 19: Natural Shocks II

Walking over to the Wayne County Central Committee meeting, I had a moment of pause. Why had I told Casey I was up to it? How blind could ambition be? True, it was an ambition to help others—but also to show I was not as incompetent as Brian. Yet this ambition would bring me into direct conflict with my own mother. At the same time, I felt a distinct pride that I had pushed myself to do this.

I had been told to arrive promptly at seven. I walked up to the Democratic Party Headquarters on Woodward Avenue, just down the street from where I worked at the bank. It was a large, ramshackle brick Victorian building indicative of Detroit's former glory. Inside was meticulously clean, if not sterile. I had to go up a grand staircase to the caucus room.

The room was already packed. On a raised podium was a central table where the committee members sat. Among the dozen or so seated at the table, in the middle, wearing a dragon-red coat, was my mother. Small in stature, her ferocity always made her seem much larger than her height. With her bobbing, flame-red hair, she was busy talking among the other committee members. She did not notice me enter the room.

At the committee table, I was surprised to see there was an assortment of familiar faces. Most of them had, at one time or another, come over to my parents' house to meet, discuss various political campaigns, and debate the politics of the day. Like Casey, they had also folded and stuffed campaign literature into envelopes or attended the occasional dinner. We had gone over to their houses for the same. I saw them just often enough that I had begun to feel like I was in my element. I understood now why Phil and Casey were so eager to have me be the DOHR liaison.

Behind the center table and against the wall was a long table where some people sat. One who was holding court I recognized right away—Sam Hauptman. He was the United Auto Workers union's chief lobbyist. Some said Sam was one of the most powerful men in Michigan. He and Mother had been best friends until she had decided to do something other than what Sam dictated. Thereafter, they had become bitter political enemies. He was as notoriously unforgiving a person as my mother was forgiving—a trait that I wished extended to myself.

There was a small audience area in front, populated by some journalists and other bored Detroiters. One board member was so bored that her head was down, fast asleep.

I joined the weary Detroiters. On each chair was a printed agenda, and sure enough, there was one, *DOHR Liaison*, with my name on it. My mother finally spotted me. She looked surprised. I was sure she was wondering what I was doing there. She checked the printed agenda and then shot a glance up at me. Anger. She had figured it out.

Nervously, I looked over the group. Everyone seemed familiar, but I wasn't exactly sure who they were. I recognized Ethel Jeffreys, the chairwoman who stood at a podium. I believed she was a good friend of my mother's, but I wasn't totally certain. It was equally likely, politics being what they were, that by now they were bitter political enemies. After a while, Ethel banged the gavel.

"We will come to order." Ethel paused, looking at my mother. She was silent until she finally realized Ethel was staring at her. Mother raised her hand.

"The chair recognizes Committeewoman Ruth Goldberg."

"I move we temporarily suspend the rules," Mother said in a raspy voice.

"There is a motion to suspend the rules. Is there a second?"

"I second!" someone shouted.

"The motion is seconded. All approved, say, aye."

Everyone said, "Aye," in lackluster voices.

"All opposed, say nay. The motion carries unanimously. The rules are suspended."

It's hard to say which rules were suspended since everyone continued to follow court-like rules of order.

"The clerk will read the opening agenda item."

"Agenda item one: the approval of the meeting minutes from last month."

"The chair recognizes Ruth Goldberg," Ethel said, this time without waiting for Mother to raise her hand.

"I move for approval of the minutes from our last meeting and to allow Secretary Anderson to take the minutes of this meeting."

"Is there any objection to approving the minutes or Secretary Anderson?" the chairwoman asked. "The motion carries," she said without waiting. It seemed suspending the rules meant completely ignoring some of them.

"The clerk will read the next item."

"Item two: accepting James Goldberg as the new liaison and representative from the Detroit Organization for Human Rights," the clerk nonchalantly read from a typed sheet. "This motion will allow Mr. Goldberg to bring in a monthly report for the chair's consideration. Further, to keep Mr. Goldberg informed of issues vital to his organization's interests."

Ethel looked around and saw me. She smiled, nodded, and motioned for me to come forward. I moved to the front of the room.

"Is there any objection in welcoming Jamie as the new liaison and representative from DOHR?" she asked. Her voice seemed friendly. I had been told they would just accept the motion and I would sit in the back with the other representatives and liaisons. "Hearing no objection—"

"I would like to make a motion, Madame Chair," said a sweet-looking, petite old lady I did not recognize.

"Excuse me, May, we're not done yet."

"It's regarding the agenda item, Madame Chair."

"Really? The chair recognizes May Harper. Ten minutes."

"Thank you, Madame Chair. Hello, Jamie. Maybe you don't remember me. I used to visit you at your mother's house when you were just an *innocent lad*. You were so sweet then. Madame Chair, I want to make a motion that we reject the representative from the Detroit Organization for *Human Rights*. *Human rights;* we know what that really stands for. It is a mockery of human and civil rights, when we, as a party, have to support the rights of sinners and criminals. You let this boy sit down here and we will be going to hell in a pothole."

Some shouts of "Amen!" peppered the room.

"What is your motion, May?" Ethel deadpanned.

"I move we not … we reject … hell, I want no association with DOHR. How do I do that?"

The crowd tittered. I felt red-faced. This wasn't supposed to happen. I had been promised that this was a simple formality. Mother stared grimly at me.

"Your motion is to ban the DOHR representative from our meetings?" Ethel asked.

"Yes, that's it."

"I second it!" another committee member yelled.

I looked at my mother. She stared at me coldly. Would she support me? She made no sign. I felt alone and attacked and no one was coming to help me, though Ethel seemed on my side. Would I even get a chance to speak? I tensed for a fight.

An elderly man raised his hand. "I have to say something here."

"May, will you yield?"

"I am through. I yield the balance of my time to Win."

"Chair recognizes Winslow Wilson for the balance of May's time."

The older man, who looked familiar, also seemed to be about to say something painful. I was certain he was going to agree with May.

"I am ashamed," he said.

I braced for the worst.

"For the first time, I am ashamed to be a member here. Look who this is. This is Jamie Goldberg, coming here to ask us for an ear. It's not just you, May. Everyone here knows this child. He was canvassing for us. We were working for civil rights together. And now that he's in need, you want to turn this man away?"

The sound of people rapping knuckles on the table rippled through the room. Much to my relief, the knuckles sounded like the majority. Then there were a few shouts of "Amen!"

I saw Mother perk up. I relaxed. This might get messy, but it was going to go my way.

"Look over there," Winslow continued. "Look at Ruth. I have never seen her so still and frozen. Why is that? You know this woman? When we came to her for help, did she hesitate?"

More knocks and echoes of approval came.

"She had bomb threats at her home; did she hesitate? She has been shot at. She has been yelled at, attacked, and abused for standing up for us. And now *you* are going to attack *her* son? That's *her* son. *Our* friend. I've had the privilege of meeting with Jamie on many occasions. A fine man. We talked on many subjects. He's a bright boy. And we sure accepted his help warmly enough—you, too, May. So I welcome this addition with arms wide enough to embrace his whole family. I understand you, May. I don't know anything about his kind. I don't know. But transgressor? Offender? Outcast? Those sound like things they said about us not too long ago."

"Still do, Win!" another yelled.

"Out of order, Mildred," Ethel said.

"Still do. But I don't care about any of that. This boy is welcome here. He deserves our ear and our concern. I can't say yet what we do about it. But he has a place at this table. Withdraw the motion, May. I yield my time.”

“This is not a civil rights issue; it is an issue with God!” May yelled.

“Civil rights?” Ethel asked. “We have a civil rights chair. Hey, Eileen, wake up; we have a civil rights issue. Someone nudge Eileen Welcomb.” People laughed. “She’s dealin’ with her daughter’s newborn, so let’s have a little compassion.”

“Oh, sorry, Ethel. I must have dozed off there.” The gray-haired woman who had had her head down stirred. “Did I miss anything?” Some board members laughed.

“Yes, we have a civil rights issue—”

“We do not!” May yelled.

“We have a civil rights debate issue,” Ethel continued. “Are you familiar with DOHR?”

“Doors?”

“DOHR, the Detroit Organization for Human Rights.”

“Of course, they them faggy rights group.” That caused everyone to laugh, and my face turned hot red.

“Well, Eileen, standing before us is one of their representatives. Jamie Goldberg.”

“Jamie? Really? Oh sorry, sorry there,” she said, gathering herself together and then looking pointedly at me. “Oh, Ruth’s son. Sorry, Ruth; no offense. Welcome, uh …”

“Jamie,” Ethel said.

“I know—welcome. Welcome Jamie Goldberg to the team. Welcome indeed, young man.”

“I take it that means you have no objections to this man representing DOHR to this body?”

"None whatsoever."

"Thank you, Eileen."

"She don't know what she's sayin'!" May yelled.

"Okay, let's see," Eileen shot back. "Do I object to an organization for human rights? No. Do I object to the five thousand dollars they gave us last year? No, I don't. Do I mind adding a bright young mind to our caucus? Do I mind the two dozen-plus volunteers DOHR contributed to the mayor's campaign? You see, May, I know more about what I am talking about sleeping than you do awake."

"Human rights, my eye! Human sinners is better."

"Out of order, May. Chair recognizes Ruth Goldberg. Ten minutes." I hadn't noticed she had raised her hand.

"Thank you, Eileen, and thank you, Win; you're still the beautiful man you've always been. Eileen, you're doing an excellent job watching out for civil rights—when you're awake." The crowd chuckled. "May, Draymond, and Lisa and everyone else, you think you are attacking homosexuals, but you are not. You're not just attacking my son. You are attacking democracy, which relies on discourse to flourish. Unless you let him talk, we can't have the discourse that you are trying to bring prematurely to the floor right now." She took a breath and looked at me. "Another thing we risk is our relevancy. If we start shutting out our supporters—and DOHR is a major one—we risk becoming irrelevant. Motion is out of order, out of line, and immoral: banning a supportive organization's representative, honestly. I hope May revokes this motion or that everyone votes to reject it. I cede the rest of my time." She sat back down without looking at me.

In the back, Sam stood up. Everyone's head turned to face him.

"The Chair recognizes Sam Hauptman, UAW representative. Ten minutes."

"For once," he said, "I agree with Ruth."

There was a burst of tension-relieving laughter.

"May, this is a counter-productive and divisive motion. While the UAW hasn't taken an official position, it's worth noting that DOHR members are overwhelmingly loyal Democrats. Stop this discussion now." He looked me right in the eyes. "Welcome, Jamie. I look forward to a lively debate on lesbian-gay issues with you and your organization."

Mother's mouth dropped. She looked at me, managed a Mona Lisa smile, and nodded her clear approval.

"Call the question!" a voice shouted.

"One moment. I don't think that will be necessary. Any objection, May?" Ethel asked.

"Motion withdrawn," May said, listlessly capitulating to Sam.

"Committeewoman Harper withdraws her motion. The rules are still suspended, aren't they? Is there further objection to the main question? … No further objection. The main question passes unanimously," Ethel said, finally letting her emotion show with a broad smile. "Jamie, welcome. It's nice having another Goldberg in the family. Looks like they are breaking that mold after all. Please, take a seat—take that one right next to our esteemed Mr. Hauptman."

I moved over to a seat behind the committee table. Sam shook my hand with a smile and a look of regard.

"Great to see you again, Jamie."

"Thank you, sir." I could feel the heat from my face, this time from joy instead of embarrassment. The handshake was noticed and caused a bit of a stir. Mother turned to face me. She cracked a full-on smile.

After the commotion, Sam leaned over and whispered, "You don't need to take after your mother in everything, okay?"

"We're different people," I replied.

"Well, you both got guts," he winked.

Before the meeting ended, my mother got up and left early, not saying anything to me. I waited for her to contact me. Call me or write a letter. She didn't. But she had supported me in the meeting, and that held some promise for the future.

◆◆◆◆◆

Casey and Phil, on the other hand, were delirious when I told them what had happened. Just by showing up, I had delivered the goods with a huge bonus. I had the political acumen to score the goodwill of the UAW, which had never been a solid supporter of LGBT rights, into their hands. They met me at a gay bar that night, and together, we raised our glasses.

"To Ruth Goldberg," Phil said.

"To Ruth? You mean Jamie!" Casey said. "Jamie, you delivered us the Wayne County Central Committee and the UAW."

"To Jamie Goldberg," Phil said. He was particularly glowing. "The UAW. Sam fucking Hauptman."

"You know, I have a confession to make," I said.

"You do?" Casey asked.

This was the moment to come clean. "I'm actually not studying political science."

"Oh, I don't think we knew what you were studying, did we, Case?" Phil said. "But what are you studying?"

"Yes, what are you studying?" Casey asked.

"Theater," I replied, expecting it to be a bombshell. No reaction from either Phil or Casey. "I am going to be in a play."

"No kidding. Which one?" Casey asked.

"*Hamlet.*"

"Shakespeare? That's impressive," Casey said. "Are you playing Hamlet?"

"Oh no, but I'm playing the role of Horatio. I'm playing him as a gay character."

"Great! I'm impressed, Jamie," Casey said. "That takes a lot of courage. Has there been any blowback from your fellow students—and faculty?"

"Better believe it." I sighed.

"You need our support, then."

"Yes!" Phil interjected. "You should know we all have your back. If they do anything that even smells of discrimination, we're ready to pounce."

"You'll have to tell us when the play runs. I know Neil and I will definitely go there to cheer you on."

"Yes, Ken and I would love to see it, too."

It seemed my life was turning a corner. Maybe it was finally time for it all to come together.

Chapter 20: Outrageous Fortune II

We weren't ready for the final dress rehearsal. There wasn't a single run-through where we didn't have problems of one kind or another. I felt very unsure of the support for my part and even less sure about how to interact with Ben: In one moment he would be kind, and in another instant aloof, if not angry. At this rehearsal, the rest of cast seemed disorganized as well. Dwight had already established himself as prone to immobilizing panic. Without Mr. Nathan—Arthur—present, Dwight was chaotic. At this late stage he kept going over blocking and seemed to change his mind constantly, making it impossible to know what to do except to improvise.

We were near the end of the dress rehearsal, with everyone standing around. We were waiting for the set to be finalized. Instead of a dry run of the performance, it was deteriorating into just another rehearsal. It took about double the time to make it this far, and tempers were a bit edgy. When Mr. Nathan entered, everyone was relieved by his appearance.

"Haven't you finished?" asked Mr. Nathan.

"Almost," said Dwight trying to sound upbeat.

"Almost? Dwight, what was there to do except exactly what we did I the last rehearsal. This is extremely disorganized," he said, trying to talk as softly as he could. With no one making a sound, he was easy to hear.

"We can't have a dress rehearsal with no set!" Dwight cried.

"Settle down and just get going. The only thing missing on the set is …" Mr. Nathan looked around. "Is the table for the poisoned cup, really."

"And the backdrop."

"That doesn't matter, does it?"

Dwight didn't reply but looked ashamed.

"Don't worry about it. We're all learning. Ben, will you grab that small table offstage? Place it where the regular table would be. Put the wine goblet there, and everything else. I spoke with Casper; he said the shop promised a delivery tomorrow, and he hasn't failed us yet. Just start. Where did you leave off?"

"We left off where Claudius poisons the wine because we didn't have a table."

"Oh, we're almost done. Dwight, let's go out in the hall. Everyone take a break." Mr. Nathan and Dwight went out.

Ben walked over to me. "I don't want you to touch me, get it? Not while Hamlet is alive or dead. I don't care, leave me alone."

Hearing that, Alec and Barb came over. Alec looked particularly intimidating dressed as the king.

"Everything all right?" Alec intoned.

"Yeah, we're good. Just talking," Ben said.

"I can't even kiss your forehead?" I asked loudly enough for Alec to hear as he was walking away.

"You can still do that, as agreed."

"I'm sure that makes sense to someone."

"Understood?"

"No, I don't understand. A kiss without a touch—but I'll do it."

"Thank you," he added with as much sarcasm as he could muster.

"Ben, I thought we got past this."

"Ben, you got to chill," said Alec. "For the good of the—"

"Attention, everyone! Attention, people!" Dwight cried, doing his best Mr. Nathan imitation. "I have an announcement to make. First, I apologize for waiting for the set to be finished. It won't happen again. Next, the musicians are excused. They can practice if they like in the small theater for the finale. Otherwise, they'll still have two chances to rehearse tomorrow."

"The orchestra went home an hour ago," Alec said as sweat dripped from under his crown down his face. "Can we just finish where we left off? I think everyone needs to go home and put this one behind us."

"That's exactly what I was planning," Dwight said. "We'll just cross the finish line on this one. I realize Osric had to leave, so Arthur will step in. Let's start with Osric, 'Aye, my good lord.' Laertes and Hamlet, have out your swords, ready to duel."

"And one quick word," Mr. Nathan said. "Ben and Simon, this match isn't to see who has a bigger cock."

This sparked some laughter.

"Do not strike each other hard with these stage swords. It looks really awkward from the audience. You're noblemen, and at first, the way you fight is genteel and with grace like the ballet instructor showed you in the practice room. Only strike hard after Simon draws blood with the cheap shot to spread the venom."

"All ready?" Dwight asked. "Starting with, 'Aye my good lord.'"

As the rehearsal commenced, I would like to say I was concentrating completely on the action, but I was in my own head worried about Ben until Mr. Nathan, as Osric, said in alarm, "Look to the Queen there, ho!"

"Oh—They bleed on both sides. How is it, my lord?" I asked Osric.

Osric bent down to Laertes, who had fallen on the ground. "How is't, Laertes?"

"Why, as a woodcock to my own spring, Osric," Laertes replied, then quickly added, "I am just—justly killed by my … treachery—fuck!"

"Simon, call no attention to it. No one will notice. Keep going," Mr. Nathan said.

Hamlet looked over to Queen Gertrude.

"Gertrude, you should be on the ground now," Dwight prompted.

"Oh right. Sorry," Barb said, falling down but hiding her hand behind her back to break her fall.

Hamlet, flustered, blurted out, "How does the Queen?"

"She swoons to see them bleed," King Claudius added quickly to cover his guilt.

"No, no, the drink—O my dear Hamlet—the drink! I am poisoned," Gertrude seemed paralyzed.

"Die," Dwight directed. "Close your eyes or fall still."

"O villainy! Ho! Let the door be locked," Hamlet bleated as if nothing was wrong with him. "Treachery! Seek it out!"

Mr. Nathan climbed down off the stage. "Dwight?" he asked. "Go on!"

"Hamlet, you're mortally wounded. Even if you don't know it yet, you still need to act it. You don't know what's wrong, but you should sound breathless or struggling, remember? Simon is doing it right—and you're both killed by the same poison."

"I know!—O villainy! Oh! Lock the door. Treachery! Seek it out," he repeated.

"It is here, Hamlet," Laertes groaned from the floor, "Hamlet, thou art slain. No medicine in the world can do thee good. In thee there is not half an hour of life. The treacherous instrument is in thy hand, unbated and envenomed. The foul practice hath turned itself on me. Low, here I lie. Never to rise again. Thy mother's poisoned. I can no more. The King, the King's to blame."

"The point envenom'd too? Then, venom, to thy work." Hamlet stabbed Claudius with the retractable prop as if he was still a vigorous man.

The courtiers all yelled disjointedly, "Treason!"

"Hamlet, you're dying, remember?" I whispered to him.

"O, yet defend me, friends. I am but hurt," Claudius said in shaky voice and staggering to keep his balance.

"Here, thou incestuous, murderous, damned Dane!" Hamlet rushed to the cup like an olympic sprinter and forced the liquid down the King's throat, who really choked on it. "Oh, sorry—Drink off this potion. Is thy union here? Follow my mother."

Claudius collapsed.

"Jesus, you're dying too!" Dwight whispered at Hamlet.

"He is justly served. It is a poison tempered by himself. Exchange forgiveness with me, noble Hamlet. Mine and my father's death come not upon thee. Nor thine on me." Laertes, having delivered his lines flawlessly, collapsed dead.

"Heaven make thee free of it. I follow thee," Hamlet said as if suddenly remembering he had been poisoned about forty lines ago. He then faced the audience—not any cast member, certainly not me—and said, "I am dead, Horatio. Wretched Queen, adieu! You that look pale and tremble at this chance, that are but mutes or audience to this act, had I but time—O, I could tell you—but let it be. Horatio, I am dead, thou livest. Report me and my cause aright to the unsatisfied."

"Never believe it." I tried my best to be choked up, but I was really pissed at Hamlet's bravado. He still looked toward the audience. I grabbed his face and turned it to me.

"Fuck!" Ben yelled.

I then grabbed the cup of poison over the king's body. "I am more an antique Roman than a Dane. Here's yet some liquor left."

"As thou a man, give me the cup," commanded Hamlet, forgetting half the words. The line was supposed to be a plea. "By heaven, I'll have it. O Horatio, what a wounded name, things standing thus unknown, shall live after me! If thou didst ever hold me in your heart, absent thee from felicity awhile, and in this harsh world draw thy breath in pain to tell my story ..."

Hamlet lay there awkwardly supporting his arm, waiting. The offstage gun hadn't fired yet.

Impulsively, I ran toward Hamlet and lay down with him.

Ben was about to complain, but Dwight screamed, "For Jesus Chrissakes, Eula! The shot! Now!"

"Chill, Dwight! Something's wrong with the switch," Eula yelled from backstage.

Finally, we heard a shot offstage, followed by some hearty guffaws, incensing Dwight and Ben. "I'm trying to stay in character, assholes!" Ben yelled.

Mr. Nathan leaped onstage to refocus everyone. "Young Fortinbras, with conquest comes from Poland, to the ambassadors of England gives this warlike volley."

As Osric brought this news, I put my hand cautiously on Hamlet's shoulder. To my surprise, he permitted it.

"O, I die, Horatio." Finally, Hamlet's voice trembled with some emotion—even if it was hatred, it felt like a step in the right direction. "The potent poison quite over-crows my spirit. I cannot live to hear the news from England, but I do prophesy the election lights on Fortinbras. He has my dying voice. So tell him, with the events, more and less, which have solicited." Hamlet impulsively grabbed my arm. My heart jumped as he fell back, dragging me to the floor. "The rest is silence."

"Now cracks a noble heart." I could hardly speak because I was so angry he had pulled me down. "Good night, sweet prince ..." The last words wouldn't come. I totally forgot them. The pause seemed excruciating, and then finally, I remembered the line. "And flights of angels sing thy test." I flubbed the line but ignored it. I bent over Hamlet, caressed his forehead gently, and kissed him there.

"Stop it!" Ben got up.

"Fuck! Ben, can you just wait until the end!" a thoroughly frustrated Dwight yelled.

"No, we didn't rehearse it like this before! Jamie's trying to steal the scene lying near me."

"He can't steal the scene. You're dead," Dwight said.

"It's bullshit, anyway," I said. "You pulled me. I'm supposed to bend down over you—without your help."

"Well, you weren't going to do it. And you aren't supposed to touch my cheek, just my forehead. That's what we agreed—"

"Stop it!" Mr. Nathan interrupted. "Believe me, it's no scene steal. Both of you are fine! From now on, these improvs are to be tolerated. They just happen. Jamie, that was a nice and appropriate addition. But Ben, for the tenth time, look at Horatio when you talk to him. React to his emotions with yours. Play off each other."

"Great, so now we're adding stuff at the last minute?" Ben whined.

"Ben, it wasn't an addition any more than you pulling Jamie down—both impulses worked. It might not work every night; you two need to communicate more clearly and watch each other's lead. But that was a fine adjustment and this is live theater, not a taped play."

"So I can add shit, too!"

"I wish you would," I said. "Be a bit spontaneous."

Ben walked up to me. "You're dead."

"You were great when I was next to you, you know that?"

"Fuck you!"

"I am putting you both on notice," Mr. Nathan was angry, "Anyone who does something on stage to the detriment of this production will watch the rest of the play from the wings. You both have understudies. Do I make myself clear?"

"Yes," I said immediately

"Yes," Ben added softly.

"Fine, you're done, Ben. You can go. We'll finish without you. You had a long, hard night, and you gave it your all. This wasn't easy, now I think we're all a little frustrated."

Ben walked by me and hissed, "And you better behave, bitch."

"Ben, you can call it a night," Dwight said. "Simon, lay down where Ben was. Okay, Jamie, let's bring it home."

I was tired, and my voice was choked up and strained. "Now cracks a noble heart. Good night sweet prince: and flights of angels sing thee to thy rest!" I softly kissed Simon's forehead. He did nothing but lay there as a dead Hamlet should. "Why does the drum come hither?"

Dwight yelled, "Pretend there are noises offstage!"

Kevin Hack playing Fortinbras walked onstage alone, his retinue having already gone home. "What is this sight?" Fortinbras looked me right in the eyes. I heaved a sigh of relief.

"What is it you would see?" I asked as grief-stricken as I could, "If aught of woe or wonder, cease your search."

Fortinbras, astonished at the bloody sight and playing off my grief, responded sadly, "This quarry cries on havoc. O proud death ..."

Afterward, Mr. Nathan came up to me as I was taking off my makeup.

"Jamie, it has not escaped many people's attention how fluently you were at the end when Ben left. You were at ease, emotionally intelligent, and the warmth you played off with the others was very clear."

"Thank you. Can you tell me how I can do the same with Ben?"

"The strain between you two is not entirely bad but it isn't working either. Simon is Ben's understudy and it looked good with you two together. But I hope it doesn't come to that, but Ben's continual rudeness is something I didn't count on."

"Am I still being rude to Ben?"

"I'm glad you asked that. No. You were doing slight variations; that's fair. Ben did the same. I think here the problem is with Ben, and we need to find a solution. I think the way forward is for you to tone down the intensity of the friendship—even though we agreed to it, it seems to be more than Ben is capable of handling. That might settle him down. Think about it, okay? Onstage, see if a lighter touch draws a better response from him. I'll talk to him about it. Let's see if we can meet somewhere in the middle. Okay?"

"Whatever it takes," I said, very disappointed that it seemed I was getting pushed bit by bit back into a traditional interpretation of Horatio.

No sooner was Mr. Nathan gone than Dwight sat down next to me. To my alarm, I realized I was alone.

"Jamie, can we talk?"

"I need to go home. I have a class early in the morning."

"I'll make it quick. Look—sorry about the misunderstanding in the tech room. Except to you and Casper, I am not out to anyone. I can't advertise that I'm gay in this school."

"Okay, so you want me to play Horatio straight as can be."

"No, I don't deserve that. I want you to do Horatio just as you did him tonight."

Great, I have a coward for a director, I thought. since he hardly lifted a finger to support me. "And how will that work?"

"You made very good progress with Ben, more than I thought possible. I think you should meet with him. You two have good chemistry whenever he relaxes but every time you get close to him, he freezes. Find a way he can get comfortable with being close to you. Offer to do some extra rehearsals—I can have Arthur suggest it to Ben if it helps."

"I'd gladly do rehearsals, if Ben wants to."

"Great." Dwight ran off.

Alone, my only conclusion was this wasn't working: this Ben-Jamie cooperation. I wondered what I could do to sustain some kind of emotional response from Hamlet so he would be playing at the same level as Laertes, Fortinbras, Gertrude and Claudius. I had to think of something.

Variation: Black Pearls

Early Spring 1982

Chapter 21: Too Sullied Flesh

Now that we seemed to be getting along, I convinced Casper to meet me at the school cafeteria. I occupied a corner table to have some privacy so we could clear the air between us. So long as he didn't know my side of the story, I kept dreaming we could be together. In my dream, he would come to my door with flowers and ask forgiveness. As he came toward me with his tray, I realized this was my last chance.

"Hi, Casper."

"Hi, Jamie. What happened to your face?" he asked as he sat down.

"Oh, the bruise?" I lit up at his concern. My smile must have seemed an odd way to respond.

"Did Ben do that?"

"No, I fell … a while ago. I cover it up with makeup during rehearsals … Great to see you again," I said as I took a spoonful of my shepherd's pie.

Casper, staring down at his salad, speared some greens and ate them. He first glared at me, which then melted into an equivocal stare. "I'm glad to see everything finally coming together—in the play."

"It is? I mean, I'm really glad to hear that." My heart was about to burst with joy. "That's important, coming from you."

"Is it?" he said, spearing more salad. His cute little twitch in his eye softened my heart.

"Of course, especially if it means we can be—"

"Jamie, let's stick to the play, okay? That's what you said you wanted to talk about. That's why I'm here."

"The play?" I didn't remember that condition. "Do you think I'm arguing too much with Ben?"

"You're sticking up for yourself. It's not like you're just blowing off air like Ben does. Especially now, you're less combative and like more of a team player."

"I'm glad to hear that. I'm not always aware what effect I have on people."

For some reason, Casper thought that was funny and laughed out loud. I forced a chuckle, hoping he was laughing with me, not at me.

"You're doing all right, Jamie." I blushed at the compliment. "You, Barb, and Alec are particularly strong. And your patience with Ben is ... impressive. I think you have him intimidated in a good way. Especially since the kiss—by the way, I wouldn't do that again—but you showed what you're capable of–and he's off balance because of it. That was ballsy."

"Really?" I was so relieved. I could not help fantasizing that we could be more than friends.

"Ben is a lot of work," I said dreamily. Looking at Casper's beautiful face was such a guilty pleasure. "I wish someone had my back, was there to support me."

"You've had support."

"I know, but Mr. Nathan isn't as involved as he was in the beginning."

"Arthur's pleased with what we've attained so far."

"It seems like a real mess to me. Still, I have to figure out Ben when he gets so ... bombastic. I don't know what to do."

"Don't push it. Ben is Ben. He's really self-centered, which will probably take him very far in the regional theater." Casper chuckled and looked up at me. He looked kind.

In a flash, I remembered the things I had done to myself because I had thought Casper hated me. He kind of stared at me, now making me feel self-conscious. His face twitched and he smiled. "Don't sweat it, Jamie. I think you're a good guy."

"I thought you hated me."

"I don't hate you. Just be real about things, okay?"

"We can be friends, then?"

"We can be ... *just* friends," he said reluctantly.

"I wish it could be more," I dared to add.

"Do we have to go into that now?" He rolled his eyes.

"No, we don't. But you wanted me once ..."

Casper shot me a hostile glance.

"Okay, I get it. But I just don't understand—"

"Just leave it alone."

"You don't believe me, but you were—are—so important to me. The last thing I want to do is screw *this* up."

"There is no *this*, Jamie."

"Can I at least learn what I did wrong? I did what you wanted. Didn't I?"

Casper grimaced.

"I did!" I could say nothing right anymore. "I mean, I know mistakes were made, but which was the worst?" I realized that didn't come out right. "I mean, what did I do first … that was wrong?"

Casper had now donned a "If looks could kill" face.

"Can't I make it up to you somehow? You never returned my calls or my letters."

He grimaced again, this time with a nose flare. I should have stopped. But I was just dying to understand the subsequent hostility after, as far as I could tell, my only crime had been sucking his cock like he had demanded.

"Jamie, your letters kind of freaked me out."

"They did?" *Perhaps they were a bit of adolescent, opera-infused romanticism,* I thought but didn't say.

"They were very unrealistic."

"Sorry, but I guess I was in love with you," I said with a sarcasm, which did not help my cause. "I didn't know what else to do. I've never loved anyone before. Perhaps they were a bit adolescent—"

"Stop it. You don't even know me."

"Your mother's a registered Democrat!"

Thank God, he laughed at my joke. "Really? I would have guessed she was a Republican."

"Casper, I was inexperienced, but—" He shot me an angry glance. I couldn't imagine what I had just said that was so wrong. "I really loved you." I wasn't listening to the voice inside of me saying, *Shut up about it.* "I mean, despite it all, I love you. I never loved anyone before … Can you forgive that I was clumsy about it? Can I get another chance?"

"Gall!" Casper rose furiously with his tray.

"What did I say now?"

"Sicko!"

"Wait! Why? Please!"

He stood and glared at me. "Do you think I was born yesterday?" he seethed in a whisper. He must have known more about my reputation than I had realized. I felt compelled to explain that had happened after we had met. But some people in the cafeteria were already staring at us.

"What are you talking about?" I pleaded as softly as I could manage.

"Why are you pretending?"

"I made some bad judgments ... afterward—"

"Asshole!"

"You're partly responsible!"

"What!"

"Forget it. But please, all that stuff happened after we met."

"Who do you take me for, anyway?"

"I never loved anyone before you. It's a fact." I hushed my voice as more students around the cafeteria started to notice. "I never even *did it* before—er, before we," then I remembered Gary, "er ... okay, it's complex."

People were staring.

"Jamie, lower your voice. How stupid do you think I am?"

"I don't think you're stupid—"

"You fucked one of my friends!"

I cringed. Making it worse, more eyes stared at us. I wanted to crawl under the table or, preferably, a rock. For too brief a moment, I wondered, *Which friend?* I had blocked Dara out of my memory, but unfortunately, the rest of the world hadn't done the same. I assumed he was referring to Dara.

"You mean Dara? I can explain," I blurted out.

"What!" He looked shocked. "Dara," he repeated evilly.

Wrong assumption.

"Oh yeah. I would have mentioned that, but I forgot. Or who did you mean?"

"Dara, too," he said sarcastically.

"Oh no, who did you mean? It wasn't what you think." *Oh God, what have I done? He knows everything, even things I've even forgotten.*

Casper turned and started walking away, napkins flying off his tray. I pursued him with my tray. My fork flew to the ground.

"You don't understand, it was—" I tried to add while picking up the fork and the napkins.

Casper stopped and turned around. "Your only time!" As I stood up, he got right into my face. He added in a hushed, bitter invective, spitting on me as he spoke, "Come on, you sucked me off like a pro, kid. You didn't need a single lick of instruction. Get away from me." He turned and briskly walked away.

His hatred should have been arresting, but I couldn't stop. "But—like a pro—that's different. You mean Gary?" I asked stupidly.

"Gary. Great, another one," Casper dropped his tray on the conveyor belt, salad flying off the tray. I threw down my tray with the half-eaten shepherd's pie on the belt, too, and rushed after him. I was overwhelmed, so much beauty and so much anger and so much humiliation, but I felt I had to tell him the rational explanation.

Despite the budding trees lining the campus walkway, it was wintery cold. I followed him shivering because my jacket still hung over my chair.

"This is really different!" I pleaded. "Just let me explain."

"Oh, fuck you, Jamie. You tried to screw your own straight roommate." He walked on ahead.

"How did you hear that? And I did not!"

"You think everyone doesn't know? You have a *reputation*."

"I can explain that ..."

He stopped and turned back to me, furious. I was prepared to confess everything about my past. But I could see the frustration; he clenched his fists. I looked on in horror, thinking he was going to hit me.

"You cannot explain, Jamie. You wouldn't know the truth if it smashed you in the face—oh, this is useless. Why did I bother?" He turned and walked away.

I just had to explain. Something told me not to. But in desperation, I did it anyway. I trailed after him. "And what do you mean I was like a pro? You think I did it before?"

"Obviously." He walked faster.

"Dammit! Okay, I did. But you don't realize who—"

"Of course it was Dwight—but of course there were others."

"What others!" I cried as I slipped on some old dead leaves and almost fell.

"Everyone knows you slept with Dwight to get your part," Casper might have said. I wasn't exactly sure because he was farther away. I picked up the pace.

"What? You know I never slept with ... Dwight." I had to think about that. I shivered. The wind was chilly. Saying I slept with him was a lie. But how could I explain our probable meeting in Palmer Park? But all that was after Casper. "That was hardly sleeping together," leaked out of my mouth as I caught up with him as he crossed a bridge from campus over a busy street.

"Don't pretend with me. It's disgusting. You slept with him, more than once."

"That's an outright lie. I did not! And whatever it was, it was way after I met you—where did you get this from?"

"Jamie, the community is a small world." Casper stopped walking and turned to face me. "Especially in the Theater Department. You've turned more than one head and bent your knees more than once!"

"I have? But don't you see I didn't know him then—oh *shit*—we never slept together, dammit! I never met him *before I knew you*, honest!"

I slipped on a patch of ice and skidded on my knee. Frustration boiled over as Casper looked at me with such damning hatred.

"I don't like being lied to. And Jesus, stop following me."

"Okay, I am ready with all the truth!" I pleaded as I got up.

He turned off the bridge to Woodward Avenue. "Goodbye, Jamie. Don't talk to me again." He started walking away faster.

"You're my first love. Before that—"

"Oh right, and you were the most experienced virgin ever. This is useless. Goodbye!" He sped up on the vacant avenue.

We were passing a strip of burned-down buildings. In blind panic, as no one was around, I yelled to say the most important thing.

"Don't you see, I learned it from Gary! When I was a kid, don't you see?"

He walked even faster, and I tried to run to keep up.

"Okay, I sucked! But I was just seven!" The farther away he got, the louder I yelled. Then I noticed people staring. Other people were walking down the street as we reached an open convenience store.

"It was my ... brother's friend. There! Are you fucking happy!" I was screaming and gasping for breath as I chased him. "I was just a poor ... fucking defenseless ... asshole ... kid."

He kept walking very fast.

I screamed louder, "For God's sake, doesn't that count for anything?"

Then he turned his head and stopped. I thought I had finally reached him.

"Beat it, Jamie," he hissed and ran off.

"Are you blind?" I was so winded I could barely talk. "I was ... only ... a kid ... Casper!"

He ran for a stopped bus. I ran and kept screaming as he jumped into it. I ran to the bus window where he sat.

"You happy now? Happy now, Mr. Right All The Fucking Time?"

The bus drove away.

"Oh God. You happy now?"

I sank to the curb, whimpering to myself, shivering and unable to move. Some students passed by staring down at me. I bristled when one said, "Look, it's that faggot again."

Emotionally exhausted and freezing cold, I got up and walked back to the cafeteria for my jacket. I bitterly realized as I did the math that Casper could not have possibly known Gary. I had confessed all that for nothing. But at the same time, Casper's callous behavior had finished my puppy crush on my first love for good. That was an empty feeling.

On the shivering-cold walk back, I wondered if my outburst in the cafeteria would get me kicked out of the Theater Department. And if it did, I had to laugh, would that make me a bigger celebrity than Brian Kitson?

Chapter 22: Get Thee to a Nunnery

I was fortunate that the bank was a world isolated from my own. They knew little about me. What they did know wasn't true anyway. They thought I was in prelaw. They knew nothing about my theater major, sexual adventures, or my political sympathies. I felt protected—until the day came when all those things came back to haunt me.

"Morning, Jamie." Caroline had just come into work. "Don't you see him? Walter is here for his check."

"Oh, sorry, I'll take care of it."

Walter was a sad case among very sad cases. A very cute Vietnam veteran. His face looked soft and sensitive, but he was cranky and he had a horribly foul mouth. He also smelled extremely bad. He was missing his right leg, but not because of a war wound. Rather, I found out he had lost it after shooting up with a dirty needle. He had become addicted to drugs while in Vietnam, apparently following an evil cocktail of neglect, brutal trauma, and hanging out with the wrong people. Eli had met him by chance in the hospital and helped him get his VA benefits to qualify as a trustee. We were just a bank, but at least the people here helped him as best they could.

I walked over to the booth, fighting the strengthening stench with every step I took.

"Yo, can't you fucking see me standing here, you cocksucking nigger-loving bitch? Bring me my goddam check, faggot!" His incongruously gnarly voice was like a croak, more offensive than usual. I winced at being called faggot; the N-word had less force since he himself was Black.

"Stop that cursing," Eli intoned in his weary, routine way. "You don't get your check talking like that in here."

"But he's the real thing: a real cocksucker. I've seen him in Palmer Park at night, on his fucking knees!"

It felt like a gut punch. This ivory tower wasn't as safe as I had thought it was. I knew, in that instant, he had really seen me. I was turning red.

He kept on shouting, "Go on! Tell him, fag boy! I ain't lying. You sucked my noodle."

"I did not! I am getting your check, Walter, so stop it."

"Cocksucker!"

At once, I panicked. My hands started shaking as I looked for his check. I knocked over the strongbox, and checks fell across the floor. I hurriedly picked them all up.

"Don't worry everyone, I got 'em!" I yelled to assure Eli and Caroline. "I got all the checks."

"Fag boy lost my check!"

Eli got up from his desk and angrily walked to the booth. "You shut that foul mouth of yours, you hear me? You don't say that about no man! Now you apologize to Mr. Goldberg. Go on, apologize or you ain't gettin' no check."

I found the check and then stuffed the others into the box. Eli took it from my hand. I put the box back on the ledge next to the booth. I tried to quickly put the checks back in order, but they were a hopeless scramble. To stop making a scene, I went back to my desk.

"But he *is* a fag! He really is! He did me for money," he went on.

I broke. "I did not! I never did!"

"I am about to tear this up," Eli warned.

"No!" Walter shouted, "I gotta have my check ... I'm ... sorry, Mr. Goldberg. I don't mean nothin' by it. Please let me have my check." Tears started streaming down his face.

I was totally discombobulated by Walter, of all people. I was still blushing and shaking. I could have just let it slide and everyone would have thought nothing of it. But with Eli's anger and Walter's cowering retreat, I was visibly shaken no matter how much I tried to cover it.

Eli tried to calm me down. "Don't take that personally, James. He don't know what he's sayin'."

"I'm sorry, Mr. Goldberg; honest, I am. Just give me my check, please."

"I don't want to hear you cursing in here no more, you get me?" Eli scolded him. He handed Walter his check. "Goodbye, Walter."

I couldn't help but think of my last panic: that scene with Casper. I wondered whether they saw Walter's tirade as just another outburst from our troubled vets or if they could hear the self-hate screaming in my mind. I felt guilt was oozing out of every pore of my body. It wasn't just the accusation of being gay, but being told I was some degenerate who had sex in the park—someone who would pay that filthy man for sex. Add the school cafeteria—it was all building up inside. Part of me wanted to run away; another part of me couldn't move.

Impulsively, I ran into the bathroom. In a stall, I gnawed the back of my hand to keep myself from screaming. I couldn't go back to my desk until I pulled myself together. I walked over to the sink. In the mirror, I looked deep red. I splashed water on my face. Until then, I had thought I was doing so well. Arrogantly, I had been sure I was better than Walter. Yet I had totally let him get to me.

I knew deep inside that Walter couldn't control what came out of his mouth. I should have been able to control my own reaction; then nothing would have happened. In an instant, the bank job seemed to crumble in front of me. I splashed more cool water on my face.

"Poor troubled head," I said to myself, thinking about Casper and now the bank. I dried off and stood up straight. Mustering all the dignity I had left in me, I walked back in the room.

Eli and Caroline stared at me. I had panicked at the wrong time. I looked at them. They looked down at their work.

Judy walked in and looked at me. "Are you all right?"

"I'm fine," I mumbled. Caroline looked up and glowered at me.

"Don't worry about him none. He just got yelled at by Walter," Eli muttered, his pity clearly showing.

"Jamie, listen to Eli. Don't let that guy bother you any. He never says anything that makes sense."

I walked back to my desk. A pall seemed to settle over the office. The silence was broken by the ringing telephone.

"Good morning. Veterans Trust. May I help you?"

"Hello, hello, James, is that you? I am so glad it's you, yes, really glad, aww, this is Bryan O'Ryan. I am here on the ground floor of the Veterans, aww, Trust Division how are you, James Goldberg?"

"Bryan, sorry, I can't talk right now." I hoped he would just stop.

"The other evening he salutes me and I salute back and he asks: 'How do you rate?'"

"Bryan, I've gotta—"

"How do you rate? Big trouble. It was going to be an evil day, the mean-looking colonel said, an evil day. What a—"

"Bryan, I can't now."

"… the doughnuts at Lafayette Coney Island, and the lady at the counter asked me about my bag … and if it was heavy. How do you rate? … Well, goodbye." Click.

I put the phone down.

Caroline got up with a big stack of folders and approached my desk.

"Hi, James," she said with a nasty smirk on her face. "I have some files here you need to take to the court. They're annual reports we need to file."

My heart sank. I had a bad feeling about getting sent out of the office at this moment.

"Here are the case request forms. You'll have to fill out a request for every file. Probably they'll ask you to go look for them yourself. I hope you're a good detective because even though there are case numbers, the filing system there follows its own logic." Caroline forced a wide smile. "Good luck."

I took the folders. Leaving the office, I felt very paranoid and guilty. Walking to the courtroom, I told myself that it was just paranoia. I had had so many bad experiences coming out to people. I had to remind myself I hadn't really come out to them. I had just been accused.

Chapter 23: The Insolence of Office

I walked into the court building and headed in the direction of the clerk's office. There was a long line. Standing in it, I couldn't help but overhear a nearby conversation as I filled out the file requests.

"Mr. Van Horn," a lawyer was saying to his client on a nearby bench, "we really shouldn't do that."

"Well, I got my rights." Mr. Van Horn was irate.

"I know you do, but we want the judge to go easy on you here."

"I don't care. She don't deserve the house. What did she do but sit around eating bonbons all day? The expensive kind, too."

"I know, but if you don't show some contrition, they won't overlook the beatings as easily."

"Fifty bucks! Fucking bonbons."

"Young man!" a belligerent clerk hollered from behind the desk. I hadn't noticed it was my turn already. "Any day you're ready. I am sure the people behind you will appreciate leavin' before lunchtime."

I rushed up to the desk and gave her the first form.

"Okay, you want case number 345–284 … all right, we'll have that out for you in a minute. Just have a seat."

"Wait, I have a few more."

"You do? Let me see 'em." She looked through the requests. She grabbed a stamp and started loudly slamming it on all the requests. When she was done, she looked at them. "You're with the bank?"

I nodded.

"You didn't say you were with the bank. Get back there in the stacks; I ain't got all afternoon to be your servant. Go on!"

She shooed me into the back. And there they were: wall-wide and ceiling-high—rows and rows of folders.

Case numbers were often mixed helter-skelter. The random streaks of logical order were short-lived. Quickly finding the case documents was out of the question. I'd have to use the sliding ladder to navigate the honeycomb of hanging files. Caroline was right; I felt like a detective: case 1156 could be next to case 1155, or next to 115–255 or even 6511. It was hard for me to fathom that something this important could be kept in such disarray. To file just ten reports took until two-thirty.

Walking back from the courthouse to the bank, I saw a disheveled-looking young man carrying a dirty blue cloth bag, hobbling along on one leg. As he walked closer, I recognized him. It was Walter. Out on the street, stripped of his veteran status, he blended in with the other homeless denizens of Downtown. He stared blankly at me with no look of recognition, even as I tried to make eye contact. I realized then: He most likely had not seen me at Palmer Park. He had just been ranting and raving, and I'd taken the bait. Palmer Park was a notorious enough spot for all kinds of things.

Back in the office, I could hear everyone talking until I opened the door. As I walked in the room, they fell silent.

The ensuing tension was terrible. I couldn't stand it anymore. I had to talk to someone. I waited until Judy and I were the only ones in the office and then walked over to her desk.

"Judy, can we talk?"

"James, sure. Come here. Sit down."

I saw a picture of children on her desk, and picked it up. "Oh, what wonderful grandchildren you have."

"James!"

"What?"

"How old do you think I am?"

"They're not … your grandchildren—oh, I'm sorry." She started laughing. "They're your children?"

"How old do you think I am?"

"Thirty-five?" I guessed with a forced smile.

"How do you think a thirty-five-year-old could have grandchildren?"

"It's a miracle?"

She laughed more. Eli walked in.

"Hey, Eli, do I look like a grandmother?"

"What the? You look like my niece."

"James here thought my kids were my grandchildren."

Eli's laughter boomed through the office. I felt awkward. But it felt good. People were talking to me again. Maybe this thing would blow over after all.

"Young man, let me tell you something about the ladies," Eli said. "Even if they are her grandchildren, you always say, 'What lovely children you have,' and if they are older kids, you call 'em the sister."

"Amen, brother Elijah," Judy said. She then turned to me and added very quietly, "You know, I have a cousin. He's a schoolteacher. And he lost his job last month because he … lived with his friend—male friend. Can you believe that? That was so unfair." What she said was very sympathetic, yet I had a feeling it was going to be prescient. She continued. "I think that was very unfair." I looked over to Eli, and he seemed to have heard nothing.

Toby stuck his head out from his office.

"James, could you come into my office, please?"

"Yes, right away," I answered.

I walked over to his office and sat down in front of his desk. He looked at me very sternly. I had a feeling I wasn't going to like this.

"How is it working here?"

"Okay, sir."

"We've been very pleased with your work. And I want you to know that you can rely on me to write you an excellent reference for your future."

"My future?" I squirmed.

"Yes, we need someone full time in this position … and we don't expect you to be a receptionist all your life, James."

"No, we don't." I was being fired.

"It's time for a change, don't you think?"

"I'm fired."

"No, absolutely not fired. Any recommendation will not say that, nor will the employee records, nor what we say to your agency."

"What will it say?"

"What should it say?" He looked at me with those gorgeous brown eyes. I hated that he was attractive.

"I left to go to Los Angeles," I said.

"Oh, that's great news." He sighed in relief. "You weren't going to apply to be a full-timer anyway, right?"

"No, not at all."

"Humph. Much to do about nothing, then. Oh well. When are you leaving?"

"My … academic adviser is probably going to recommend a transfer to UCLA next year."

"Well, well, well, that's a good school. A lot better than Detroit State, if you don't mind my saying so." He was suddenly quite happy. "Excellent news."

"When's my last day here?"

"Sadly, today."

"I couldn't finish the week?"

"I am afraid not. We have someone coming in tomorrow. Your recommendation, I can give it to you now."

"I won't need it. I think I already have a job." I wondered how much my old boss, Sheldon, was going to enjoy my begging for my job back.

"You might need it anyway. Good thing to keep for the future. Go ahead, clean out your desk. Stop by here, and I will have it ready before you leave."

"Thank you." I felt thoroughly humiliated. Somehow it was more acceptable being humiliated by Casper than by this guy or Caroline.

"No reason for you to stay the rest of the day. You can pack up your things and go now. Oh, and don't worry about the money. I've decided I'll approve your time sheet for the time period. Consider it severance pay. Do you need any help? We can call security."

"No, everything will fit in my backpack," I said, wondering what I had in that desk; at most, there were some books I'd brought in.

"And thanks for all your hard work."

"You're welcome. Can I ask a question off the record?"

"Depends."

"Is this related to my being gay?"

"I'm sorry? I didn't know that." He seemed genuinely surprised. It made me ill to think about who wanted me fired: Caroline or Eli. I was sure it wasn't Judy. I thought better of Eli, too.

"You know, I've done a good job here—better than any other receptionist has done."

"Yes, I do know that, Jamie. I hope you understand that and we can leave on an amicable basis. I don't need to call security, now, do I?"

"No, of course not."

"Good. Please don't speak of *it* again. Agreed?"

"Agreed. Can I just … say one more thing?"

"I have a meeting."

I suddenly developed a lump in my throat. I couldn't talk. The last thing I wanted to do was lose it in front of this asshole. But suddenly, I felt overwhelmed. A telltale tear streaked down my cheek, but I held it together.

"Jamie," Toby said flatly.

"It's about Bryan O'Ryan," I said.

"Eli told you not to get emotionally involved in your work here. You made a difference in their lives."

"Can you at least ask whoever replaces me one thing? To talk to Bryan O'Ryan. It only takes a half hour or so."

"If they're not busy, I will insist on it—take it easy, James. I have to go to a meeting. Stay here until you collect yourself."

"Thank you. One more thing." My hands started shaking. My voice started to crack. Toby leaned forward. "I am in a play."

"You're in a what?"

"I am in a play. I'm a theater major."

"Is that a fact? What's the name of the play?"

"*Hamlet.*"

"When is it?"

"Opening night is next Thursday."

"I'll tell the team. Sounds like a good team outing."

"Thanks."

"James?"

"Yes?"

"It's my turn for a comment. It is unfortunate you have to lie to get along in life. I can't do anything about that. Good luck, James. I am sure you're gonna be okay."

I was being fired because I was gay. Yet he seemed nice about it.

When I walked back to the office, they all were at their desks: Caroline, Judy, and Eli. No one asked me why I was leaving. They all knew. I felt ashamed, embarrassed. I wondered if they all had gotten me fired. Bitterly, I thought at least one of them probably had. I assumed it was Caroline. I packed my stuff. I was surprised by how many books and papers had accumulated.

Eli got up. He grabbed a box from behind his desk and helped me fill it up with all the stuff I had accumulated. Then the others walked over to me.

"Good luck, young man." Eli stuck out his hand. I shook it.

"Goodbye, James," Caroline stuck her hand out stiffly, and I also shook it.

Judy hugged me. "Goodbye, James. It's not fair," she added adamantly. Caroline walked back to her desk, leaving Judy and Eli, so I knew who was responsible.

"I am going to be in a play. I'd be honored to have you come see me at the DSU Theater Arts building. The opening is next Thursday."

"Why, of course, if we can get away," Judy said. "What's the play?"

"It's *Hamlet*."

"I love that play," Eli said.

I walked over to the door. Eli got up and opened the door for me. A vet walked up to the booth asking for his check. My eyes shot over to him. It was General Grant.

Eli stared at me. "I told you not to get emotionally involved."

"Take care of them."

"We do our best, Jamie," he whispered, using my real name. "But that's all I'll do. Don't let the world eat you alive, understand? You take care of yourself. I'm going to enjoy that play of yours."

Toby leaned his head into the room as I was leaving and handed me an envelope. "Here, Jamie, is a well-earned recommendation. Caroline, I want to see you in my office."

I walked out and jumped on the Woodward bus back to my house. I stopped at the Bagel Factory. I wanted to see if I could get my old job back. Luckily, Sheldon was in.

"Mr. Goldberg!" a surprised, mustachioed Sheldon Kaufman said. His potbelly seemed to have only grown with time.

"Hi, Shel."

"Long time no see, Mr. Goldberg. Well, well, well, you're looking quite the dapper man. Swell-dressed. How is the bank?"

"Great. I just got fired."

"Fired? What did you do, cash someone else's check?"

"No ... I don't know how to say this ..." I realized I was coming out to Shel. I braced myself for the worst. "They found out I'm ... like those guys ... at the men's room. You know, at the Sassy Cat." The strip joint Shel had taken me to on my birthday, where a group of down-and-out gay men hung out to suck off anyone who strayed there.

He let out a belly laugh that seemed to bounce off the walls.

"You aren't like those losers. Those morons fired you for that, just for being queer? What a bunch a' fuckin' morons, Jimmy. Yeah, goddam fuckers; that's what I call them. They're dumber than dirt, and you're the best employee anyone would be lucky to have."

"You … you knew? You knew I was gay?"

"Fuck yeah, Connie told me you're queer after your first day at work. Fuckin' a. Don't pay any attention to those bank assholes. I hate pig-headed people like that … Jimmy, what's the matter?"

"I'm sorry. I didn't mean to lie to you."

"Don't worry about it. That night we went out there, I hoped the Sassy Cat would loosen you up a bit—just loosened you up in a different way than I expected, ha ha ha!"

"You're far kinder than I deserve."

Sheldon laughed again. "Bullshit, fruitcake, but what can I do for you? I assumed there was a method to your madness in coming here."

"Shakespeare! Did you know that's Shakespeare?"

"Of course I do. *Hamlet*. You think I'm ignorant?"

"Did you know I'm a theater major?"

"You are?"

"Yeah. I'm in a play." There was something about that sentence coming out of my mouth that seemed so incredible, but it was true. It made me suddenly proud of myself.

"Is it possible to see you in it?"

"Absolutely."

"Sure, let me know when it is. But I have to go now. Time to make my deliveries. That bank is all fucked up …"

"Thanks. There is something else before you go: Any chance I can get my old job back?"

"You want your old job?"

"Yes, but I have to level with you. I need it to save up for a trip to LA."

"LA? That's great. We missed you here!" he boomed with pride. "Why LA?"

"I might be going to UCLA next year."

"Wow, big fucking deal. LA. You're gonna be in Hollywood. Okay, as long as you don't forget us little people you climbed all over on your way to the top." Shel let out a bellowing laugh. "LA. You'll have a great fucking time with all those fudge packers they got there. I gotta run. I'll tell Sydney to get you back on the payroll—he should give you a raise; you have more experience now. I'll need you Sunday morning. Come in at four-thirty and open the place. Ask Connie up front for a key. You remember the store-opening rigmarole?"

"Like I never left."

"Welcome back!"

Chapter 24: Every Man Thy Ear

Brian was the unforgiving sort. Consequently, I had to take the notoriously slow Detroit public transit to the next DOHR meeting. I was eager to get there. I needed a place far away from Casper, the bank, or any other confrontations with my past. Somewhere where I was not going to be rejected. The meeting was noncontroversial and I needed the mental rest. I brought an oversize bag of bagels for everyone at the meeting.

I walked into the bleach-and-cigarette-smelling lobby of the Pontiac Hotel. The comforting energy of gospel music greeted my ears: *"Tryin' times don't get me down! I can't see where I am walking, but I have faith in the Lord!"*

I walked into the Penobscot Room and was stunned by what I saw. The smoky haze was like a dense cloud. There were well over two hundred people crowded into the space, way more than I had bagels. I could not imagine what could account for this sudden spike in attendance but immediately suspected the worst: They were going to ask someone like Casper to be the new student rep.

Onstage, Casey was seated at a table, sweating. Phil was standing near him, spouting off again, lecturing him. I was overwhelmed. I thought I had been the peacemaker between show for an election for uncontested officers."

"Hey, who's side are you on?"

"I don't even know what the sides are."

"The race is contested now, and you have to pick sides between inclusion or exclusion. As for the crowd … when word slips out that there's a contested election, people show up." Ken was making a lion's effort to sound relaxed.

"How did it get contested? And is it just Casey? I don't understand. I thought no one wanted the VP job. That's why the term limits were lifted."

"That was just for contingency."

"Hey, down in the front!" someone yelled behind us. I maintained my focus on Ken, who avoided my gaze as we sat down.

"Jamie, don't get defensive. It's just politics, and it's for the betterment of the organization. Stick with me."

"Who's running against Casey?"

He turned to me. "We have a wymyn's candidate—and that's spelled with two Y's. They're joining thanks to our affiliate membership program both you and Casey approved. This is a breakthrough."

"Yeah? Looks like a real coup. An affiliate member can run for office?"

"This one can. Read your bylaws. The deal with Casey was no term limits in exchange for affiliate membership, and he got that deal. That's what that other meeting was all about. Anyway, it's all according to Hoyle. So are you for women's rights or not? That's the contest."

"Since when is Casey against women's rights?" I asked.

"He's in the way. Got any cream cheese in that bag?" Ken

asked, munching on his bagel.

"No, I don't."

"Just listen to Casey bloviating up there."

"Why are you doing this?" Casey exclaimed as he stood up and confronted Phil. The optics were bad: Phil, tall and neat; Casey, short and sweating. "This can tear the group apart." If the sparseness of cheering was any indication, Casey was in for a rough night.

"This is to DOHR's advantage," Phil said. "It's only divisive if you fight this."

"You set me up, buddy. How is getting rid of me to DOHR's advantage? More like *your* advantage."

Casey got a few more cheers. Phil snapped his fingers and glowered at Brian.

"Casey, you're out of order," Brian said. "Phil still has five minutes. I have you on the list. You'll get your turn." Other people's hands shot up in the audience. "Yes, Craig, I see you. I have Casey. Let me just get the other names," Brian was overwhelmed by the number of hands going up.

"Why is Brian doing the secretary bit and not Neil?" I asked.

"Long story," Ken snapped. "Why are you making an issue of this?"

"'Cause it feels like you're stuffing the ballot box?"

"Okay, listen, we should have talked to you before, but this all happened quickly and is the result of a long negotiation. This is a major breakthrough. We should be very happy getting the Wymyn's Collective on board, and Casey, instead of being on our side, is trying to blow the whole thing up. Now, what do you want: a men's club and support Casey or a real progressive movement that includes the entire community?"

"Did you talk to him beforehand?"

"Of course we did. You try and talk to him. No one wants him making a fool of himself up there."

"I should talk to him?"

"Please."

I looked around the room for Neil. It was so packed that people were standing in the back. "And what are all these people doing here?"

"Jamie, they're just motivated by the election."

"Point of order!" someone cried.

"Point of order recognized by Justin," Brian said.

An older man in the audience got up from his chair. "This isn't the way we handle things. When Henry was president, we always used consensus. Forcing things is mean and divisive. I don't even know half of these people. Let's stop this."

A few people shouted in agreement.

"It's a lost cause, idiots," Ken muttered.

"Lost cause? But he doesn't seem to think this is the normal membership."

"That's because it's a lost cause. He doesn't have the numbers."

"Whaddya mean?"

"Look at all the people here. Justin's complaining about not following consensus because he's outnumbered."

"These aren't members just showing up?" I challenged.

"Okay, Jamie, don't be so naive. Phil, Brian, and I called the membership ... and managed to sign up ... some new ones. Casey and Neil were doing the same."

"But you're the membership chair."

"What's that supposed to mean? Look, we have to move forward. We have to involve women. To do that, we have to share the top executive positions. You know this. Casey should have realized that and not taken it personally. Jamie, don't get angry. You and Casey are important members of the organization." He took my hand and looked me in the eyes. "We need you."

"I try to do what's right."

"That's all we want from you. You have to trust me here. Just talk some sense into him."

There was a break. I walked up to Casey and Neil but they would hardly let me get a word in edgewise as they vented how evil Ken and Phil were.

"Casey, please let me just say you're right this is unfair but this is happening and you see how many people there are."

"I know what you want. You want me to roll over and play dead. I saw you with Ken."

"Oh please, I just want to save you from any more embarrassment."

"Go away, Jamie, I need to talk to Casey since you are abandoning ship."

"Just so you know, Jamie," added Casey, "They never explained their motives to me."

"But now you see what they are. Can't you see this is a lost cause."

"You're not supporting me?"

"What are you trying to achieve? Block the Wymyn's Collective from joining?"

"Aha! That's what's going on. The last thing I want is to stop that. I want a delay so this is talked out honestly."

"Sounds fair, but it also sounds like it ain't happening. Look at the numbers. You'll come across as being divisive."

"Divisive! You got some nerve!"

"I am not saying you are. But that is how it will look to some who don't know what's really going on."

Casey shot an ugly glance at me and walked over to Neil. When the proceedings reconvened, I took my seat in the front row with Ken.

"Casey said you weren't upfront with him about a new VP candidate."

"What else is he going to say? You're not telling me you're against empowering women?"

"No, but you weren't telling me the truth."

"You're being petty." Ken sighed.

I saw Neil, a few rows behind Ken, waving at me. "Yoo-hoo! Hello, Jamie."

"He doesn't need to talk to you," Ken said with bare hostility.

"You said I should talk to them." At this point, I was just exhausted. I was not in the mood for this internecine struggle after getting gut-punched by Casper and kicked by Caroline. I didn't go back to Neil, but he walked up to me anyway. I stood up and hugged him.

"Thank you for that talk with Case. It was a trove of information," he said while staring right at Ken.

"Neil," I whispered, hoping to defuse the situation, "do you want a bagel?"

"Sure. Do you have an egg bagel?"

"No, I have almost every other kind, though." I searched the bagel bag again. "How about poppy seed?"

"No thanks, egg is the only kind I like."

"I have a raisin?"

"I'll take the raisin," Ken said and took the bagel out of my hands.

"Bialy?" I offered Neil.

"Okay. Thanks."

We stood listening as members of the audience took turns opposing or supporting the proceedings.

"Sit down, Neil," I offered.

"Here?"

"Yes, of course."

I nudged Ken to get over. He didn't budge at first, then reluctantly moved without acknowledging Neil's existence. My two opposite friends munched on their bagels, looking rather sour. My attempt at neutrality was making both angry at me.

"Phil, don't go for a vote now, " said Casey, seated and looking more dignified than before. "Don't do this to our organization. We can find a win-win, but let's talk first."

"We *are* talking, Casey. We need to progress, to grow. And it means giving up the past. We'll find something else for you."

"What am I, a spoiled child?"

"Yes, you are!" Ken screamed.

"I didn't mean it that way!" Phil said.

Neil looked forward to the podium and raised his hand. "Point of order!" he yelled.

Brian looked out and then up at Phil. Phil nodded his head.

"Okay," Brian said, "point of order—Neil."

"I think it's a little obstructive and unnecessary to insult and humiliate members of our organization in the name of inclusion and empowerment. Affiliates are essential to our growth—everyone agrees—so it is imperative that we show to our *future* affiliates that we do things with integrity."

"That's what my mother would say," I said to Ken, who rolled his eyes.

"Neil, that's not a point of order," Phil said.

"Fine. Then I move we table this discussion to next month."

"I second it," Casey said hastily.

"That isn't a point of order either," Phil shot back.

"There's a motion and it's been seconded!" someone yelled.

"The motion isn't a point of order. Look around the room, Casey, and I think you'll understand. By my count, only three of the women here are DOHR members."

"And I'm a fag hag!" someone cried to general laughter among the crowd.

Casey lit a cigarette, puffed away on it nervously, and then took the microphone from Phil, looking every bit the sad victim. Nevertheless, I could not help feeling Casey had landed on the wrong side of the optics.

"We have a motion to table this discussion," Casey said.

"It's been seconded," Neil pronounced.

"And I am saying, to do that is to attack women's rights," said Phil, who got quite some applause.

"No, it's not, Phil. I want to include more women and minorities. Our charter has all the women's rights covered: pro-choice, ERA, equal pay, all that crap!" Casey was flustered, but it was a poor word choice, and he knew it. "You're just sidelining me. We extended the nominations to affiliates for future elections. That's what you told me."

"You just said, 'Pro-choice, equal pay, and *all that crap!*' That's exactly the attitude I am talking about," Phil said loudly. The crowd erupted with applause and my suspicions were confirmed. He had packed the meeting.

"Oh, come on." Casey was foundering. "You know what I mean. Women's issues are vitally important. I am talking about you going against our agreement."

"This isn't the time for backroom agreements. I know what you said. You said women's rights and '*all that crap!*'" Phil yelled. The crowd hooted.

"Your petty tricks." Casey took a long drag on his cigarette. "You know damn well this isn't about women's issues."

On my left, Ken was livid. On my right, so was Neil.

"Ken, what are *you* getting so upset about?" I asked.

"Baby, Casey is being a real prick."

"He is not!" Neil snapped. "You're pissed off because he's not rolling over and playing dead."

"Only because he's dead and doesn't realize it," Ken quipped. "Why draw this out? Are you a masochist, Neil?"

"Cunt! Ken, you didn't talk about this ahead of time like you told Jamie. You blindsided Casey."

"Then, Jamie, you're on his side?" Ken asked.

"Are you on their side?" Neil asked.

"I want Casper for vice president."

They both looked like they wanted to kill me. "Who's Casper?" Neil asked.

"Look, both of you, don't shoot the messenger. There's two things going on here. One is a step toward inclusion and the other a political coup. I don't think the coup was necessary."

Ken glowered at me.

"Ha! You get it, kid," Neil said. "See, he's on our side."

"But Neil," I added, "I don't see how Casey can win. I'm not going to support him against the Wymyn's Collective joining the group."

Casey and Phil were standing face-to-face again. "You can't get over yourself, can you?" Phil exclaimed.

"Look, I have had it up to here," Casey said, pointing to his nose. "And we're up to about here." He turned his back and put his hand to his butt. Everyone laughed. The joke worked.

Casey lit another cigarette, took a puff, and blew it in Phil's face. "You think you're the only one who knows discrimination because you've read about it in some law book. You all know I lost my job at the Detroit National Bank just because I'm gay. I think you want someone with my kind of passion and direct experience than some political hack."

"I hate seeing these two friends fighting," I said.

"They're not friends!" Neil and Ken said simultaneously.

"What goes up the chimney?" I asked lightly.

"What?" Neil asked.

"Never mind. Bad joke."

"Jamie, he's getting what he deserves for being so stubborn," Ken said.

"Fuck you!" Neil snapped.

"Ken, can't you do something?" I asked. "This is so divisive. Even you two are fighting over it."

"I know exactly what to do!" At that point, Neil resolutely stood up. "I would like to make another motion!" he screamed.

"What?" Brian asked.

"I have a very relevant motion. I'd like to make right now."

"We already have—okay, what's your motion?" Brian asked, exasperated.

"Don't let him do that," Phil hissed to Brian.

"I'd like to nominate Margo Perez for president of DOHR. Yeah, president. Let's put our money where our mouths are. The head of the Wymyn's Collective should be leading this group! Sends an important message."

"You bastard!" Ken yelled. "Where did you hear that name!"

"I second the motion!" a woman yelled.

"Wait a second!" a suddenly defensive Phil yelled. "Margo can't do this—I mean, Margo can run for any office she'd like, so I have no problem with her running for president. But let her decide which office she wants to run for—not some backstabbing attempt to divide us."

"Backstabbing!" Ken agreed.

"*That's* the Sam Hauptman way," I quipped.

During the ensuing chaos, I got up with my bag of bagels and moved to the back of the room. There was nothing to be won sitting with them. But I had to say something, so I raised my hand to speak.

"The chair recognizes ... is that you? Jamie?" Brian asked. "James Goldberg for two minutes."

"I am really concerned here," I said. "I don't know why you two are fighting. I know where this leads: Someone or some group will be cut out. We need to be inclusive of everyone, so let's set aside our differences. We have common enemies: Republicans, homophobia, and discrimination. Why are we fighting among ourselves and not aiming our energies where they should be—at the people discriminating against us?"

I thought that was a reasonable thing to say at a gay rights organization, but it did not have the desired effect: Everyone laughed derisively.

"What would you have us do, Jamie?" Casey asked.

"Let Margo decide which office she runs for," seemed a good thing to say. Except right after I said it, I realized she had probably already made a deal with Phil.

"If you stay on the board, I am not going to another meeting!" someone shouted.

Neil walked up to me. "You see? Phil's being unfair to Case."

"Sort of." I squirmed.

"Sort of? Isn't it obvious?"

"It's not obvious," Ken snapped. I jumped in shock, not realizing he was right behind me. "There's two sides to this."

"Traitor!"

"Moron!"

"And let me tell you ..." Neil added.

"No, let me tell you!" Ken said.

And they proceeded to talk over each other, so I couldn't make out anything, though it was easy to figure out.

"Will you guys take this outside? I'm trying to listen," scolded a man seated in front of us.

"Anyway, it was decided long ago that we would renominate Case." Neil said.

"We also decided, just as long ago, to add a major feminist organization to our group?" Ken countered and walked off.

Neil turned to me. "She is so full of herself. Can't you see Phil got a friend of his from a different organization to run against Casey? Vote with us. Look, your vote carries weight. Margo will be a great president."

"This should have been decided before it ever came to the floor," I said.

"Exactly. We thought it was decided until over a hundred of Phil's *friends* showed up."

This was what I hated about politics: the personal sand traps people got themselves into. It sounded like the addition of the Wymyn's Collective was essential to the organization, more important than one more male executive. And while a packed meeting left a lot be desired, a packed meeting was what we had.

"Let me talk to Ken real quick. Neil, I'll see you later."

I walked back. Ken was still very upset.

"I am confused! Who's running for what?" someone cried from the crowd. Huge applause followed.

"Want another bagel, Ken?" The bag tore a little more.

"No!"

"Why are you so upset? Phil is making mincemeat of Casey."

"What side are you on, anyway? Look, baby, that bastard is getting only half of what he deserves—"

Ken's voice broke off as about twenty women entered through the back door. The hostility in Phil's voice seemed to evaporate. Casey was furious and Ken was suddenly relieved. I was sick to my stomach as I sensed the trigger was about to be pulled.

Casey started pacing the stage, sweat pouring from his forehead. "Phil, I am trying to keep some continuity in our leadership."

"Everybody, please, in the interest of transparency, I want to introduce who I want to be our new vice president, Margo Perez," Phil said, motioning the women at the door to step forward. "So Casey and I are now in agreement! Margo and I would make a great team. We would bring two organizations closer together and assure DOHR does not become just another men's club. Margo, can you come up?"

Everyone started hooting and cheering. Casey was dumbstruck. He stood there looking sad and defeated.

Margo was wiry, cute, and energetic. She was introduced and then walked onstage. "Thank you, Phil. That's right: Boys Town is over!" she cried caustically.

Casey was completely humiliated. The debate had been over when his own surprise nomination had turned on him. Adding salt to the wound, while still standing center stage, he was forced to smile and even clap along with the crowd.

"Is there still a motion on the floor for debate?" Phil asked.

"I withdraw the motion," Neil listlessly said. He walked by me. "Thanks for nothing."

Ken walked by and said, "We didn't even need you. I think we need a new representative to the WCDCC."

I turned to talk to them, except at that moment, the bag of bagels tore apart and all the bagels fell out, rolling all over the floor.

I was batting a thousand: Casper, the bank, and now DOHR. I feared what horror story awaited me when the curtain went up on *Hamlet.*

Chapter 25: Unbated and Envenomed

It was opening night. Backstage in our communal dressing room, I stared long and hard at myself in the mirror as I put on my makeup. I thought my costume was silly. I wore an outlandish mustache designed to make me look older. Instead of traditional Renaissance clothing, we wore turn-of-the-century costumes. I was dressed like someone from the cover of the Sgt. Pepper's Lonely Hearts Club Band album.

How many lines will I blow this time? I wondered. I knew there was no such thing as a perfect performance, but I just hoped I'd keep my flubs to a minimum. I started imagining what new way I'd find to humiliate myself. I might trip over my feet. Or twist my words on my most important lines. I'd burp in the middle of a speech. Or worse, break out in uncontrollable laughter at the wrong moment: Once, I'd made a joke of the way Simon, who was playing Laertes, stumbled to his death, and thereafter I couldn't help but laugh whenever someone pretended to die.

I noticed Hank Minton who was playing Bernardo walk by. I looked and saw Hank's short roly-poly body was flanked by the stick figures of Billy Thompson who was playing Marcellus and Evan Bennet who was Francisco. Dressed up in costume they looked like two bowling pins flanking a bowling ball. I didn't know Hank or Evan well but I noticed they were nervous and rehearsing together very earnestly, even with their small roles.

Then I turned and noticed Ben. He was seated at the table next to me. He was in deep concentration with his own makeup. Barb came by, already dressed up as Gertrude.

"Break a leg boys!" she said as she walked past.

"Thanks, you too!" I said. Ben merely grunted at his girlfriend's greeting.

I forgot my stage fright. Here we were. Opening night. The rest of the cast was giving a hundred and twenty percent, and Ben, despite some concessions, still wanted the macho spotlight. He refused to let his one-dimensional Hamlet display any vulnerability. I felt I needed to do something—not just for him, but for the production. But I had no idea what to do.

Ben smugly applied the last touches of makeup to his penciled mustache. In an uncharacteristically weak moment, he turned to me. "How do I look?"

"Can I say one thing?"

"I'm trying to concentrate now. Do I look good or not?"

"Well, it's just the speech you give right after meeting with the players in act two."

"What about it?"

"You still just play it angry. But I think it's frustration with himself, like this, 'O, what a rogue and peasant slave am I! Is it not monstrous that this player here—' Do you see?"

Ben was looked at me quizzically. "Weird. Can you just tell me if my makeup looks okay?"

I got closer to see him better. But instead of stopping, I inched closer and closer. I asked myself, *What are you doing?* As Ben's eyes opened wide in alarm, his mouth agape, I answered myself, *Shut up and just do it.*

"You're sweet, Ben," I said. "You can never hurt me as much as I love you." Then, with his mouth open like it was, I planted a French kiss on his lips. To my surprise, he kissed back for an instant. Then he caught himself and stopped. I stopped immediately.

"Jamie, in the wings in thirty seconds!" Dwight yelled from outside the dressing room.

"What was that? What was that for?" Ben said, bewildered. I had no time to think of what I had done. Before I knew it, I was off to the stage for my entrance.

I was back in the wings, waiting for the orchestra prelude to end. Then came the fanfare. I was trying to get into character and live Horatio's personal history. In this moment, he was annoyed that he had been called into this unpleasantly cold night watch for some stupid story about a ghost; he would rather be inside with Hamlet. Someone tapped my shoulder and I jumped.

"Sorry," whispered Alec, dressed as Claudius. "You got some nerve, kiddo. Break a leg." He walked away, and I wondered how fast the news had traveled—a distraction I didn't need. I lost my focus and then heard a voice onstage announce, "Not a mouse stirring."

◆◆◆◆◆

Marcellus kindly grabbed my elbow and smiled at me. Bernardo glanced at the wings to make sure we were there and then finally told Francisco, "Well, good night. If you do meet Horatio and Marcellus, the rivals of my watch, bid them make haste."

Onstage, we went almost arm in arm. I felt surprisingly confident, thanks to Marcellus's unexpected support.

Francisco looked at us. "Stand, ho! Who's there?"

"Friends to this ground," I pled.

Marcellus added, "And liegemen to the Dane." I concentrated hard by making eye contact with each speaker.

Francisco, gathering up his gun, said, "Give you good-night."

"O, farewell, honest soldier, who hath relieved you?" Marcellus asked.

"Bernardo has my place. Give you good-night."

Marcellus turned to look at Bernardo. To do this, he actually had to look above his head. Mr. Nathan had instructed us that the auditorium seats had been installed too steeply. Consequently, to appear as if we were looking at one another, we actually had to look up just above our heads.

"Holla, Bernardo!" Marcellus cried.

Bernardo smiled at me. "Say, what, is Horatio there?

"A piece of him." I smiled.

Bernardo smiled back; any bad feelings from the confrontation during rehearsals were gone. "Welcome, Horatio. Welcome, good Marcellus."

"What, has this thing appeared again tonight?"

"I have seen nothing," Bernardo replied.

Marcellus gave me a gentle jab with his elbow, "Horatio says 'tis but our fantasy, and will not let belief take hold of him touching this dreaded sight. Therefore, I have entreated him along with us to watch the minutes of this night, that if again this apparition come he may approve our eyes and speak to it."

"Tsk, tsk, 'twill not appear." I was in the groove and in character.

<hr>

I watched Hamlet's entrance from the opposite wing. He looked shaken as Claudius walked over to him. Gone was the anger he always projected; he now seemed very ill at ease, which looked perfect for Hamlet.

"But how is my cousin Hamlet, and my son?" Claudius asked.

"A little more than kin, and less than kind," a moody Hamlet replied.

"How is it that the clouds still hang on you?"

"Not so my Lord, I am too much in the Sun." Hamlet's reply was reluctant, not angry.

Someone passed me in the wings. "It worked," he whispered. I turned and they were already gone.

Barb, playing Gertrude, could not help a very broad smile. "Good Hamlet cast thy nightly color off, and let thine eye look like a friend on Denmark."

The play seemed to be in good hands. But as word traveled fast, I was nervous Ben would get angry with me and try something onstage. When Hamlet was alone, it was my cue again. Marcellus stood comfortably near me with Bernardo behind us, and we walked onstage.

"Hail to your lordship!"

Hamlet was at first perfunctory and joyless. "I am glad to see you well." Then I looked again. He was at once cheerful and happy. For the first time, he smiled at me onstage. "Horatio, or I do forget myself." This smiling improvisation set the tone and kept me in the moment. I needed to catch any new nuance Hamlet might throw my way.

"The same, my lord." I smiled back at him and added, "And your poor servant ever." Perhaps my searching gaze was less confrontational for Hamlet since it was actually aimed above his head in accordance with Mr. Nathan's direction.

The scene went eerily well. Hamlet spoke to me like he was joking with a long-lost friend. It was unlike any rehearsal we had ever had. "What is your affair in Elsinore? We'll teach you to drink deep ere you depart."

I felt a breezy, friendly rapport. "My lord, I came to see your father's funeral."

"I prithee do not mock me, fellow student," Hamlet said in jest instead of anger. He even put a hand on my shoulder. "I think it was to see my mother's wedding."

"Indeed, my lord, it followed hard upon …" I was astonished by the absence of any sense of tension between me and Hamlet. *Did the kiss do that?* I wondered.

⊷⊶⊷⊶⊷

At the end of the first act, I hid out backstage during the break to avoid seeing Ben. If he was going to hit me, I would rather it took place after the performance.

Alec came up to me and confirmed my suspicions. "Don't

go to the main dressing room. Use the back one. You two need to stay separated. We all need to stay focused—just do it."

"Of course. Ben's pissed at me?"

"I think he mentioned giving you a black eye."

"Oh shit—"

"Chill, Jamie, just joking. He didn't say anything except he wanted to see you, but given your history, it can't be good. We all have a lot to concentrate on, and you have some long speeches coming up. Don't worry. You two are great onstage— really good. Like, way better than during rehearsals. And he hasn't snapped once at me either."

"Wow, he's relaxing into the part."

"The magic of the theater, Jamie. This is your first play, but this always happens: the fighting, the struggling, the personalities, and then the razor focus when the curtain rises."

"I'm doing okay?"

Alec just put a hand on my shoulder and then walked off.

Backstage, what I feared most were the scenes where Ben and I would be intimate. But once onstage, those fears were minimal. Backstage, I became overwhelmed by my lines; sometimes I didn't even understand how I remembered them. But onstage, my body was transformed into a conduit for Horatio. Interacting with Hamlet now felt like the most natural thing in the world. Sometimes I even felt like I was talking with my lover.

Before the play within the play began, we had an intimate scene together. As I entered, I embraced Hamlet. He just naturally returned the embrace.

"Here, sweet lord, at your service," I said as lovingly as I could.

"Horatio, you are even as just a man, as ever my conversation coped withal," Hamlet delivered pointedly.

"Oh, my dear lord—"

"Nay, do not think I flatter, for what advancement may I hope from thee that no revenue has but your good spirits to feed and clothe thee? Why should the poor be flattered? ... Give me that man that is not passion's slave, and I will wear him in my heart's core, yes, in my heart of heart." Hamlet put his arm on my shoulder with a firm grip. He looked toward me, not the audience, in as generous a move as I had ever seen since working with him. "As I do thee," he continued.

He felt like a truly different person, inhabiting a Hamlet who cared deeply for his friend. The give-and-take was perfect.

◆◆◆◆◆◆◆

During the last intermission, Mr. Nathan came up to me. "Jamie, how's it going?"

"How do you think it's going? I can't tell—part of me feels like I'm in overdrive. Onstage, I've got such intense concentration, sometimes I don't even remember what happens."

"I think that's because everyone is really letting the play take shape onstage and feeding off one another. It's getting there. Keep up your concentration. Your big scene is coming up. You rehearsed it a lot of ways, but just pay attention to everyone, feel the pulse of the room, and go with it, as I think everyone has. We've got a much more sensitive lad onstage than I'd expected. Break a leg out there."

Getting ready for the last act I joined Simon in the wings with a theater professor, Dr. Hart who was playing the English Ambassador and Kevin Hack who was Fortinbras. We were smiling at each other, as the collegiality among us was energizing.

Then came my big moment at the end. When Hamlet realized he had been poisoned and finally avenged his father—that was my moment, but how effective I could be all depended on what Hamlet did.

Hamlet, staggering, slashed Claudius with Laertes's poisoned sword.

"O, yet defend me, friends!" Claudius desperately cried. "I am but hurt!"

Hamlet staggered right up to him. Claudius seemed overwhelmed, and with his mouth naturally agape, Hamlet grabbed the cup of poison and then got tongue-tied, but no one seemed to notice.

"Here, thou incestuous, murderous, damned *Dame*! Drink all this potion. Is thy union here? Follow my mother." Hamlet poured the fluid into Claudius's mouth. Then Claudius sank to the floor beside the prone, dead queen.

"He is justly served," Laertes croaked, near death. "It is a poison tempered by himself. Exchange forgiveness with me, noble Hamlet. Mine and my father's death come not upon thee, nor thine on me."

Laertes sank down in front of the king. When Hamlet finally slumped to his death, downstage from Laertes, I knelt behind Hamlet, giving him space but the option to slide onto my lap as I had wanted him to, but he had always preferred the floor.

"Oh, heaven make thee free of it. I follow thee. I am dead, Horatio. Wretched queen, adieu." Hamlet looked at the queen, which he had never done before. Then, to my surprise, he looked me. "Horatio, I am dead," he announced and sunk into my lap. I was so moved that I burst into sobs—just the sobbing Horatio needed. "Thou livest," he said, "report me and my cause aright, to the unsatisfied."

"Never believe it," I said through a hoarse voice as tears streamed down my cheeks. "I am more an antique Roman than a Dane." I realized the cup was now out of my reach, so I improvised, "In that cup there's yet some liquor left—"

"As thou art a man, give me the cup. Let go! By heaven, I'll take it." Hamlet leaned on my lap, not missing a beat. "O God, Horatio, what a wounded name …" The recording of offstage guns brought me back into focus. "What warlike noise is this?"

Osric entered. "Young Fortinbras, with conquest come from Poland to the ambassadors of England gives this warlike volley."

"O, I die, Horatio! The potent poison quite overtakes my spirit. I cannot live to hear the news from England—the rest is silence." He then completely relaxed into his death. I gently caught his head so it could land softly on my knee. I kissed his forehead and gently leaned his head back on my thigh.

"Now cracks a noble heart. Good night, sweet—" I couldn't say it because I was crying. I swallowed and tried again. "Good night, sweet prince, and flights of angels sing thee … to thy rest."

When Fortinbras, the ambassador of England, and soldiers entered, the magic intimacy between Hamlet and I dissolved. I gently placed his head on the floor and rose for the ending. Before I knew it, I was reciting my closing lines: "Of that I shall have also cause to speak, and from his mouth whose voice will draw on more." I knelt down to Hamlet and delivered the rest of my speech looking at him.

The orchestra played a fanfare, and a bass drum played the shots off. Lights out. Curtain.

I couldn't hear any applause. And then there were a few claps. Gradually, more arrived. It seemed like forever until the crowd really applauded.

Alec shouted, "Places!" Everyone got up and formed a line.

Ben yelled, "Yes! We fucking nailed it!"

When everyone was aligned and holding hands, the lights went on. After a moment, Ben stepped forward and everyone in the audience yelled like crazy. We all yelled, "Bravo!," onstage, making Ben blush. Alec stepped forward next. The lights went out again, and the rest of the Cast joined us along with the crew.

The lights went on again, and we took a collective bow to typical wild student-like applause, complete with whistling and hooting. Ben squeezed my hand. I looked at him and he smiled at me. I heaved a sigh of relief.

We quickly faced the audience and stepped upstage. The lights came back on. The principals—Ben, Barb, Alec, Leslie, Fred, Simon, and myself—stepped forward. The applause was like a drug. I looked at the audience, but I was blinded by the lights. In some ways, it had been the most intimate yet impersonal act of my life. I couldn't even see whom I had just shared it with.

"Bravo!" a familiar voice shouted from the audience as we stood in front of the stage. The lights went out. The applause continued.

"Hands!" Alec yelled.

We all rejoined hands and the lights went up again. The applause started to dwindle.

Can't this go on forever?

The curtain came down, and instantly, the applause stopped. Without thinking, I kissed and hugged everyone in sight, even Mr. Nathan. Then, turning to Ben, I hugged him, and he hugged back violently. My guess was he wanted to make sure I didn't kiss him again. He tightly held the hug until Barb came up to hug him.

The dean of the Theater Department ran up to us. "Arthur, you pulled it off. Why do I even doubt you? Brilliant, Arthur!" Mr. Nathan was beaming.

The dean turned to us. "I am proud of you! That was stunning! And absolutely brilliant, Dwight. Having Jamie here succoring his dead friend. A stroke of genius. Alec, you were magisterial—that was an evil Claudius. Jamie, I loved your Horatio—quirky, tasteful, but such a loyal friend. And your Hamlet—well, Ben, I hope you're satisfied. No Olivier imitation. You were really fresh compared with the dress rehearsal—just magic. That shows a lot of character in my book."

I smiled and felt proud. I gave myself credit for helping to make Ben look good. The dean looked back at Mr. Nathan and pointed at him. "And you! You are a genius! That was fresh. I look forward to the adjudication after the run."

Just then, Casper ran up to the dean. "Dean, we have a problem."

"What's the matter, Casper?"

"There's some homeless guy running around backstage here, and no one knows what to do."

"How did he get here?"

"I don't know."

"Excuse me everyone, but great job!" the dean said as he and Casper rushed off.

Chapter 26: All That Glitters

It was exhilarating backstage. Members of the audience came pouring in. Alec, Ben, and the rest broke off into their own for-the-moment fan clubs. I was standing alone, but I didn't care. It was the happiest I had been in a very long time. I could do something right. It hadn't been a perfect performance: I had flubbed my share of lines, and Ben had really bailed me out by finally befriending me onstage and not making a big deal of the cup I couldn't reach. Still, I had taken the biggest chance of my life, and it had paid off. I had acted in a play, I had recited the lines of a major role, and I had kissed a man onstage. I wondered if Ben felt something for me and that was why he had suddenly been so giving, why he had taken so much care to land his head on my lap. I wondered whether that was all because I had French kissed him before the play had started.

I looked at Ben's admirers and thought that maybe, for the first time since Casper, I had fallen in love with someone new. But why Ben?

Just then, Dave appeared from the corner of the stage curtain. He came walking in with a new hippie girlfriend in tow. I was so glad there was at least someone to congratulate me; I was happy, too, that the Theater Department would see me with someone so obviously heterosexual. It would be a double victory, establishing I can both act and act normally.

"Dude, congratulations! You were fucking fantastic," Dave said.

The joy inside me became almost overwhelming and overwhelmingly egotistical. It seemed obscene to enjoy something this much. He hugged me with the ease of being my best friend.

"Yes, you were just fantastic," his girlfriend gushed. She hugged and kissed me. I blushed with joy.

"Thank you—" My voice trailed off when, from the corner my eye, I saw someone else approaching.

Casey was wearing a dark suit, looking surprisingly very much the part of a lawyer. I had never told Dave I was working in party politics again. As Casey approached, my stomach tightened.

"Jamie! Yes, you were just fantastic!" Casey hugged me and I tried to stay loose.

Okay, a gay man is hugging me, but no one knows that, I thought. *He's here to congratulate me, not talk politics.* "Thanks, thank you." *How do I introduce him?* "Hey, Casey, this is Dave, my roommate."

"Oh, hello, I'm Casey. I'm a civil rights lawyer."

Thank you, God. Please just please don't mention the Democratic Party!

"Civil rights? Far out."

No sooner had this edgy yet benign exchange taken place when Neil showed up. He took his spot in our little circle very close to Casey. Where Casey's dark suit announced being a lawyer, Neil's mauve-and-pastel-green suit spit homosexuality in the face of everyone nearby. He turned to me and put out his arms.

"Jamie, you were just *faaantaaastic*! You *were* Horatio!" he cried in a shrill voice. Neil gave me a huge hug and a wet, sloppy kiss on my mouth, then removed his face from mine trailing a thin line of spittle.

I quickly wiped his spittle from my lips with my hands. But I was so happy it meant Neil had forgiven me since our last meeting.

"Incredible, wasn't he Neil?" Casey asked. "Certainly more lively than that Gordon Jackson."

"And more intimate," Neil added salaciously. I winced. "That Hamlet was a sweetie. No wonder you two looked so in love—and who are your little friends here, Jamie dear?"

"Neil, I want you to meet my roommate, Dave, and his girlfriend, Jennifer. Dave, this is … my … friend Neil." *Just no Democratic Party, please,* I pleaded in my head.

"Cool, man. Great to meet you, guys."

Everyone exchanged pleasantries. But no sooner was that fire out when a worse danger appeared: Judy from the bank came up and hugged me.

"James! Hi! You were just amazing. Really, you played that so …"

"Intimately!" Neil added.

"Yes—intimately," Judy turned to the flamboyant Neil and then looked at me with a wink, "Thank you."

No one there knew I had worked for the conservative DNB bank. From the corner of my eye, I saw another weird sight: a short homeless man in a dingy-yellow raincoat running around backstage. Casper and some other guy seemed to be chasing after him. In my distraction, I realized Judy was still talking to me, offering what I assumed were compliments.

"Really? Thank you. That's so kind of you to come ... from so far."

"What are you talking about? You know I live just a mile away, and I have a special treat—"

Not tonight! A stoner roommate, a flamboyant homosexual, a self-identified civil rights lawyer, and now my banking *collaborateur*. What else could happen? In my triumph, I was a trapped animal. But I had to think of some smart and subtle way to introduce Judy.

"Hi, everyone, I want you to meet ... Judy."

Judy shook Casey's hand. "Oh, hi. I'm Judy. I used to work with James." Near miss.

"Hi, I'm Casey. You worked together? What—"

I backed into someone right behind me. "James, that's my foot!" Eli cried out. The torment was not over.

"Oh, look!" Judy cried. "I didn't know you would be here."

I swung around. Eli was dressed in a lavish suit, far more colorful than anything he ever wore at the bank.

"Are you kidding? I wouldn't miss our little man's debut. I was really surprised, James, you were just fantastic," Eli said, entering the circle of hell that was forming—they were all bombs waiting to explode. "You were such a different person up there. It was like I didn't know you."

Eli made a move toward me. I stepped back in fright, bumping into Casey, who stumbled. While I was off balance, Eli wrapped his arms around me in a bear hug. "Hold on! I am so proud of you, James." He hugged me and steadied me, then he mussed up my hair. "You were talkin' Shakespeare tonight!"

The bank! Don't mention the bank.

"Are you okay?" Judy asked Casey. "Let me help you up, dear."

I walked over to Judy. Eli was suddenly face-to-face with the just-risen Casey.

"Oh, hi, I'm Casey. I'm a civil rights lawyer."

"Really? Honored to meet you, sir. My name is Elijah."

"It is? Since when?" Judy asked.

"Am I talking to you now? No, I am talking to this gentleman here, if you don't mind." Then Eli turned to Casey. "My name is Elijah Pepper. I used to work with James."

"Oh, with Judy here, too?"

"Yes."

"That's interesting. Where did you work—"

"Sir, I just wanted to say how glad I am to hear that you're involved in civil rights! I'm glad to meet you, sir!"

"Thank you, Elijah."

"Civil rights is just music to my ears. It seems to be a dying breed around here."

"For me, it is very much alive," Casey said. "So where did you and Jamie—"

"I am so glad you guys came!" I interjected. "Ah, wow, Eli; Judy. I didn't expect this at all. Here's my roommate, Dave, and Jennifer ..."

"My name is Gay."

"What!" I shouted too loudly.

"Calm down. I just said my name is Gay, not Jennifer."

"Oh, of course," I said.

"I exist too, sugar. Hello, my name is Neil."

Knots in my stomach tightened.

"Jamie!" came another shout from behind.

"What!" I turned around.

"Jamie! Yes, you were just simply fantabulous, dear. Mind if I?" an aged but elegant figure said. With outstretched hands, she enveloped me in her arms and a cloud of perfume. It was my movement professor and the department Norma Desmond, Katherine Crawford. She quickly turned around, revealing a giant, tall column of billowing chiffon and silk and flaming-red hair. While hugging me, she kept on addressing the rest of her audience. "I am so proud of him. He moved out there like a true thespian—"

"Yes, a real trouper!" Neil cried, eagerly.

"No, more a proto tragedian. Almost like I have never seen Jamie before. Under my tutelage, you have come such a long way, my problem pupil. Ha ha ha. Yes, you were difficult, my child, but did we give up? Oh no. Really, Jamie you were—yes, you were—most wonderful. Yes, a real thespian—"

"Yes! He is!" an enthralled Neil shrieked. "What an honor to meet you, Ms. Crawford!"

"Oh, thank you, young man. I'll introduce myself since Jamie boy here seems a little out of it. As you already know, obviously, I am *the* Katherine Crawford. And Jamie is one of my more *surprising* acolytes. I am so proud of this little *luvvie.*"

Beads of sweat formed on my forehead. She didn't know about my being gay, and I was counting on a recommendation from her.

"We're proud of our darling, too," Neil said, spellbound by The Katherine Crawford Show while proudly cuddling up to Casey.

"It's a pleasure to meet you, young man, and who might you be?"

"Let me introduce myself. I am Neil." He must have thought he was talking to the real-life Gloria Swanson.

"Lovely to meet you, young man. How do you know Jamie?"

He put his arm around Casey. "We—my *friend*, Casey, here and I, we're—"

"Oh! Dear, aren't you both adorable. Hello, Casey. You two are just darlings. Casey and Neil: a nice ring to it, like a movie title. *The Adventures of Casey and Neil*." Katherine had forgotten her question.

But Neil had not. "Like I was saying, both of us know Jamie from DOHR. I'm the secretary of the organization."

No!

"Door?" Katherine asked.

Stop!

"Yes, and Casey, my … other half—he's the vice president, or former …"

"How charming is that, and what exactly is this *Door?* I have *never* heard of Door before—oh, a rhyme. How ludicrous."

"Yeah, Door, what's that?" Eli asked.

"I never heard of it either," Dave said.

"Jamie, did I make a faux pas?" asked Neil.

My knees started to shake.

"Oh, it must be a gay organization," Dave said.

"Really? How is that, dear?" Katherine looked at me with melodramatic surprise.

"Oh God." *Make this all stop!*

"DOHR stands for the Detroit Organization for Human Rights. It's a gay rights political pressure group," Neil said.

Political pressure! My life is over.

"Strange, Jamie. I thought you said you weren't politically active anymore," Dave said.

"Indeed, Jamie is apparently more active than even I could imagine, and I'm his movement teacher, darlings."

"I didn't know that either. I mean, I knew you were gay, obviously, after the other day," Judy said.

"What happened the other day?" Dave asked.

"Let's not exaggerate here. I don't really do much; really nothing, ha ha. Nothing at—"

"Jamie, you're so modest. He's none other than Ruth Goldberg's son, the absolute diva of the Wayne County Democratic Party."

"Neil, you can't call my mother a diva."

Dave was finally getting angry. "Democrats? I thought you called them sellouts."

Casey was surprised. "You called us sellouts?"

"Of course not. I wouldn't call anyone—"

"You said it," Dave said.

"I know I said it, but that's not what I meant—not about DOHR, which is really nonpartisan, isn't it?"

"But your mother is a Demo—"

"Well, well, well, it's quite simply *The Many Lives of Jamie Goldberg*. Sounds like a Broadway hit all on its own, and I can't guess who's going to be the star," Katherine said, savoring the drama.

"I am impressed, Jamie," Elijah said.

"Speaking of which, where did you work with Jamie?" Casey asked.

"I worked with Jamie at *the bank, of course.*"

"Yes, that's right. We both worked with Jamie at the bank," Judy added.

"*The* bank? Which bank?" Casey asked.

"The Detroit National Bank," Judy and Eli said together. They laughed.

"What's goes up a chimney?" Eli asked.

"Smoke."

He and Judy curled pinkies. "May yours and my wish come true," they said and then laughed.

"I thought you baked bagels?" Casey asked.

"No, he hasn't done that for a while." Dave said.

"No, I work there—I mean, again–now."

"Not just any bank. The DNB?" Casey asked.

"After all you've been through there." Neil put his arm back on Casey's shoulder. "Oh Casey, that's the bank where your ..."

"Wow, really," Dave said. "You told me you hate banks, didn't you?"

"I know I said bad things about banks," I said and then I turned away, trying to bounce my attention from Neil to Dave, "but it's not as bad as you think."

"Did you say bad things about us, too?" Eli asked.

"Well, yes—I mean no—I mean, politically—you see, not about you. I mean not personally—Judy and Eli, you guys are great—and gals, too." I turned to Casey, adding defensively, "They're great people, not the banks—the banks aren't great, but I had to fit in—I mean, I had to work. With school and everything."

"The Republican right arm? You worked at *that* bank?" demanded Casey.

"What's wrong with DNB? They're a great employer," Judy said.

"How can you say that!" Neil yelled.

"After all you said, you work for a bank?" Dave was now turning very hostile.

"What's wrong with a bank, my dear young man?" Katherine asked.

Why is she still here? I could not help wondering.

"If Jamie is contributing to our local economy," Katherine continued, "I couldn't be more pleased with our thespian *en gestation*."

"Hey, lady, get off my back," Dave said.

"I beg your pardon; do you know who I am?"

"Wait a second," I said. "I know I said all those horrible things about banks—"

"You said bad things about us?" Judy asked.

"No! I just—"

"Oh, look!" Eli yelled. "Is that who I think it is?"

Oh fuck! Who can this be now! I turned again.

My worst nightmare was getting worse. That homeless man in the yellow rain jacket, wearing ragged clothes underneath, was coming right toward me. A bad smell emanated from him. He was scampering, not unlike the guy who had played Osric. Another man was right behind him, chasing after him.

Judy's mood completely changed. She started waving to the old man. "Bryan! Bryan, over here!"

Katherine was appalled. "What is a homeless man doing in here?"

I looked closer. Underneath the dirty jacket, his clothes were the soiled remains of a threadbare but expensive suit. His face was covered by a scraggly gray beard. The man chasing the homeless man was winded and wheezing. But I noticed right away that the homeless man had an impossibly youthful sparkle in his eyes.

"James, you know who this is?" Judy asked.

"How did he get in here?" Eli asked.

"James, this is Bryan O'Ryan," Judy said. "And this is his grandson, Patrick O'Ryan," Indicating the out-of-breath man who was chasing Bryan.

"Bryan O'Ryan!" I exclaimed.

"You can't tell me you know this … this *vaurien*? This rapscallion?" an incredulous Katherine declaimed.

"Bryan, this is James—you know, the one who talked with you every morning," Judy explained.

"James!" Bryan rushed at me and held me. I felt trapped under a dingy yellow tarp and bristled beard—the polar opposite of the cloud of the great Katherine.

"Bryan what?" Katherine asked. "I demand to know, who let this … this *person* in?"

"Oh, thank God, you're here." I sighed and hugged him tightly as if my life depended on it. "Thank you—thank you for coming, Bryan!" I had never been so happy to see such a distraction in my life.

A circle had gathered to watch this bizarre tableau: I, dressed up like a soldier in Sergeant Pepper's Lonely Hearts Club Band , hugging a yellow-rain-coated homeless man. Only when I stepped back from my embrace did I appreciate seeing what he actually looked like.

"Wow, Bryan. This is … you."

"I have never seen such a thing in all my life," said Katherine, gaping.

"Awww! Awww! How do you rate?" came the friendly, familiar prattle from the elderly man. He was much more haggard than I had pictured him.

"This is Bryan," Judy said, turning to everyone else. "Jamie spoke with him every day at the bank."

"Really?" Neil and Casey asked.

"What goes up the chimney—"

"Don't, Eli," Judy interrupted.

"He's dirty," Katherine said.

"I think he's cute," Gay said.

"So, who is this?" Dave asked.

"Exactly. The question of the moment," Katherine said. "I've heard Jamie has done some weird things before, but now I see it with my own eyes. Is this your … lover?"

"Of course not—" Eli interjected as I wondered how she could even think of such a thing.

"Oh, don't look at me like that. Everyone knows he's queerer than a three-dollar bill."

"Katherine!" a scandalized Neil yelled. I should have been horrified; yet with Bryan and his grandson in front of me, Neil coming to my aid, for once, I didn't care about my reputation.

"This is Bryan O'Ryan, one of the vets we take care of, we're like their *parents!*" Eli said. "And our friend James here was very kind to him."

"Yes, James talked with Bryan on the phone almost every day he worked. Bryan is always so lonely, and James always made time for him," Judy said. "But they never met. So I asked Patrick here if we could all come see the play together."

"I thought you said you guys worked for a bank?" Dave asked.

"We do, where we take care of mentally incompetent vets," Eli said.

"What kind of bank is this?" Dave asked.

"Legally, they are mentally incompetent, but it means people who were mentally damaged while they were in the military," Judy added. "It's sad. And Bryan is one of our vets."

Neil's face perked up. "Oh, *that* DNB? You mean the DNB Veterans Trust Division?"

"Yes, that's right," Judy said.

"You must know Caroline de Graff?" he asked.

"Of course. She's our main trust officer."

"Casey, that's hardly the bank—I'm Neil Bradley."

"Oh, Social Security office Neil?"

"That's me."

"You guys do amazing work. Jamie, you should have told us earlier. They are amazing. Casey, this isn't a normal DNB bank you're thinking of."

"That's for sure. We're no vaulty, marble-floored department," Eli said. "I can tell you stories that would make your hair curl. But we do our best to take care of our guys."

"Far out, that's … awesome work," said Dave, now softened by the overwhelming confusion. "Why didn't you say anything?"

"Yeah, far fucking out. Hello, Mr. O'Ryan," Gay said, shaking his bewildered hand.

Katherine swept by. "Oh, what an honor to have such special people enjoying our theater. Mr. O'Ryan, a pleasure to meet you, and now I must take my leave of you. I believe the dean is calling me." Katherine swept herself away with Neil's eye following her exit.

"Awww, hello, James! Awww, how do you rate? Great news, a Tennessee play, really, how do you rate? This is a beautiful *Hamlet* morning I was at the first floor of the Veterans Trust Building—to be or not to be …" he continued to babble.

"You are *the James*?" Patrick asked. "Great to meet you. Judy told me quite a bit about you. About how you would speak with my grandfather for an hour a day."

"He never gave me much choice."

"Don't pull that one on me. People hang up on him, walk away from him all the time. You didn't. Just want to, just …" to my surprise Patrick choked up, hugged me.

"I was just … doing my job." Suddenly, I was crying.

"James, thank you. Not many people take the time to understand my grandpa. You know, I just want to tell you, you are also a fantastic actor. That moment you embraced Hamlet before he died, I cried."

"I did, too," Judy added.

"He had me in tears, too," Eli said.

"I completely bawled," Gay said.

"Aww ... tears, tears, tears, how do you rate, General Kolonsky bad day well behaved, awww," Bryan continued.

I turned and took in the group. I felt like I had a courage I had never had before. I was so proud of these friends of mine.

"Awwww, Tennessee, Tennessee, loved like a brother. Chaplain, that's the profession for you, awwwww ..."

"Patrick, do you mind my asking what happened to him?" Casey asked.

"It's a long story. I'll give you the short version of it. Grandpa didn't fit into the army's image of what a man should be." Patrick sighed. "I think he was always a soft-spoken man. But he also had a ... a ... a friend he always palled around with."

"Awww, Tennessee, Tennessee, loved like a brother. Chaplain, is the profession for you, awww—"

"In Tennessee. You can guess what the army thought of that. They thought they could ... make a man out of him. He was given electroshock therapy, to cure him of his *brotherly love*, as my grandpa now calls it. But they ... botched it ... sorry, still gets me. Anyway, he's been like this ever since. He was in an institution for a while. But when I bought my first building, I had room for him, so we got him out of there. And then these guys here," he motioned to Eli and Judy, "have helped me to take responsibilities over my granddad, and he's a free man now, or as free as ... he can be."

"That's what I feared," Casey said. "Maybe we can see him every now and then. Hear what we can of his story."

"I know he'd love the company."

"Who do we have here?" asked an enthusiastic Mr. Nathan, joining our increasing circle and looking kindly at Bryan and me in the center.

"Hello, Mr. Nathan. That is Bryan O'Ryan, a veteran of World War II and a real inspiration to me."

"The sources of enlightenment will never cease to amaze me," Mr. Nathan said. Turning to Bryan, he asked, "How might you be doing, sir?"

"Awww, I am here with all, how do you rate Gold-Goldberg—great show, Caroline. A great—a great news, big day, awwww ..."

"Glad to hear that, Mr. O'Ryan." Mr. Nathan then turned to me. "Now, Jamie, sorry to interrupt your friends here." He took my hands into both of his. "But I have to say this, and in front of your friends, too. I know your imprint is all over this play. While the dean congratulated everyone, I just want you to know I noticed your generosity."

"Wow, thank you so much, Mr. Nathan. I'd like you to meet my friends."

"Hey, is that Rock fucking Hudson?" Shel's voice boomed behind me.

Chapter 27: Closing Night

I stayed backstage long after everyone had left the closing-night party. Walking in the abandoned dressing areas, I quietly basked in my own personal triumph. My first play, a major role, and nothing too embarrassing had happened. The audiences had apparently enjoyed what we had to say about *Hamlet*.

I looked back at how far I had come from an almost suicidal slide into perversion to this theatrical redemption: the coming together of so many parts of my life. Each night a vociferous audience had told me I was okay. I got it: why theater people were addicted to the stage.

I went back to a dressing table to take off my makeup. There was one last plastic cup of the contraband champagne. The dizziness from drinking that night made me feel released, as if a shackle had been removed and I could bask in my own self-love. I took another sip as the lights went out. Whoever had turned them off didn't know I was still in the theater. Thanks to a small lamp on the table, I finished wiping the last of the makeup from my face.

Then I noticed on the table there was an envelope with my name on it. Probably another congratulatory note. I stuck it in my pocket. Whoever had turned out the lights would soon be gone. I realized I would then be alone. Without a trace of self-hatred, I thought about what perverse acts I could get away with once I was safely alone in the theater. I rubbed my crotch and fingered my ominous belt, but this time it was with a devil-may-care attitude.

I stood up from the dressing table and walked onstage with my cup of champagne. I took another gulp, beginning to feel wild. The theater was empty. The sets of *Hamlet* had already been taken away. A bare, harsh light stood on the stage. Everything else was dark.

I jostled with my pants' zipper—when, in a flash of embarrassment, I saw someone was sitting on the edge of the stage, looking out at the theater. I quickly zipped up my pants.

Shakily, I walked over to see who it was. He looked so alone, so overwhelmed by the emptiness around him: a shadowed figure surrounded by a world of darkness.

I walked stiffly over to the shadow when he turned to me and spoke.

"What took you so long?" Ben asked with a trace of sadness in his voice.

"That's the question I really keep asking myself. I've lived in a shell, haven't I? No one really knew who I was until now, until this production—"

"That's not what I meant. My note. I left you a note to meet me here."

"You did? Sorry, I didn't see it." Then I remembered the envelope I had stuffed into my pocket. The fact he had left me a note filled me at once with delight and fear. Did he finally want to beat me up for kissing him on opening night? Given his emotional state, that was unlikely. In my current mood, I wanted to suck him off.

I just couldn't imagine what he wanted. We had avoided each other offstage through the play's run even as we were the deepest friends onstage. I had feared he would hit me. But I had never seen him like this before: He looked sad. Who was he? Ben the bully, Ben the actor, or some other Ben I didn't know?

"I almost punched you in the face opening night," Ben choked out. His voice disappeared into the echoless darkness.

He was facing the seats, so I couldn't see his expression. I took a tentative step forward. I couldn't help a perverse smile, a strange feeling of inebriated self-satisfaction. I had been able to hurt him like he had hurt me. Except I had also been able to open him up and have him deliver a great team performance. Nevertheless, I also felt a twinge of guilt; it must have been for the kiss. I needed to explain it all hadn't meant a thing. I had just … what? Been making a point? That sounded worse. I took another drunken step closer.

"I didn't get a chance to thank you for letting me do my Horatio. About opening night, I don't know what came over me, Ben—maybe I thought it was the only thing that could help you. I didn't want to harm you in any way." I was babbling. I wanted to know his reaction, but he still faced the darkness.

"You had your reasons," he said. "I'm a jerk." I realized then that he was a little drunk as well. "But that first intermission," Ben spoke wistfully, "I thought if I gave you a bloody nose, that would teach you not to fuck with me—I saw you down the hall … but then I didn't want to hurt you at all."

I stepped closer. Perversely, I wanted to mess with him and see what happened. Ben stayed seated on the edge of the dark theater, one leg folded under him while the other dangled over the edge of the stage. As I approached him, I reasoned with myself, *He admitted being a jerk, so don't be one yourself, Jamie.*

"I was afraid you'd hit me," I admitted. "Alec told me not to go back near your dressing table. But I figured if I got a black eye after the second intermission, you'd feel bad and let me be for the rest of the run."

He laughed. "You're something else, you know that? But that night, I didn't know what you were doing for me."

I looked at our shadows on the front seats. I saw the back of Ben's checkered shirt and the backside of his blue jeans. His arms were folded in an invisible lap.

"Want some bubbly?" I merrily offered him my cup.

He waved his hand away. I took a large gulp for courage, sat down next to him, and dangled my feet off the stage. He still didn't look at me.

I offered him the cup again. He took it, gulped it empty, and threw it away. The cup crashed with a hollow sound in the darkness.

"I can still hear the dean say it," Ben said. "'Your Hamlet was like nuttin' I'd seen you do before.' The dean. But I didn't need him to tell me. Around the second act—that first night … with Alec and Barb onstage, doing what you wanted me to do, everything changed. It all became more fluid and easy. With every performance after that, it got even easier." Ben turned and made eye contact. His face looked soft. His eyes were moist. "I've been waiting for you. Where have you been?"

I shrugged and slid a little closer to him. "Ben, I like you. Can I be your friend, at least?"

I waited to see what he would do. He did nothing. Overcome with desire, I allowed myself to put my hand on his shoulder. "I know you're straight ..." I was hyperventilating and couldn't finish what I was going to say.

He flinched and pulled his shoulder away from me. He slid behind me, then made me turn around, his legs now folded onstage. Facing each other, he looked angry. Then, impulsively, he grabbed me by my hair and pulled my face to his. "What are you trying to do?" he seethed.

I was in shock that he had grabbed me. I wasn't even aware of the pain at first; I was more intimidated and excited by the anger. Then, as if nothing had happened, Ben let go and looked out at the invisible audience. I was smarting in pain, confusion, and a deep sexual arousal.

"I deserved that," I said. Yet I didn't dare ask anything about what he had meant. It suddenly occurred to me I should have read that note. Trying another, more dangerous route, I wanted to bare my soul to him—for what reason only God, champagne, and my erection could say. "You know about my reputation?"

"Are you kidding? Everyone knows—believe me, we know more than we want to know."

Ben slid farther away. I put my hand nearby, but he batted it away. I retracted my hand into my pants pocket and felt the envelope.

"You know *my reputation*. It's why people hate me."

"Don't say that."

Did my ears deceive me, or was Ben now being protective? "Okay," I said softly, completely confused. I felt tenderness for Ben and some mysterious excitement. I felt some desire to be self-destructive: sacrifice myself to him.

"Faggot," Ben said, but I could hear the smile in his voice.

"Breeder," I countered.

"Is that what you call us?"

You don't hate me, do you? I waited for a response until I realized I had only thought it in my head. My inebriated arousal kept egging me on to lay it all bare. "I needed this play—my friends told me that. I needed you. I'm babbling, aren't I?" I didn't know what I was saying.

He looked me right in the eyes. My heart jumped and began to palpitate. His face shone in the bright glare like a star.

"You're fucking with me, and it's making me pretty angry. Don't look stupid. You've been fucking with me."

"Me?" I asked.

"You needle me, you flirt with me, you make passes at me, you help me, you buddy up to my girlfriend. And you still are trying to embarrass me—why?"

"Oh my God." *I love you,* I thought as my lips couldn't say it. "I had no idea I was doing any of these things to you."

He turned his face back to the half darkness, not waiting for an answer. I slid closer to him. Had I tormented the one who had bullied me so dominantly? Perversely, I moved my arm toward him. I hesitated at first—and then, I rested my arm on his shoulder. His shoulder was stiff as a rock at first, but it slowly relaxed and accepted my touch.

Thinking of my reputation, I fumbled for words. All that came out was, "Slap me, Ben. Yes, hurt me, if I hurt you."

He said nothing. My heart pounded.

"Do it," I said so softly. He turned and slapped my face. Then turned back.

Far from any pain, I felt a sexual energy I had never felt before.

"I'm sorry." I swallowed, hardly able to talk. "I really didn't mean—to mess with you."

"Okay, then, that kiss on opening night. Did you mean that?"

The question surprised me. "Yes, I meant it," I said, really unsure.

"You did? ... You think I'm a fag, then?"

"I think you're beautiful."

"Does it make me a fag?"

"What?" With my arm around him, it seemed a moot question. But then he pushed me away.

"You kissed me. I kissed back. I liked it—for a moment. Am I ... gay?"

"Are you gay?" I thought I had just been provoking Ben, but the kiss had hit its mark much deeper than I had ever dreamed. I had also put my arm around him. That must have meant something, too. "Ben, do we have to call it something? I got myself in a lot of trouble because I thought I was gay."

"You're not gay?"

"That's not what I mean. I *am* gay, but I am not *gay*. Being gay doesn't mean you have to do certain things. I let it define me. I don't know if you're gay, Ben. You love Barb. All I do know is ..." My mouth was gaping open.

Ben lunged at me, grabbing my face. "What are you saying?"

I felt cornered. "I love you, Ben just as you are," I blurted out.

"Oh. Okay ... You don't think I'm gay?"

"Experimenting, maybe? Bisexual?" I offered.

"Do people think that—in the cast?"

"No. No one has ever said anything like that. I'm the one with the bad reputation. They probably think more that it's me, Mr. Faggot, being a jerk."

"Mr. Freak is more like it." He laughed. He looked away off into the audience again. I wished I could see his expression.

Mr. Freak? Is that what they call me? I shuddered. But here I was, allegedly fucking with someone's mind. I didn't know how I could set the record straight. Or was the record different than I had thought it was?

"Do people call me that? Mr. Freak?"

"You're not Mr. Freak," he said defensively. "I'll hurt anyone who calls you that again."

"I love you. What do I have to do, Ben? Tell me. I'll do it."

He reached out a hand that landed on my thigh. *Maybe he is bi?* My heart started racing. A wild desire overcame me: I wanted to tear off my clothes for him.

"You like me, then?" I could barely ask.

"I do. But I have a girlfriend. I have Barb ... it's different."

"I know Barb. She's amazing." I slid closer so we touched sides. His hand stayed on my thigh.

"Yes, she's amazing. But I get strange … *dreams*. Fantasies, I guess. I don't know what to do with them. They involve … you. But I don't know you."

"The way I behaved … my reputation."

"Don't apologize to me."

"I'm not apologizing. But I have done a lot of bad things I'm not proud of, Ben."

"Well, that's too bad. But it doesn't bother me."

"It doesn't?" I gulped, wondering how far I would go to explain this. "In the past, I did stuff because I thought it was the gay thing to do. I read the wrong books. But that so-called gay thing got mixed up in other … stuff. Shoot, kissing you wasn't like that. Opening night, that was good. I was just afraid how you'd react. So I kept away."

"It was okay. We're talking now because you gave me space. I thought you wanted to humiliate me, but you kept your distance. That meant a lot to me."

"It did? That was good? Wow, I did something right?" I looked between his legs, and I could see an erection in his pants, too.

"How can I believe you, Jamie?"

"What?" I no longer knew what the stakes of this conversation were. Ben looked away again.

"Believe? I need to believe in you, too."

I moved closer. Our thighs touched. Our eyes met again; his looked so beautiful and alluring.

"It's about trust …" I noticed mid-sentence that he didn't move his face away. I leaned closer until my mouth was near his. I moved to kiss him again but he pulled away.

"Sorry—I didn't mean … are you angry at me?" I asked desperately. I felt a flash of shame. I had blown it. "You're angry. If you want to hit me, please, I deserve it."

"You're pissing me off again … jeez, I am not going to hit you, who do you think I am? There's a difference between being a freak and … and being you. Just … you really *want me* to hit you?"

I felt a flash of sobering shame. I regretted that I had confessed something so blatantly masochistic. He looked at me oddly. I wished I could take it back, but it was out there. To take it back would be like fucking with his mind again.

"I guess I do." I shrugged. Not sure what to do, I sang softly, *"Hurts so good …"* from that John Cougar song.

I felt like I was offering myself up like a sacrificial lamb. Time seemed to stop in the silence after my admission. I was in awe of myself that I had dared to say this to another soul, let alone Ben.

"I don't care if you're gay. We can just do whatever it is you want—we want—and let's not call it anything," I offered.

As I inched closer, he inched away. I realized I was sitting in the spot where he had been sitting, and he was now pressed uncomfortably against the corner of the stage.

"Still, it has to change you, being gay—or discovering you like Mr. Freak," Ben challenged softly.

It felt like ice was cracking beneath me. I was about to sink and drown. I'd started something very serious without realizing it and had no idea where this was going.

"Ben, maybe you're just curious? A phase? Whatever fits you, I'll believe it. I won't judge you. But I admit, discovering what I wanted was one of the biggest reliefs of my life. It was liberating—you know that?"

"I am beginning to ... "

"I'm playing no games, Ben. The choice is yours. You want me, you can have me," I dared. "I just want to satisfy you."

"I don't want to be gay." he said.

"Being gay doesn't change you. But sometimes when people come out, they start acting in a certain way—"

"Yeah, like acting all effeminate, like they were girls."

"Or they start behaving like ... Mr. Freak."

"Stop. I don't want to hear that from you. Don't put yourself down."

"You called me Mr. Freak."

"Fuck that. Don't you do that."

"Let me just explain? Let me tell you something no one knows, but maybe you can understand. I have to tell you this in confidence. I was in love with ... Casper."

"Casper? The asshole set designer Casper?"

"Yeah, not the best judgment on my part, but I loved him."

"Is he queer, too? Figures."

"No, let me finish. I was closeted until I fell in love with him. After that, I couldn't ignore being gay anymore. He was the first person I ever dared to love."

"Did he love you?" Ben turned to me. "Well, did he?"

"No, he didn't."

I leaned slowly toward him again. I wondered if he was ready. As my mouth came closer to his lips, I urged myself, *Do it!*

This time he was against the wall. He couldn't really resist. When I realized that, I backed away a few feet. In the glare from the stage light, he made a gentle silhouette. The sharp light on one side and dark shadow on the other softened his face. I saw such sweetness now. His skin was so caress-ably soft. He had a tenderness I had somehow missed before. How was this the bully who had terrorized me?

"I think I get where you're going. Maybe you interest me, Jamie. All of you, not just the parts you selectively show me. The things you're afraid to show me, show me those, too."

"Oh my God, Ben. I promise I will."

"The things I want to do to you. I don't know whether to—" Ben's voice trailed off. At once, he looked at me with revulsion. "I hate you more than just about any living thing on this planet. I don't know why I put up with this shit from you. A month ago, I would have just hauled your ass out of ... okay. Enough. That was before ... "

He stopped talking and stared at me. Then, in an impulsive movement, he stood up and walked behind me.

"Get up, Jamie."

It sounded like a command to me, and I obeyed. I stood up and faced him.

He raised a hand. I flinched, expecting to be hit. Instead, Ben stroked my cheeks. "Soft like a girl. I'm going to do something, okay?"

My mind was swimming with the most outrageous fantasies. I nodded my head yes.

He put the back of his hand to my cheek again and stroked it. He slid his hand down my face, my neck, and put his palm against my chest. "We're okay?" Ben asked.

"We're okay," I said. I was scared but thrilled about what would happen next. Impulsively, I moved my face decisively to his. He was surprised. His mouth opened and we kissed.

It started soft and tentative; it was more erotic than any kiss in my entire catalog of sex partners combined. He put his arm on my shoulder to balance himself as he leaned over into me. Pumped his lips several times against mine. His other hand went to the back of my head, and he painfully grabbed my hair again and pushed me to his face as if we would melt together. The pain sent shivers down my spine and an energetic excitement between my legs. The kiss became wild. Each pump of his lips was exhilarating, sharp then soft. Sharper, then softer. He disengaged and leaned back into the darkness. I cocked my head back in ecstasy, and he sunk his teeth into my neck. I felt like a virgin again. I felt a love and a pain that was cleansing, purifying me like I had always wanted it to.

"That's what I've wanted to do since opening night." Ben looked away and out again at the imaginary audience. He looked for a long time. His cheek wrinkled, making me believe he was smiling. "Wow, I just kissed a fucking guy, and it's Mr. Freak himself … I think I might be … I wish I could tell you all the things I want to do to you right now."

"Do them! I swear you can trust me, Ben. I won't tell anyone no matter what you do to me."

"I want to see you cum and scream in ecstasy."

And I knew I had hit the jackpot.

"I love you, Benjamin!" I yelled. "Nobody's here, no one can hear us. I love you, Ben!" My heart started to pound again.

"Love?" He kind of chuckled to himself. "Ha. And think all the time I wasted hating you. I hated you so much during all those rehearsals. How did I know what you were really trying to do for me? Shit, you heard what the dean said about me— us?"

Ben stepped back and stared at me. We both stood on the stage, the lights casting long shadows onto the floor and into the darkness. I looked down at Ben's crotch. It was the sexiest thing I had ever seen. I felt a magnetic attraction to it and slowly went to my knees.

Ben suddenly looked repulsed.

Not again! I though thinking back to Casper.

"You're lucky, Jamie. You know I should have punched your fucking lights out. Don't ever do that again. And forget what we just did. Forget it."

Incredulous at myself, I stood up and stepped toward Ben, but he jerked back. Ben looked even angrier and I was even more confused.

"I said don't," he warned. Suddenly, he was dangerous, but I sensed I was equally dangerous. I smiled.

He slapped me in the face much harder than the first time. "Mr. Freak."

It smarted. The pain sent old recriminations through my body but with a new excitement. The torturer I needed to wipe out my sins had arrived.

Ben was suddenly furious. He looked down on me, his nose flaring. *Homosexual panic,* I thought. I could swear he was about to kick me. "You don't have the guts to," I dared senselessly.

I could see on his mouth the thoughts churning in his mind.

"I am not fucking with you. You said you wanted to see all of me. Here it is. All the cards are on the table, Ben. I love you," I protested. "Tell everyone. I won't deny it. Even if you humiliate me."

"Who do you think I am, anyway? I am not a faggot like you." Ben turned around and jumped down off the stage. He glowed in the direct light. "Good night, Jamie ... You better stop fucking with me, or so help me ... asshole."

Before I knew it, he was gone. For a moment, I buried my face in my hands, horrified at what I had just done. I feared what terrible new gossip would come of it. I touched my cheek, still hot and tingling in pain. This was far worse than any bullying he had ever done in school, yet it had turned me on. It felt like the slap of a belt during one of my rituals. Suddenly, my sexuality didn't seem so bad after all. I was even proud I had had the nerve to admit what I wanted. I remembered that exciting tension between us. How I wanted to feel that again.

I straightened up and smiled, self-contended, until I looked out at the void and heard a distant door slam. Though there was no audience, I still took a bow.

Variation: Finale, Like a Conduit

End of the School Year 1982

Chapter 28: Farewell, Fantasy

With my welcome-to-UCLA letter, I realized time was running out. And while I savored my escape from Detroit and a possible career in the theater. That excitement was tempered by my desire to see Ben alone one last time. The lack of resolution really bothered me. Ben was avoiding me. Tantalizingly, in class I noticed him looking at me from time to time from the corner of my eyes. He would look away if I tried to make eye contact. I reached out to him a couple of times, but he ignored me.

I wanted some communication. Yet as far as I could tell, we had reached a détente: He wouldn't acknowledge me, but he also wasn't bullying me. Since closing night, I had had such great fears and high hopes; but with the passing of time, hope was running out but there was still plenty of fear.

Then came an unlikely surprise: a phone call from Casper. He was suddenly quite eager to talk to me. We set a date to meet at the music practice building. For over a year, this was the moment I had been yearning for.

It wasn't the best day for this meeting: I had a massive hangover from the night before. The day before, I had received my welcome packet from UCLA. Dave and I had celebrated with cheap sparkling wine and shots of tequila that he had bought for the occasion.

Despite my headache, my heart beat wildly the day we were to meet. But I was not as excited to see Casper as I should have been—I was more agitated with myself. In my present state, would I sing to him "Hurts So Good"? That seemed ridiculous: Casper was so ordinary. After that school cafeteria debacle, he seemed to belong to another time, a time when I was innocent and naive. A time when I idealized him. I couldn't claim any of that now.

Meeting him in a music practice room was a long-held fantasy. There, I had imagined we could secretively make out without anyone seeing us. But now being with him, I felt awkward. Yet Casper was still the man of a long held dream.

There he sat on the edge of a scratched wooden chair painted yellow. I sat on a creaky piano bench in front of a baby grand. The piano's shiny black front had *Schimmel* written on it in gold letters. Casper's presence was intimidating—but not in the sexy way I had thought. Instead, I worried what he had heard from Ben or what other terrible judgments awaited me.

Casper sat there in a floral shirt and green-and-blue striped pants. He had his trimmed blond hair, his blue eyes with their dear little twitch. Before me was the one I had wanted all this time. Yet I couldn't stop wondering, *Did he always wear such tacky clothes? ... What has happened to me?* I looked at him and I didn't see my Casper anymore. He had shrunk down to real life.

I greedily took hold of the hand I had longed to hold for so long. I hoped it would reignite something in me. Casper was receptive. His hand warmly greeted mine.

Casper put his other hand to my face and caressed my cheek. My heart began to pound with awkwardness. He leaned over and hugged me. With my arms around him, I was swirling into a forgotten dream. Then, with a sudden shiver, I jerked my body away. It spoiled a very tender moment and made my poor head a little dizzy. I let out a little groan.

"I heard you were leaving, Jamie," Casper said sadly. I was so touched he had finally come around.

"I'm going to UCLA next year." My voice sounded hollow. I leaned toward him, my hungover body needing the support. "I guess word gets around."

Casper laughed. "No, I talked to Arthur."

"I got in maybe because he pulled strings."

"If he pulled strings, it's because he knows you'll succeed. He puts his reputation on the line, recommending us. But don't knock yourself. You're good, Jamie." What I would have given to hear him say something like this months ago. "You deserve UCLA, and I think you'll do better there."

"With a fresh start," I added distantly.

"Can't hurt, but I didn't mean that."

"A clean break," I muttered, wanting to rest my head against something.

"I didn't say that either. Let's face it: UCLA is a better school than DSU."

"I know, it's a rare opportunity." I didn't recognize the bitterness in my voice. "I just need to get out of here."

"I don't want to leave things the way they are right now."

"What things?" I snapped out of my malaise.

"I don't like the way we left things ... last time we spoke."
He looked deeply, intently at me.

It seemed ironic how the tables had shifted. I didn't like feeling so distant from someone I had wanted for so long. I wanted to get close again, at least for some intimacy. I touched his shoulder. But all I could do is catalog the sensations: a soft shirt, soft skin underneath, nice muscle, firm bone.

"I behaved like a fool," I said. "I humiliated myself ... and you. Screaming, carrying on like that." I took my hand away.

"It wasn't your fault."

"Pretty Mr. Freak of me, wasn't it?" I tried to laugh it off.

"You're not Mr. Freak." He put his hand on my shoulder.

"I couldn't be sorrier."

"Will you stop apologizing?" I was getting tired of hearing that from various people.

He squeezed my shoulder as we spoke. How I wanted to want that. But I had lusted after him for so long, I didn't mind. I felt like I owed it to him.

"Just listen," Casper said

"Okay." Evidently there was more shame to come.

"I was wrong. You were a top-notch Horatio."

Casper and I made eye contact. His blue eyes seemed so hard compared with Ben's softer brown eyes.

"No one wants to be associated with me."

Casper put his hand in his lap. "I do. I'm proud of you, Jamie."

"Proud? Why? ... say, you must be graduating soon. Do you have any plans yet?"

"Jamie."

"Enough about me. Let me hear something about you, please."

"Me? Yes, I'm graduating." He smiled hesitantly.

"What will you do?"

"I was accepted at USC, but I might not go for an MFA. I might go right to New York. It depends whether I want to go into theater or film. I don't know yet. But if I do go to USC, maybe I'll see you sometime?"

"You still want to see me?"

"That's what I'm trying to tell you. When you said to me that stuff about your, you know, childhood. I didn't hear it. Until I was on the bus."

"Great. Poor, pathetic Jamie. You were sexually abused, and I feel so sorry for you." My sarcasm surprised me. "Well, if it's any consolation, I have literally been whipping myself for that disgusting display."

"Don't say that, Jamie, not even in jest." He stroked my cheek. I loved how that felt and how he wasn't put off by my attempts to put him off. I didn't have the heart to tell him I wasn't *jesting*.

"I feel responsible for that, walking away like I did. That was callous of me. It took time for your story to sink in."

"You were angry at me before that. I was being a pest. You never really liked me, and I didn't want to accept that."

"Jamie, I … I really love you."

"What? You hate me."

"In the past, but that's only partially true. Even before we met, I heard a lot of talk about you from people who claimed to know you. I thought they were good friends. So when we met, I didn't believe you. I look back now, and I see things I didn't see before. This 'friend' didn't know you at all. Now I know I shouldn't have believed him." He put his arm around my back. I loved the touch. "It was hard to match what they said about you with your letters to me. I thought you were playing with me, and I didn't like you very much because I thought those letters were hurtful. And then ... well, now I know it was unfair."

"Unfair." I moved away from his arms. My left elbow hit the keys of the piano, and it made a tinny chord.

"I was lied to. I thought all you were interested in was sex."

"That was when I was a freshman. You were so beautiful and pure. After that I just became this freak—you weren't being unfair," I said blandly. "You saw what I became—"

"Don't, Jamie." He leaned toward me and took my hand with a firm grip. It felt sad to feel the hands I had dreamed of feeling after I had awakened from the dream. This time I noticed how surprisingly calloused and muscled his hands were. "It was shocking for me to hear, what you said that last time in the cafeteria. It explained a lot. I haven't been able to think of anything else since."

"Why wouldn't you talk to me, then?"

"I didn't think you wanted to talk to me after our last meeting. But I heard you were leaving, and I thought it was my last shot. I can't take things back, Jamie. I hurt you—I wish we could hit the rewind button."

"Really? We could have had a chance, then?" I gratuitously put my hand on his thigh and stroked it.

"Do we have a chance now?"

"A year ago, it certainly would have saved me a lot of trouble … or maybe not. I would have found a way to destroy it anyway." I squeezed his thigh and let go.

"You don't know that." He looked at me with such arresting sweetness.

"I am who I am. As my hero once said, 'You can't live life backwards.'"

"If I go to USC, would you like to see me?"

Finally, he wanted me. How ironic only after the light I had held for Casper had gone out. "Of course. I hope we can be … friends."

"Friends." Casper frowned in sadness. He stared at the pedals of the Schimmel piano. "It must have been awful … having to do that … and as a kid."

I looked down, too. At the school cafeteria, I had tried desperately to gain his pity. Now having it, I realized pity wasn't a good thing to have. Then I looked up and our eyes met.

"I have to admit, it wasn't … it wasn't so horrible. But you're too late, Casper. And I am just too weird. I am a different person than I used to be."

"I don't care. If I go, can we see each other in LA?"

"Sure."

"If I go to New York, you can come see me."

"I'd like that, I love New York. Can you let me explain something to you?"

"Sure. You don't have to."

"Yes, I do. I need to clear the air. I want you to understand me and my actions.

"Way before we even had met, I fell in love with you and only you. I built, in my mind, this whole wonderful world where we could be together. Just seeing you appear walking down the street from my dorm, it made me feel so happy. Getting you to glance my way, my heart skipped a beat. Every romantic dream I stifled about loving another man, I let loose falling in love with you."

I smiled and Casper blushed. I couldn't help smiling, thinking of those distant, innocent days as if they were decades ago and not just a couple of years.

"You know I met your friend Dara when I was living in the dorms. I didn't plan to have sex with her," I continued. "She seduced me. I had sex with her because—it may sound crazy—but as much as I loved you, I didn't want to believe I was gay. And Dara helped me lie to myself. That's the power of Dara."

"I understand, Jamie. It wasn't bad of you to have slept with her. She's great. I just took it the wrong way because people lied to me about you."

"Wow, they did?" I said. It was finally sinking in what he was trying to say. "Are you saying people were talking behind my back even before I was out to myself?"

"Yes. But it was just one person who was jealous of us, even before we could ever be anything."

"So you know I'm not such a bad person after all?"

"Yes, I do. I hope you see I am not either—except I trusted the wrong person."

"Okay. Another thing I want to explain: You once said to me I 'sucked like a pro.' Well, I did learn, when I was eight. As I told you before, I used to suck off my brother's friend, Gary.

I really believed he loved me. I mean, he showed more outward concern for me than anyone else ever had. He stopped people from beating me up once. He made me feel useful. All I want to say is, that's how I learned to suck like a pro. And then I blocked it all out. Everything about sex. I created little boxes of my life and kept them all separate from one another. Then, when I met you, I found a new box. In that new box, I lied both to myself and you. I really believed ... I was a virgin. The clean, innocent boy I never was but always wanted to be. That's why I don't blame you for not believing me. I did lie."

"You don't have to go on. I get it."

"After we finally met and did it and then you walked out, I grasped for any comfort I could find. I told my roommate, Tim, I loved him. I shouldn't have done that. I got thrown out of the dorm. Then I came out to my parents and they kicked me out of the house. Even my own brother wouldn't talk to me. That really started a tailspin that created the Jamie you see now."

"Oh Jamie ..." He stroked my cheek again, and I was transported to a time that never had been: a time we were together and in love with each other.

"In that tailspin, I lowered my standards beyond all redemption. I wanted a forest of faces—penises—asses—whatever to hide you from my memory. If I couldn't pick someone up at the bar, I went out to the park—Palmer Park, you know?"

"I've heard of it, but never been. I heard it's pretty dangerous."

"Well, I went there. I also often went to Dreamland ... maybe you went there, too?"

"From time to time."

"You saw me there?"

"Sure did."

"You saw some of things I did, Casper?"

He nodded.

"I didn't see you, but of course, you must have been there … others, too. You … and I … lost all respect for myself. One night, I was at Dreamland as usual. About to give up on picking up anyone and I saw this oily, ugly guy."

Casper laughed.

"I remember him as some ghoul-like creature, just like the rest; that's why I never thought of him being anyone I knew. And I scarcely knew Dwight then. Anyway, this guy was staring at me with those hungry eyes, but I didn't do anything then. Later … oh, it was Dwight."

"Yeah, he's the one who said those horrible things about you."

"Oh. I thought so. After that night, once in a while, I would run into him in the park. I was such a disgusting whore—"

"Don't call yourself that." There were echoes of the same protective voice Ben had used.

I pulled away from Casper. As my elbows hit the piano keys, a loud dissonant chord played from the piano. Casper sat next to me on the bench and took me in his arms. I felt smothered into his body. My tired hungover head could only rest on his shoulder.

"I have to learn to be easier on myself … but the fact is I used to let anyone do anything to me there. I suppose that's how my reputation started and how Dwight did it with me. Anyway, end the confessions of Jamie Goldberg. I wanted you to understand." The smothering started to feel good. I wrapped my arms around Casper, living the fantasy of being with him.

"Thank you, Jamie. I can only say I am so sorry I played a part in all this." He kissed my forehead. "I don't know quite how to tell you this. I have my own confession."

"I think I know." I wanted to pull away but didn't.

"Know what?" He kissed my head again.

"You said some unkind things about me."

"You knew that?" He kissed my head again as if it was a penance.

"I don't know specifics. But I could tell by the way ... some people reacted to me. They knew things only you knew about me."

"I'm sorry."

"Don't be. I forgive you." My hands felt his body and caressed it. Then I told myself, *Enough,* and disengaged, causing another slight Schoenberg-like sound from the piano.

"But it wasn't me. Dwight's the real bastard. He lied about you to many people—and betrayed confidences."

"He did?"

"According to him, you were quite a feather in his cap. He ... told ... a lot of people. But, by your story, he put that feather in his cap way before it was possible. He said he had sex with you way back when you used to look at me from that bench outside—your dorm."

"Outside my dorm?"

Casper nodded.

"Did you notice me?"

"Of course I did. To tell you the truth, I was falling for you, too. Anyway, I was sure what you told me about love and all was just bullshit because Dwight told me you both had sex all the time."

"You were falling for me?"

"Of course. You're very attractive—and very kind. That asshole ruined it."

"He sure did."

"Yes, he must have been jealous. When you helped me TA *A Long Day's Journey Into Night*, I thought you just wanted some quick sex—well, that's what Dwight said, and I believed him. Then came your impossible letters. You were being honest; I see that now. I harmed you when I should have been there for you."

"Then it wasn't you." I was relieved. I felt so much better about Casper. "Okay, so Eula freaking out on me because she thought I knew about gay bars back then was because of Dwight? Geez, that makes sense now. She thought I was ... what did she call me?"

"An old pro."

"Yeah—oh, right."

"That's how Dwight described you."

"I proved him right, eventually. I was so convinced there was—is—something wrong with me. After everything I had done, everyone thought I was some kind of freak."

"Only because we didn't know the truth—and it was hardly everyone. I hope you're not pissed off at me?"

"On some level, I guess it was all true, in anticipation. This sounds weird, but I can't tell you how happy I am. It means you weren't spreading the stories."

"You have every right to be angry." He looked at me with such longing in his eyes. He hugged me tightly and felt my lower back.

Oh Casper, you're too late.

He took my head in his hands and brought it to meet his. Then he kissed me, and I kissed back passionately with all the damned-up love I had ever felt for him. I think we kissed for several minutes. It didn't feel good; it felt empty and awkward. I felt I was taking advantage of the situation, but somehow this prolonged kissing was helping me get him out of my system. After a while, I leaned back to the piano, which made a comic trill.

"God, I needed that. I'm glad we can close this on a nice note."

"You don't understand what I'm really telling you, Jamie. I'm only realizing now what a beautiful person you are. I mean your behavior on the set, the way you worked with the cast—Ben and Alec. It showed a lot of class."

"Strange. Dwight did occasionally support me."

"He had no choice."

"No choice? Mr. Nathan?"

"No, Eula and Alec cornered Dwight."

I put my head on his shoulder. I was so tired. He caressed my back. I liked the feeling of sweetness even if it wasn't love.

"Really? They did that for me?" I put my hand on his thigh. It felt warm and soft.

"Mostly Alec. But Eula told Dwight if he valued his balls, he'd leave you alone. I had heard about it just before opening night."

"How did you find out?"

Casper leaned back and started stroking my hair like he was petting a dog. I continued fondling his thighs. I was getting to make out with him in the music room after all. "Dwight bragged to the wrong person. Alec told me what Dwight said about you."

"God, I'm grateful to Alec and Eula—I can talk to them about this?"

"Yes, of course. Even to Mr. Nathan. When he heard about this, he had Dwight expelled—or rather, Dwight left the Theater Department. Anyway, I'm sorry I missed my chance with you, little sweetie."

We snuggled like loveless lovers, it was still beautiful.

"It wasn't the chance we thought it was, though." I disentangled myself from Casper. Time for the dream to come to an end. "I just loved you so much that I thought you could cure me of my self-hatred. But you couldn't. No one could."

"You've got nothing to be cured of, Jamie."

I started laughing.

"What's so funny?"

"A therapist once told me I had nothing to be cured of. But this time, I believe it."

"Then I'm glad to be of some help."

We both stood up. "Can I have a last hug?" Casper asked.

We embraced. His arms, his body against mine. I was transported back in time, to when I first looked out of my dorm room at the intimidating beauty to whom I dared not speak, let alone touch. How generous he was now, touching me and caressing me. And I thought Casper was right: Had it not been for Dwight, we could have at least had some fun—for a time. Then it slipped out.

"I love you, Casper—excuse me, I wanted to say that to you for so long. But I love you like a friend now."

"I underestimated you," he said with a strange stare. "You deserve hope."

"Your kindness gives me hope. Can we walk back to the theater building? I have to pick up my stuff."

We walked silently in the afternoon sun. He took my hand. For a last moment, I could lie to myself about the two of us as I walked romantically down the street with Casper the friendly ghost. I held his hand tightly so he wouldn't let go. Walking hand in hand down the street, there were catcalls from other students—"Faggots!" "Queers!"—delighting my ears with a new sense of pride. I smiled at Casper, and he adorably blushed and twitched. It was one of those rare, perfect Detroit spring days: balmy, but neither cold nor warm. I was in a light-blue spring jacket. As long as we stayed in the sun, I was warm enough.

"Casper, thanks for talking with me. It really means the world to me."

"I wish I had done it sooner."

"You can't live life backwards." I smiled.

"Thank you. Besides, I know I'm too late … you love someone else, don't you?"

"No."

"Haven't you seen Ben lately?"

"Me? No. Actually, not since closing night." *What now?* I braced myself.

"You can tell me. I won't mind hearing it."

It was stunning to hear him say that. My affections were elsewhere. Could it really be Ben? Ben, who was ignoring me? Ben who had kissed me but then treated me so roughly.

"Yes, I guess I am in love with someone else." Admitting it seemed like the ultimate perversion. "How did you find out?"

"It's a small world here, for both good and bad. I'm happy for you. I wish you all the luck in the world." He forced a smile.

"Thanks, Casper. Good luck. And I hope you go to USC."

"Maybe. Maybe there you'll give me another chance?"

"Maybe." I smiled.

We were already in the shadow of the Theater Arts Building. Casper was about to turn to go.

"Casper, I have to know one thing."

He stopped and looked at me.

"Do you pronounce your name 'Tears' or 'Tires'?"

He smiled. "It's Tires."

"Goodbye, Casper Tyres."

"Goodbye, Jamie Goldberg."

Chapter 29: Farewell, DSU

The wood underneath me creaked as I walked along the book-lined walls of Mr. Nathan's sanctuary. As usual, there were play scripts piled all over his desk.

"You wanted to talk to me, Mr. Nathan?"

"James, have a seat." Like always, we took the two seats in front of his desk. "First, congratulations on UCLA."

"Thank you, sir."

"I think at this point I've earned Arthur now?"

I laughed. "My parents taught me to respect my—well, those worthy of respect. Okay, Arthur, but maybe I've earned Jamie?"

"Fair enough, Jamie. I'm proud of you getting accepted."

It was odd hearing something from my professor that I would have given anything to hear from my own parents. "I have you to thank for it … Arthur."

"Nonsense. If you didn't have the record or the abilities, it wouldn't have happened. They were impressed by both your auditions from *Equus* and *Hamlet*. I do have to warn you, the bar will be higher at UCLA, as will the competition. It will take an adjustment; they'll be much stricter than DSU. But you can manage. Just expect to be more focused and—passionate."

"I really appreciate this—Arthur. I just have one question. I've overheard some people talk about me. Am I being kicked out of here?"

"'Kicked up' is probably a better way to put it."

"Was I an embarrassment?"

"You're not being kicked out. You know that. But after your participation in my classes, your Horatio portrayal, and your work with Dwight and Ben, I realized this is not the place for you."

"Because I'm no good here?"

"Jamie, this is one way you get very tiresome."

"Sorry."

"And can you please just ban that word *sorry* from your vocabulary? At the right time, apologizing is great, but give it a rest for now. Look around you. This place is beneath you. I said the same to Eula and Alec."

"And Ben?"

"No." He laughed. "He fits right in."

"But what about my *reputation*? Isn't that the real reason I can't stay?"

"Is it really so painful for you to receive a compliment?"

"It's not that …"

"I saw you drinking in the applause after every performance. You've got the bug."

"I know, but I fought with Dwight. I fought with Ben. And then there's my reputation."

"You keep saying that. But I don't know what your reputation is."

"You must have heard something?"

"Nope."

"Come on."

"What, are you so conceited to think that no one can get enough of the latest gossip about what you're up to?"

"I heard everyone thinks I got the role because I slept with Dwight."

"Of course you did."

"I did?"

"Do you honestly think we'd give the role to someone like you?"

"I am not very attractive, I admit."

"Appalling."

"I am?"

"If it was a bigger role, like Hamlet, you'd have to sleep with the entire cast and be our permanent whore for the entire run. Plus, you and Dwight would have to perform at the Eight Mile Adult Male Cinema in order to graduate."

"Okay. I get it."

"No, Jamie, you just about anything but get it. I took a huge risk putting you in as Horatio. And you ran with the role like it was your birthright."

"I tried to quit first."

"That was the old Jamie. We're not likely to see him around anytime soon. I don't remember a class on Stanislawski in the curriculum, but there you were, building an emotional memory for Horatio. No one told you to badger Ben into being a great team player. And I have no idea what you did with Dwight, but he seemed bent on getting rid of you and then flipped overnight."

"I can't take credit for that. Some people stood up for me without my knowing about it."

"Whatever happened, he became easier to work with. We fought a lot less."

"Fought?"

"Yes." He chuckled, "You and I—and your three guardian angels—we all indeed made Dwight's life miserable. I hope he learned he is not a director, despite being Ms. Crawford's darling. He wisely chose to leave the department for another field of study. Lastly, and you know this, I picked *Hamlet* specifically for Alec, Barb, Ben, and you. I knew if I got you four onstage, *sparks* were going to fly."

"But what about the auditions?"

"We have to do them. And I was open for someone else to do a better job, but no one stepped forward. I knew what I wanted, and no one came close, as I suspected."

"You did it for me?"

"No! Of course I didn't. *Hamlet* wasn't even my first choice until my budget was taken away. But lucky for you, I had to change plays. My neck was stretched across the guillotine for this one. So I thought, 'Who are the best actors, and what outrageous roles can I give them?' I had to prove what utter incompetent morons they are in this department. It was pure, unadulterated ego, Jamie. *My* ego!"

"But you refused to take a bow with us."

"That's the beauty of it, isn't it? Who is the first person the dean congratulated?"

"You?"

"I did this project for my own career, and it served me very well. Of course, I helped you, Alec, Barb, Ben, Casper, Eula, and even Dwight. That's my job. A job I happen to love."

"Why me?"

Mr. Nathan smiled and shook his head.

"I thought Ben and Alec would make a great team. And Simon would be a serviceable Horatio. But when you showed up in my playwriting class, I immediately saw the spark between you and Ben. After a while, I knew you two hated each other—at least, at first—but were serious enough to do a good job. I wanted that tension onstage, mixed in with the mutual dependency between Hamlet and Horatio. The way you read in class, I knew you'd be fine. But you threw everybody a curve. No one expected how you would handle the role—or Ben. The love, the loyalty, and the compassion you poured into Horatio was a marvel. But actually, I was most impressed with the straightforward and single-minded honesty with which you pursued your love for someone."

"My love? Of who?"

"Come on."

"Was it that obvious?"

"Of course it was. To everyone on the set. Except possibly Barb, who's blind to everything around her."

"We're talking about Ben, right? Everyone knew I loved Ben? But he's straight."

"Yet you won him over."

"He really loves me?"

"Oh, come on, you need to wake up. That kiss made it pretty obvious. Why are you looking at me so blankly? You know! The one on opening night before you two went onstage."

"Did he tell you about that?"

"What? No one had to be told about. Everyone saw it."

"Everyone?"

"Jamie, come on, you were in an open room, twelve seconds before you had to be onstage. Two boys kissing: The entire backstage crew and cast saw you."

"They did?"

"Of course."

"So that's why Ben was so pissed off?"

Mr. Nathan guffawed so loudly it could be heard in the courtyard below. "I imagine you and Ben are pretty tight now, right?"

"Err … actually, I haven't seen Ben since closing night."

"That's too bad. I'd have thought you'd be at least the best of friends by now."

"I tried to call him at first. He was … always busy."

"Do try and call him again, Jamie."

"Part of me is afraid."

"I don't want to trivialize what you have been through; it was certainly harrowing. But you have to live your life. You have to stop apologizing for your existence. '*We know what we are, but know not what we may be.*'"

"It just seems like everyone is judging me."

"That which doesn't kill me makes me stronger."

"Friedrich Nietzsche! Arthur, he's my favorite philosopher."

"One of mine, too. He's amazing. You know that scene from *Zarathustra* when he looked out over the horizon and saw that God was dead and that man had killed him—a powerful insight, isn't it? And of course, it was true."

"Wow, I just love Nietzsche ... and also opera. Richard Wagner."

"Then you must have seen my *Parsifal* last year, didn't you?"

"You mean 'The Magic Garden'?"

"Of course, and with your background, you must have understood the internal struggle Parsifal had with Kundry."

"Wait—your *Parsifal*?"

"Yes, I did that with Eula and Casper. The Music Department invited me. That's why we had to delay the *Hamlet* production. The department got members of the Detroit Symphony to donate their time. It was an offer I couldn't resist."

"That was amazing. It was the most intriguing opera I ever saw. I could swear Parsifal was a gay character."

"You mean his repulsion for women? I can't take credit for that. That was the Brian Crowley's idea. He played Parsifal. Oh, I see now. You must know Nina Hudson. She played Kundry. Oh—you're *her* Jamie?"

"Oh, don't tell me she hates me, too."

"Far from it. You're the *lover boy* she was pining about—you're the one who went to all her recitals. Of course it was you."

"Of course? Me?"

"She had a crush on someone named Jamie. It must have been you."

"She had a crush on me? I am crushable? Who knew? Oh, that's too bad. I really liked her—not that way—but we could have been friends."

Mr. Nathan looked at his watch. "I must go to a meeting. I'm glad you came by. How are you getting to LA?" He got up and put on his tweed jacket.

"I'm saving for a bus ticket."

"When are you leaving?"

"Next weekend. I want to settle down there over the summer. Maybe explore the country a bit on my way there. Alec has a friend in San Francisco he wanted me to meet before I arrive in LA."

"Good idea. Do you need any money?" Mr. Nathan had already taken out his wallet.

"No, I should be okay."

"Think of it as a scholarship. It's to help you to get to UCLA. How much is the bus ticket?"

"Fifty dollars."

"Here's sixty."

"Mr. Nathan, please, I can't take it."

He shoved the money into my hand. "Let me know when you get safely to LA or San Fran. And Jamie, keep in touch. Plenty of people back here want to hear how it's going with you."

"Okay, but how do I repay you?"

He said in as theatrical a voice as possible, "Succeed ... and stop calling me Mr. Nathan!"

Chapter 30: Farewell, Detroit

I was waiting in a gay restaurant, which was a New York Broadway-themed deli called The Backstage. It was near the DOHR offices. In the late afternoon, the eatery could have been anything: an empty restaurant with standard-issue effeminate, skinny gay waiters. I was sitting at an empty table wondering what to say to my mother.

Casey had engineered the meeting. She had met with the DOHR board, a group that no longer included me. Not knowing how my mother would act, I readied myself for combat.

Then she came through the door, dressed in another outrageous designer jacket: strips of black sequins alternating with a plastic-like gray fabric, making her appear like a space invader crossed with a beer can. She looked around and then, seeing me, walked grimly in my direction.

She was not her usually energetic self, but looked like someone who had not gotten enough sleep. Her eyes were tired and ragged. She had aged since I had last seen her. My need for a fight drained away. I stood up tentatively.

She hugged and kissed me on the cheek. In my family, that was a downgrade from being kissed on the lips.

"Jamie, glad to see you," my uncharacteristically weary mother said.

"Hello, Mom." I felt awkward.

"What happened to you?" she asked, noticing a bruise on my forehead.

"Oh, I fell."

"Be careful. You can be such a klutz." She looked at me with contempt, then softened. I could tell she regretted it, but she wasn't the kind to acknowledge regret. "Want a late lunch or early dinner? My treat," she said flatly. She looked comfortingly fierce again.

"I'd like that very much," I said. "How did the meeting go?"

"As meetings go, it went well," she said distantly as she picked up her menu. "I was disappointed you weren't there."

"I had a disagreement with the wrong people."

"I know. I heard about it from Casey."

"Are you going to help them?"

"I am going to help them," she said without relish. "Pastrami?" she asked herself.

"Then you're supporting our side?" I asked tentatively.

She was still hiding behind the menu. "Since when did everyone start putting soup in a loaf of bread? How idiotic is that?"

"You're supporting our side?"

"What do they do with all that scooped-out bread? Throw it out? ... They assume that because I'm the liberal and you're my son that I am naturally on their side. The discussion lacked nuance, but that's politics. I don't like being taken for granted."

"It takes away the bargaining chip."

She put down her menu. "No, it takes away my voice. I didn't want to air out my family ... laundry, and they took advantage of—yes, I am going to help them out." DOHR had known how to play the parent card on my mother. "I am doing this partly because somehow it got me back in the UAW's good graces, but we'll see how long that lasts." She stared at me hard. She had a quizzical look like a smile that was stifled. "I am supporting DOHR because I don't understand it. I can't even say it, let alone accept it, Jamie. But I look around and there *they* are. There *you* are. Neither of you are going away."

"Going away?"

"Your cause needs me. I don't understand, but it's the best I can do for you right now," she said. "You are the new underdogs."

"Have you all decided?" our effeminate waiter asked.

"I'll have a cheeseburger and French fries," I said.

"How do you want it cooked, dear?" the waiter asked, and my mother winced.

"Medium rare."

"Gin and tonic as usual, love?"

I blushed. "No, just a ..."

"Go ahead and get it," my mother said. "I'll have the veal liver with bacon. Cook it just in a flash on one side and then quickly on the other, you got it? Seared, not overcooked: It gets like shoe leather, and I don't like that. I'll have a screwdriver."

"Right away," the waiter said and pranced off.

I always had a sinking feeling whenever she ordered liver. Why she ordered it, I never knew. The chefs of Detroit just could not accept her wishes and always overcooked it.

"Casey's just a friend," I said, hoping she didn't think we were together. It didn't work. She winced again. We hit a silence that was only broken by the arrival of our drinks. I raised my gin and tonic.

"Cheers," I offered with a forced smile.

She smiled back, then said, "Look, you want me to accept you." She stared at me. "Well, try and accept me. And if you can't accept me like I can't accept you, then let's at least listen to each other," she said, sounding like we had more in common than I realized. "You know, I'm also doing this DOHR thing for you, Jamie. I am putting aside my problems with it, with you, with Harold, with everything. This movement needs me. I hope you can accept the fact it's the only way I can love you at the moment ... it's all I've got to give you."

"You love me?"

"Of course I do," she said dismissively.

"I thought that was over with," I said.

She looked at me blankly. Another strained silence in the conversation.

"You've grown. You've grown big ... I saw you in *Hamlet*."

"Really? Did you like it?"

"You were great. You were. I was very impressed. I guess you have your father and I to thank for that."

I laughed and then she smiled.

"Wow, you saw me. How did you know about it?"

"I have my ways. I went with your Aunt Louise and your Aunt Sylvia. She was visiting from Florida."

"Did they like it?"

"Of course they liked—"

The waiter interrupted her. "Here we go, girls," he said, sending my mother into winces. He placed our plates before us with a queer flourish. "Bon appétit, darlings."

The waiter had no sooner left the table than my mother did her customary cut into the liver. She looked at it and threw down the silverware, a chunk of solid gray meat still on the fork.

"Overcooked."

"Did they like it?" I asked.

"No, it's overcooked, I said." She was annoyed.

"I was talking about my performance in *Hamlet*. Did Aunt Louise and Aunt Sylvia like it?"

"The play was a little over their heads, I'm afraid."

"Oh. Sorry to hear that."

"They enjoyed it—it was the language they had a hard time following. They went to see you."

"You know it was my idea to play Horatio more animated?"

"Animated, was it? I was wondering about that. You stood out from the start, but those monologues, how you remembered all those lines—I am proud of you. And that Benjamin what's-his-name. Amazing, both of you."

"I flubbed my lines more than a few times," I said.

"I'm sure you did, but no one notices those things, at least not in the audience," she said, looking for the waiter, growing ever more fierce.

"It was also my idea to play Horatio as being in love with Hamlet."

"I was wondering about that, too … I saw the play twice, you know."

"You did?"

"Don't be surprised. You're my son. I was proud." She looked at me. "Besides, I needed to see it alone without explaining everything to the *schmendriks*."

"Is Dad proud of me, too?"

"Why don't you ask him—Excuse me! Excuse me!" She flagged down our waiter.

"What is it, dear?"

"I said I wanted it cooked rare. This is like leather. Send it back, and tell them to do it right."

"Oh, I am so sorry! I will take it back immediately. Is there anything else I can get you?"

"Yes, what I ordered. Calf's liver cooked in a flash, just browning it on both sides. Can you relay that message to your cook?"

"Hmph!" Our waiter did not appreciate her imperious tone of voice. He whisked the plate away.

"Spending all their money on charm school," she said under her breath. Then she looked up at me and came to attention. She saw the tears welling up in my eyes.

"And Dad?" I tried to say.

"Don't cry on me in public; it's hard enough as it is," she quipped. Her eyes betrayed her words; they glistened.

"And Dad?"

"Your father?"

"Does he love me, too?"

"He does, but give him some time."

"Should I talk to him?"

"Look, we didn't call you. We were ... confused and upset. He didn't understand. We're still learning. But we hurt you more than was necessary. I was angry you kept it secret for so long. *Mea culpa.* I threw your things out. I also almost got you electroshocked or whatever. I'll have to live with that. I apologize, okay? ... But you didn't call us either; you didn't really prepare us."

"And Dad?"

"Let it go. Maybe call him once you're in LA or wherever you're going. Give him time. I'll have to work on him a bit," she said, sipping her drink, then looking up in the air. "But that's good because it will also help me convince myself."

Again came the blank stares. The painful silence.

"I need to tell you I am—"

"Let's skip it for now, okay?" she asked. "You know, I spoke with your Aunt Sylvia. She said she knew you were ... the way you are. I told her, 'I just wanted him to be in the mainstream.' She said to me, 'Since when was your Jimmy ever in the mainstream?'" She let out a puff of a laugh.

I had to laugh, too. "No, I've never had that ambition, Mom." We shared a moment. It was a moment I felt like I had a mother again.

"I didn't have such motherly ambitions myself."

"No, you didn't. You took me to see *Easy Rider* when I was nine."

"What's wrong with that? Next I suppose it was wrong to give you *The Autobiography of Malcolm X*."

"No, it taught me to be very guilty."

"Well, I don't see that translating into much positive action."

"Meaning?"

"Meaning working for civil rights."

"Mom, civil rights is dead: Ronald Reagan's president. Almost anyone associated with the Civil Rights Movement was voted out of office. Civil rights has been replaced with a debate over whether ketchup is a vegetable."

"The pendulum swings. You just wait."

"Wait? All the big civil rights fights are won. The Voting Rights Act, the end of Jim Crow. Hippies like Steven and his friends have all become businessmen and lawyers, they voted for Reagan for all I know. And the rallying cries sound empty."

"Your brother Steven did not vote for Reagan! Anyway, there's still *de facto* segregation and cross-district busing."

"Mom, even the Black community's lost it appetite for that fight."

"Oh, what do you know? I make that fight every day. We discuss it and make public policy about it."

"Yeah, in Detroit. That's why you're now jumping over to gay rights?"

"You don't know what you're talking about."

"You saw how powerful gay rights is. Civil rights? You're preaching to the choir here, but you saw Sam Hauptman's response when I appeared. Then when you stood up. It was probably the first drama that committee had seen in years."

"You obviously don't know what you're talking about. As if civil rights was a solved issue—you could not possibly be more naive. You attend a few meetings and you're an expert. My son, the genius. Give me a little credit. You don't even want to admit it that I am fighting for your fa—ho—gay rights for *you*."

Another heavy silence. A cute guy who walked into the restaurant caught my eye. My mother caught my distraction and turned around. She looked disappointed.

"Mom, you're a great lady ... you really are ... but a real lousy parent."

"Thanks a lot," she replied with a breezy irony. "When are you leaving for—where are you going?"

I squirmed. "I'm leaving next weekend, I meant to tell you. I'm just staying in San Francisco for the summer before school starts in LA. I'm attending UCLA drama school"

"I know. Casey told me. You two are an ... item ... aren't you?"

"No, Mom, we're really just friends. In case you hadn't noticed, he's much older than me. Besides, he has a—someone. His name is Neil."

"Whatever."

Another untruth I could not disprove, so I let it drop. Then I thought of something to say, even if it wasn't the truth. "You know the guy who played Hamlet, the one you liked?"

"Yeah, I remember."

"Well, he's the one I am ..."

"Involved with?"

I nodded my head yes.

"He's a good actor. Seems nice. He's Black."

"Is that a problem?"

"Well, I guess that means he's not Jewish," she said. I was a little taken aback that dating a Jew was still important to her. "Well, good for you. How are you making it to California?"

"I saved up for the ticket myself, and my school adviser, Arthur, gave me sixty dollars for bus fare."

"Sixty? Arthur? You mean Mr. Arthur Nathan? He's nice. I like him. I met him ... somewhere. He's a good man. Do you, what ... sleep with him?"

"Mom!"

"You called him Arthur. Sorry I asked."

"He's my professor. He gave it to me as a going-away present."

"Of course he did. I'm sure all students get sixty dollars for their good looks."

"I'm a good actor. He wanted to pay my ticket to UCLA. He got me into the drama school—oh—I guess that means I'm not studying political science."

"So I gathered. You're good. I liked you as Horatio. Very convincing ... a kind-hearted ... disturbed ... person. You could have been a good lawyer, too. I can get you a job in the city if you want to stay and study law." She stopped herself and quickly sighed. "I'd have gray hair and glasses if I waited for you to call us." Her guilt trip was as close as I was going to get to respect. "I hope you do well."

The waiter brought her another serving of liver with blood on the plate. "That looks excellent," she told him. But his feelings were apparently irreparably damaged, and he marched off. At least my mother didn't have to wince anymore.

"I know Edward Albee, and I also saw—what's it called—*Waiting for Godot*—Samuel Beckett. You know I like the theater."

"Yes."

"But you didn't know I was in the theater, did you?"

"You told me you were in New York."

"That's right. I was on Broadway. It was just before the war, so my career ended abruptly, but I did perform in a few shows—nothing major."

"So it's in the blood."

"Yeah, so it's in the blood. For that, I am happy for you." She smiled and took a bite of the liver. "Perfect! Speaking of which, I was very proud of you at the county committee meetings. I admit I was surprised to see you there that first time— and I don't surprise easily. But you were very courageous at those meetings. I am sorry you won't be attending anymore. You even got Sam on your side. That was big, but don't expect him to do anything. This Brian guy they got is a royal nebbish. I told them Casey had to be there and to lose the kid."

"DOHR had a change in leadership," I said.

"It changed back a little now. You backed the wrong horse and delivered too early. That's the price in politics, Jamie; I know that too well. But I am still very impressed."

"You got Casey to be their liaison instead of Brian?"

"I had to. They needed someone serious." She looked up at me. "Okay, and I had the power to do it, too. He's your friend and he was mine. You know he used to come over to the house?"

"Yes, I do. Casey was real nice to me. And I couldn't stand that Brian."

She flashed a perfunctory smile. "I couldn't either ... and if you stay, I can get you back on that board, too. They need you."

She took a few more bites of liver, looking at me. "You're looking good. Relaxed. Your father and I overreacted. Don't leave our lives. Stick with us. We'll make it worth your while."

I took a few swallows of the gin and tonic. I didn't speak until I was sure I wasn't going to cry. "What can I do to show you I am okay?"

"I see it. I told your Aunt Louise about you. But she couldn't handle it, even after all this time. Poor Harold. Your Aunt Louise is *meshuggah*. She could drive anybody crazy. But Harold?" She sighed. "You don't exactly have a tough act to follow."

"I don't do those things. I don't ... Mom, I don't do drugs. I don't wear women's clothes."

"Give us some time, Jamie. Can you do that for me?"

"Yes, I can do that ... for you, Mom."

"Good. In a while, you can do whatever you want. Los Angeles isn't going to be a bad place for you. You'll do fine, and let me know how it's going. Even women's clothes—I don't know that I care about that. Just don't give up on us, Jamie."

I couldn't talk. It may not have sounded like much, but it was the closest thing to acceptance I had ever hoped to hear from my mother. She could hardly eat as I wolfed down my comfort food. She looked at her watch. I looked at mine. It was five-thirty.

"I gotta go home, Jamie," she said, a tear falling down her right cheek. The tough politician humbled by love for her wayward son. I wanted to hold her, but the table was in the way. I looked at her.

She wiped the tear away and finally said, "Whatever it is you do or whoever you are, do a good job. Your father and I will come around to cheer for you. I promise."

She got up and put on her wild black sparkly beer can. "Wrap mine in a doggie bag. You can have it for dinner tomorrow."

"Thanks, Mom, but I hate liver."

She smiled at me and, after a pause, gathered her composure. "We're gonna miss you, Jamie." She left money on the table for dinner and handed me an envelope. "Take it. You need something to settle in when you get there. It won't be easy. It's not much, but it's a start. We should have helped you with college. This will make up for it. We're not cheap—just not rich. Besides, I gotta do better than your professor. There's also a name and a phone number on a slip of paper in there: Rick Fishman. In Los Angeles, he's a Democratic Party official; treasurer or something. I met him at the seventy-six convention. Maybe he can help you out. I think he's one of your ... tribe ... a *landsman*."

"Thanks, Mom. This means a lot." We looked at each other.

She shook her head and stared at me as she buttoned her loud black coat. I stood up and we hugged tightly. She put her hand on my cheek and kissed me on the lips. She didn't cry, but I could see the wetness in her eyes.

"I don't want you to leave, but I want you to be happy. Take care of yourself," she said softly. Then she turned around and left.

I looked at the envelope and opened it. Out dropped a coffee-stained business card: *Rick Fishman. Los Angeles County Democratic Club.* Also inside was a check for $1,800. Eighteen being an important family number: a variation on the Hebrew sign for life.

Chapter 31: The Inevitable Unknowable

I was in the kitchen cooking the standard student dinner fare of macaroni and cheese with frozen peas for Dave and myself when I heard a knock at the door. I was attending obsessively to the cooking pasta, so I waited for Dave to answer.

"You hear the door, Jamie?" he yelled.

"Huh?"

"Answer it! I'm on the toilet."

This was the critical al dente moment for the macaroni, which I had read about in an Italian cookbook, so I didn't want to leave the pot unattended. I dashed over to the door to let inside whichever Dave's girlfriend of the day was waiting there. I fumbled with the lock and opened it. Then I froze, bewildered. It took a moment to take in what I saw: Ben.

Insecure-looking and sharply dressed in a suit, he was holding two roses. One was red; the other, white. I could only imagine he had stopped over on his way to the prom. But there was no college prom.

"Ben?"

"Jamie."

"Ben."

The volley completed with an awkward silence. I felt a twinge of guilt because I had wanted to call him after our meeting following the closing-night party. Apparently, I had procrastinated too long. I instantly felt contrite. Yet there he was—and with flowers.

He saw me stare at the roses. He looked a little embarrassed and held them closer to his body.

"I-I-I was j-j-just … th-th-th-inking about you." Ben's stammering was so sweet that a lump formed in my throat. "I wanted to see you before you left."

"I meant to call you as well. Want to come inside?"

Ben didn't move. I was scared and excited, wondering what we would be getting into if he crossed that threshold.

"Come on in. I'm making dinner for me and my roommate. Join us?"

Ben walked tentatively into the house, holding the flowers tightly. A tense silence descended over us. He used to make my life miserable for so long, and now here he was. Was he here to bully me? If so, he certainly wouldn't have come with flowers. Besides, I had nothing to worry about. Dave would protect me.

"How are you doing?" I asked.

"Great."

"Good," I replied, lamely.

Another silence, broken only by the sound of water boiling over in the kitchen.

"Oh shit, the macaroni! Be back in a minute!"

I ran out of the room and tried to do some damage control on the overcooked pasta. I quickly strained the macaroni with a wire mesh strainer not quite big enough for the job. I threw what macaroni didn't fall in the sink into a bowl and tossed a big cube of margarine over it, then I rushed back to Ben.

He was exactly where I had left him, holding the flowers as if he was a statue. The embarrassing sound of the toilet flushing was followed by Dave's awkward, ice-breaking entrance. Ben tensed; so did I.

Dave looked at me, then at Ben. Then he noticed the flowers and was taken aback, but quickly sized up the situation.

"Hi, I'm Dave." He smiled broadly as he shook Ben's hand, then leered at me approvingly.

"Hi, I'm Ben … a friend of Jamie's."

"I see that. Nice to meet you. Sorry, Jamie, I just remembered I have to go see my girlfriend, Debbie—I mean, Sally." Ignoring my alarm, Dave made eye contact with me and winked. My protector was about to abandon me.

"What about dinner?" I pleaded.

"Grow up. I gotta go. Maybe Ben's hungry. Get it?"

"I sure am," Ben said.

"See? I'll catch you two later." Dave grabbed his coat and silently mouthed the words *rubber band* as he ran out the door. I blushed, as I had never needed to use our *Do Not Enter* sign before.

Dave closed the door behind him. We were alone. Those flowers suddenly took on the proportions of an elephant. I looked at Ben again. With his suit and neat haircut, he looked like he was on his way to a date with Barb. Could I dare think this was all for me?

"It's great to see you," I said. Unsure where this was going, my fantasies were running wild. "How did you know where I live?"

"A friend of yours told me. It wasn't hard to figure out."

"Can you stay for dinner?"

"Sure." Suddenly, he shoved the flowers under my face and blurted out softly, "For you."

My heart started pounding. *What else is in store for me?* I wondered.

I took the two flowers and smelled them. "Thank you, Ben. So sweet." I pricked my index finger. "Thorns."

"Sorry. I must have saved them for you," he said cryptically.

I sucked the blood from my finger and wondered if he had picked the flowers from someone's garden. "This is so kind of you," I said. "You don't know what this means."

"I think I do," Ben said sharply.

"Can you tell me?"

"You know."

Silence.

"Geez, what a sense of timing. I'm leaving in a few days."

"The time had to be right ... when Barb was out of town."

"She was an amazing Gertrude."

"Barb likes you."

"Oh, she does? Well, I like her, too."

Another silence fell. I tried to restart the conversation. "How do I put this ... I ... I am—well—what am I trying to say? Wait, you came here. What are you doing here?"

"I was hoping we could ..." He paused for a second. He was breathing heavily. "I'd like to pick up where we left off closing night."

"You would?" My knees shook.

"I'd like to make it up to you." And then, in a menacing tone, he said, "I want to set it right."

I felt a bead of sweat from my forehead drip down along my left cheek. Unsure if I was ready for what I thought he meant, I tried to delay what was about to happen. "Are you cheating on Barb?"

"This isn't the same thing."

"It isn't?"

"*No*," he snapped. "I'm not like you." Then he held up his hand as if to stop me from speaking, "Okay, this is still new." Then more quietly, "Besides, what if I told you she knows?"

I still couldn't discern what was going through Ben's mind. I thought I was beginning to grasp his intentions. But his tone kept switching between belligerent and vulnerable. Together with the suit and flowers, it was very confusing.

"Wait, Barb knows about me—this?" I couldn't stop wondering what that meant. What did she know?

"Everyone saw the kiss. Look, do you want me here?" he challenged.

"Of course!" And I realized the inevitable unknowable was about to happen.

"Okay, then. Stop talking—about Barb." He stared directly into my eyes. "You remember closing night?"

"I'll never forget." I looked away as my confusion lifted.

"Oh fucking God—I've been thinking about what you said to me. Look me in the eyes, Jamie!"

That grabbed my attention, and I obediently looked right into his eyes.

"I want to say—and don't give me any crap about this—you mean a lot to me."

"I do?"

"In a special way."

Jackpot. But now what? I had tried so hard to win this game I didn't know what to do now that I had won.

"I mean a lot to you *in a special way?*" I was so astonished and overwhelmed. I never thought I would be having this conversation with anyone, let alone Ben.

"Are you embarrassed?" he asked, walking closer to me.

"Overwhelmed. I'm so happy you came. You know, I couldn't stop thinking about you."

"Yes, you made that that perfectly clear."

"But what does a 'special way' mean to you?"

Ben refused to answer.

"I'm afraid, Ben."

"Me, too. I don't understand the give-and-take, Jamie, but you want me—you want me to take you. Tell me I'm wrong."

"You're not wrong." I was completely unsure what he meant but willing to take anything he would give me. "But I don't want to make a fool of myself in front of you anymore."

"If we learned one thing, it's how to make fools of ourselves with dignity. *'There is nothing either good or bad, but thinking makes it so.'*" I couldn't help but laugh at the Mr. Nathan imitation and the *Hamlet* quote. He then added softly, "Besides, you're no fool, Jamie." Then, smiling and looking at me intently, he added, "I'm as worried as you are, faggot."

I bristled in alarm. I felt triggered by *faggot*.

He walked right up to me. "Get on your knees."

I sunk to my knees without even thinking. The flowers rested on my face, feeling oddly ominous. A flash to Casper and Dwight: I didn't want this to degenerate into a blowjob. But there I was on my knees, looking up at Ben. What else could happen? Ben smiled, sighed, and relaxed.

"Now let me hear you say it," he ordered.

At first, I couldn't think of what he wanted me to say. I fumbled for the right words. Looking up at Ben, I felt totally vulnerable. I had never felt both so comfortable and so unsure in my life.

"What we are about to do is sacred, and I promise to obey you," I muttered, then looked up questioningly.

He looked down and smiled so broadly after I said it. "Good, Jamie." He sighed. "I like that. Get up."

I stood, and we looked at each other with a new fondness. I put the flowers on the coffee table, and my heart started to pound.

"Okay, Ben, we understand each other. I'm just gonna say it: I love you."

His smile broadened.

"I'm gonna let you take over … there just has to be one ground rule." My directness surprised me.

Ben stood attentively. I knew I was going to let him do some wild things to me in a way I could not predict. But he could still freak out like he had on closing night. I cleared my throat.

"We'll do this together. You'll be in charge. But whatever happens afterward—tomorrow—don't make me feel this was wrong. It will crush me, Ben."

He seemed genuinely moved in a way I had never seen before. "I get it. You're right. After tonight, it will never be the same. You can trust me, Jamie. I won't treat you like ... them."

"Them?" I asked.

"Yes, I know about *them*. They're not even worth thinking about. With me, it will be different. I told you, I love you." He actually hadn't told me that, but I was thrilled to hear it. "I know you're not a girl, but I'll treat you like a girl. I mean, the way I treat girls—with respect."

He walked closer toward me. That he had said *love* gave me the confidence to bare myself. It was time to drop the pretense. Even though the price I imagined I might have to pay could be very high, I was ready to bet the bank on Ben.

"You know about them?" I asked as softly as I could. "I don't know what you may have heard. And maybe it's because of something in my past, when I was younger—"

Ben shook his head. "Don't." He looked penetratingly into my eyes. He became more confident and larger than life. A tear fell down my cheek. *He must love me,* I thought. He gently wiped the tear from my cheek with his hand. I felt I was getting smaller and submissive.

"Maybe I have stories, too, but this isn't about that. Let's save that for later. Jamie ... you are what I want ... I am what you need." Ben's voice was increasing in intensity. I felt myself submitting to that intensity, and that clearly gave him more confidence. "Tonight, the only thing I care about is you. And

I'm just grateful for the apple I am about to bite into. I can't tell you how long I ..." His voice trailed off. Yes, he had his story, too.

"It's been too long for both of us."

He was seductively and deliciously intimidating. I started to tremble; my knees shook, too. Ben looked at me up and down, examined my fear, and smiled with approval. He moved his left hand gently to my face and caressed my cheek. "Now, can we pick up where we left off? *Closing night?*"

"Starting with what?"

Ben gazed intently into my eyes. They looked mean but also seductive. He smiled and leaned closer to my face. He began to sing softly the words to "Hurts So Good" into my ear.

My heart started to pound. I joined him in softly singing that song. Together it sounded like some sacred confession. Never was singing together so sexy. I leaned back to look at him.

"I am in charge now," he said.

I nodded yes. Ben seemed more beautiful and more danger-ous than ever before.

"Look at me, Jamie. I'm trying something here," he said with a loving throb in his voice.

I looked up and smiled. Our eyes met. He held my shoulders and suddenly looked menacing. Then he spit in my face.

A flash of terror and humiliation gripped me. His piercing brown eyes stayed focused on mine. Insecure, I went to wipe the spit away.

"Leave it," he whispered.

Obediently, I put my hand down. "Just leave it on my face?"

"I'm marking you."

"Okay." Then I remembered, during my nightmarish sexual escapades going to a gay biker bar and meeting a leather man named Kurtz. And his admonishment to me. Then I had said it in fear this time I said it with love: "I mean, yes, sir."

Ben lit up at my response. "Sir?"

I nodded my head.

"You do love me, you little thing?"

The spit on my face instantly turned from humiliation to succulence. "Yes, sir."

With one hand, he held my cheek and spread his spit on my face with his thumb. I let him do it and he smiled. "Good."

It was like he was putting me in my place and I was accepting it. He touched my crotch, confirming my excitement. Pressing it lightly, he smiled and leaned into my ear. "Still afraid of me?"

The drying spit on my face did feel like some sort of mark of what I was becoming. "I'm afraid of showing you who I really am," I said.

"And you're afraid of seeing what I am?"

"Yes, that, too."

"Then let's be afraid together. You show me yours and I'll show you mine," he said, and we laughed. Ben looked at me with such desire that he seemed at a loss for words. "I tell you what ... you can always say, 'Stop,' or 'Slow down.' Okay?"

"Okay."

"You're shaking. But I don't believe for a second you're really scared. You want me to hurt you, don't you?"

"Ben, I want you to take control of me. Use me to make you happy. That's what closing night was all about, right? But—"

Before I could say anything else, Ben softly slapped me on the face. He looked awkward, so he tried again. He slapped harder. The strike made a loud slap, louder than its force. He looked awkwardly around, afraid if someone was listening in.

My cheek vibrated from the moderate blow. The slap itself didn't really hurt, but the vibrating glow that came afterward felt holy. We stared at each other, hyperventilating. I nodded my head yes, not knowing what was supposed to happen next. I felt my cheek. My hand still quivered despite how hard I tried to stop it. Ben gently took my hand away.

"I don't want you to touch yourself without my permission." I felt an unexpected high just from being at his mercy. "Did I hit you too hard?"

"No, Ben—it was … just right." I swallowed. And without thinking of the consequences, I added, "Go deeper, please."

"Okay, Jamie. Anything else before I take over? I don't want you to talk unless absolutely necessary, understand?"

I placed my hand against his chest. He looked down at my hand. His smile was mild and gentle.

In the silence, I felt his heartbeat. His skin was warm through the soft fabric of his dress shirt. It was beating fast. That told me more than any words. I enjoyed the gentle moment. There was a feeling of romantic warmth, but the time was up.

"Well?" he asked me. "Shall we?"

"'The rest is silence,'" I said, and he laughed.

Then there was a flash of sensual anger. He slapped my face, this time harder. My focus on him became razor sharp. After the impact pain of the hit, again my face vibrated with excitement. My eyes were locked on his. It was a sign that we were beginning ... whatever we were beginning.

He grabbed me in an aggressive, tight embrace. My face rested on his shoulder and his head on mine. His chin dug into my neck. I hugged him more for dear life than tenderness. My heart pounded, and my brain went in all sorts of fantastical directions.

"Here's how much I want you," he whispered viciously. He grabbed my ass with both hands and squeezed each cheek hard, holding it. My eyes widened. "Yeah!"

It was breathtaking the way he seemed to impulsively take me. The pressure from squeezing my butt wasn't exactly pain. It was intensely erotic, sending excitement through my back-side. He released my buttocks and then pulled my shirt out from the back and placed a hand underneath, onto my bare back.

"Jamie, I am still here," he said mildly. "I've wanted to do this to you for so long."

He intently and deeply scratched my back, causing an indescribable stimulation: a mix of sexual, emotional, and sensational excitement. His eyes demanded my unwavering focus.

"That's better. Relax. Tell me if it's too much. You can trust me. I've wanted to hurt you so bad. Faggot. Faggot. Faggot."

With every repetition, he both dug his nails deeper in my back and moved his face closer to mine. The pain became so sharp I was going to yell, until he kissed me. He kissed me tenderly, the sharp pain from my back melting into a sexy wave with his increasingly tender kiss. "I don't care what anyone thinks anymore. I love you, you … fucking faggot."

I was beginning to get submerged in this wave of pain, ecstasy, and increasing fear. I broke out in a sweat. He dug his nails into my back—harder, firmer, sending more electric energy through my body with a warm moistness. I let out a painful yelp-moan.

"Stop?" he asked.

"Harder, please?" I asked automatically, feeling an arousal that seemed to take over my brain. He scratched harder. "Ow! Ben—"

"Then let's take this up a step." Ben bent over and turned on the stereo. He found a radio station playing pulsating, arousing heavy metal music and turned up the volume full blast. "Now make all the noise you want, baby," he said as the pulsating, throbbing music matched our own pulsating, throbbing excitement.

I moaned senselessly.

"What were you going to say?" he demanded.

Goodbye, Gary!

"What were you going to say?"

"I love you. Ben Geln, I love you and I submit."

"Damn straight you love me!" he barked, letting go of my back. We dis-embraced and looked at each other, panting with a longing I had never had the courage to show anyone. The burden of my true masochist sexuality had lifted.

He wore a devilish grin. "This is really new to me, Jamie." He stared at me. Then he grabbed my hair and pulled it. The pain was at once shocking and alluring. I could feel his energy taking hold over my body. "Too much?" he asked very directly, but his eyes looked questioning, almost pleading.

With a shaky voice and pain stripping my words of any weight, I said, "No, sir. I'd like more, please."

"Good," he replied. Not letting go of my hair, maintaining his control over my head, he kissed me. The pain was intense, the kiss tender.

"Ow," I squealed softly. The electric sensation of the pain from pulling my hair mixed with the dissonant erotic kiss set my heart pumping wildly with fear and excitement.

Ben let go of me. Smiling at me and enjoying my smile, he asked, "You love it, fagboy?"

I nodded yes. There was no self-hatred and no shame despite being called fagboy. I could scarcely understand the mixture of humiliation and pride, of degradation and love, pain and ecstasy that I felt. The intense stiffness and longing in my groin attested to a deeper sexual experience than I have ever had before.

There was no going back.

With the music blaring, Ben takes me. With a squeeze, he holds me tightly; the sweat on my back stings from the deep scratches. He grabs hold of my head and kisses me. Passion mixes with violence. His teeth, lips, and tongue all play an equal part in the sensual attack on my face. He bites my lips so excruciatingly, I senselessly whimper. Accepting the pain, I feel the submission to his control deepening.

I feel a vague pressure and the sharp pain in my mouth as his saliva enters and mixes with the unmistakable taste of blood. Alarm merges with surrender, and this mixture signals the end of resistance. He now looks directly into my eyes. I gaze back.

"Strip, Jamie."

Another alarm sounds off; but now, it is hollow and irrelevant. Stripping while he's fully clothed, I'll be completely vulnerable. He is still in his suit, which looks now like a suit of armor to me. I find myself undoing my belt. I feel so surprisingly sexy because he wants me to do it.

I'm undoing my belt when I think of it: the ritual. Hurting myself. Something I am so ashamed of, what I never let anyone know about me. I take off my belt and show it to him.

Ben looks questioningly into my eyes. I look back longingly. He extends his hand halfway to me, unsure. My hand with the belt meets his. When I give it to him, he smiles broadly.

"Oh yes, I have wanted to do this to you for so long." He says it with such lust in his voice that I shiver in sexy fear.

We say nothing else. I just pull my pants and underwear down to my ankles. I bend over the couch so my ass is an easy target. I feel a cool draft over my exposed skin. I shiver.

Crack! Without warning, he whips my ass with the belt.

"Aaahh!" I scream.

"Too hard?"

"No, but build up to that please, sir?" I say, unsure if he can even hear me over the pulsating music.

He whips me again. It's softer, almost gentle. He whips me again, a little harder. I moan not so much in pain as from sharing something deep and dark with Ben. I brace myself for the outpouring of shame my ritual used to invoke deep inside me.

Crack! He strikes me again—more painfully than I have ever struck myself, but I just moan softly. The pain shoots across my ass and afterward sparkles with sexual excitement. I'm afraid of how long and how intense this will be, but I can do nothing but await the next blow. When it comes, again I brace myself for a torrent of self-hatred. Instead, I hear Ben ask, "Like it?"

"Love it!" And instead of triggering hatred, it brings a sexy submissive humility. The feeling flooding my brain isn't self-hatred: It's unbridled sexual lust and an overwhelming surrender to Ben.

As he whips me, I yelp. He whips my ass harder. The world around us vanishes. A mental wound closes. He whips away shame and self-hatred. I feel in my submission both lovable and loved. I relax and soften for whatever Ben wants. He hits me again and again until suddenly something different happens: My brain floods with disorienting desire as if the pain is turned into sensual electricity coursing through my body. The strikes although harder, seem to soften into something intoxicatingly sexual.

He drops the belt and turns me over. My pants are still around my ankles. Much to my surprise, he has taken off his clothes already. His surprising sexy swimmer's build is almost too much to take in.

Without thinking, I start kissing his chest and nipples. As I kiss him, I feel my ass glow with a loving warmth. He pushes me into the couch. I trip over my pants and fall on my back. He rolls me onto the cold floor.

My back aches. My body tingles with the coolness and the hardness of the floor. He pounces on top of me. I buckle from his weight. My pants and underwear are somehow gone.

For a moment, I ask myself, *What do you think you're doing, Jamie?*

My question is answered by a flooding sense of bliss. I feel myself sinking, melting into Ben's sexual desire. My mouth explores his torso. My mind delves into satisfying him; the hungrier he gets, the more blissful I feel. He takes my head and shoves it back to the floor. I lay back and close my eyes. I feel him bite my neck as he tears off my shirt—buttons go flying.

We're transformed into an island surrounded by surging waves of pleasure and pain. Lovemaking and ritual finally join hands.

Over the throbbing heavy metal music, I am discovering my own ungraspable love of *Tristan und Isolde*. After such a long absence, I hear the soaring strains of my own version of "*Liebestod*":

> *Do we alone hear*
> *this music?*

Ben hoists my legs into the air. His hands widen my tense ass cheeks. Yielding is no question. Shivers of humility and glory shake in time with my body. Ben spits on his hand and reaches down. I tighten, but his ungentle fingers do not take no for an answer.

Singing sweetly and bitterly,
In lamenting bliss,

With one hand, he fiercely pinches a nipple. My brain soars to some new place of stimulation. He fully enters me and the feeling deepens; waves of pleasure run through my body.

All-hallowing,
piercing me,

Ben is in control from behind, with rough movements. All of the sensations intensify as I melt into a strange cocktail of pain and sex. At last, I can hold back no more: My cries release a primal howl that echoes deep and raw.

All-extinguishing
Guilt and shame

Sparks of pain melt with a new luscious sensation from my cock as Ben strokes it. Sexual ecstasy melds with sublime and submissive pain—

We soar
higher and higher.

All fear is transformed into love with strokes of sharpness and excitement—

As melodies seethe
and roar around us,

Torment and ecstasy flow as our bodies pulsate and grind together—

Shall we listen to them?

"Yes! Yes!" Ben chants with each hard thrust—

Shall we breathe them?

Senselessly, I repeat, "Yes, sir. Yes, sir."

Shall we drink them?

My mouth gapes open as Ben's saliva drips into my mouth, his spit claiming ownership of me.

*Shall we plunge
beneath the waves?*

His body and mine fuse in increasing torrents of bitter-sweet sexuality.

*Shall we expire
among sweet scents?—*

"Yes!" I encourage him. The world disappears except for Ben and his power. All that remain are his bites, his strokes, his tongue and hands—

*In the heaving swell,
in the resounding echoes—*

Everything explodes in wildness and agony, ecstasy and torment.

*in the universal stream
of utmost rapture ...*

In the moist euphoria of our exhausting world-breath, Ben strokes my face with my own cum, like a benediction.

We founder—

My lover sinks on top of me.

We drown—

Spent and damp, our bodies glow.

unbewusst—
höchste
Lust!

Acknowledgments

The author would like to thank those who made all three volumes of *The Goldberg Variations* possible. The late Morris Taylor looms large throughout them. Likewise, Linda Watanabe McFerrin helped usher this idea from a dream to a reality. Larry Brown, David Siegel, and René Capone were all essential in the ways these volumes took their final form.

Particularly for this installment, I want to thank Brian Ng for his help and support.

I need to acknowledge my muses in writing this saga. The spiritual literary muses of this book were the works of Charles Dickens, Johann von Wolfgang Goethe, Hermann Hesse, Stephen McCauley, and Lorenzo da Ponte. The spiritual musical muses were the works of Gustav Mahler, Frank Zappa, Richard Wagner, Tom Waits, Giuseppe Verdi, Wolfgang Amadeus Mozart, Quiet Riot, Anton Bruckner, John Cougar Mellencamp, and the incessant rhythms of great music of all kinds driving us all to our truths.

A word about the texts in the book:

For the Shakespeare source used for this novel, as a base reference, I employed the first folio edition of 1623 and adapted it to suit the needs of the story, including intentional misinterpretations. I modified the text to conform to how a college performance with student actors might deliver the text and reflect the novel's characters' preoccupations. In this I sacrificed the poetic beauty of Shakespeare for the dramatic purposes of my plot. I hope Shakespeare lovers will forgive this liberty, but I invite you to see a local production of *Hamlet* to reaffirm your sensibilities about the play.

The *Tristan und Isolde* passages, (mis)translated by the author, are intended to reflect the main character's state of mind, not a literal translation of the texts. And to save you a trip to your favorite German-English Dictionary:

Unbewusst—
höchste
Lust!
roughly translates as,
Unconscious—supreme bliss!

About the Author

Jonathan Arnowitz Taylor is an American-born writer and designer currently residing in Turin, Italy. His career is a rich tapestry of literary achievement and groundbreaking work in user-experience design, all underscored by a deep commitment to ethics, community, and social justice.

Jonathan's life and work are a testament to the power of creativity and community. His contributions to literature and design, combined with his leadership in the LGBTQ+ community, make him a compelling figure whose work resonates with authenticity and depth. Through his books and professional achievements, he continues to inspire and engage audiences around the world, inviting them to explore the complexities and beauty of life through his unique lens.

The Complete Goldberg Variation is now Available

If you enjoyed *Volume III: Slings and Arrows*, the other books in *The Goldberg Variations* series:
Volume 1: *The Rites of Passage*
Volume II: *The Redemption of the Damned*
Volume III: *Slings and Arrows*
are available for your enjoyment at your favorite local bookstore, Amazon.com and other e-book sellers.
And currently on sale at a discount price from Ingram:

Volume 1 The Rights of Passage

Volume II: The Redemption of the Damned